Odyssey of Revenge

ODYSSEY OF REVENGE

A Novel by
BERNARD DIAMOND

COLUMBIA PUBLISHING COMPANY, INC.
FRENCHTOWN, NEW JERSEY
1983

PS
3554
. I 23
. O 3
1983

Library of Congress Cataloging in Publication Data

Diamond, Bernard
    Odyssey of revenge.

    I. Title
PS3554.I2303   1983   813'.54   83-15191
ISBN 0-914366-21-1

COLUMBIA PUBLISHING COMPANY, INC., FRENCHTOWN, NEW JERSEY 08825

To Ruth

Chapter 1

HE PURCHASED HIS new electric razor for its gentle contours and delicate balance, so it would glide over the deepening lines of his face. To cut himself, to suffer an abrasion, could set in motion the reflexes of old tragedy long buried. His own blood, but a drop of it, made him uncomfortable, as if the drop enlarged and hung down, gathered torrential velocity, and somehow worked its way beneath his flesh to pour out at his crotch. This was the dream, the body of it buried with the torn figure he had seen as an adolescent, the tail of it thrashing at him in odd moments like some prehistoric monster he must subdue.

Yet the blood he saw in his surgical practice was not bothersome. He did not particularly enjoy that first incision; he feared those problems which he might encounter. But this was in line of duty and some good might come of it. He was obsessed with that gratification, the status given him by his ability to perform a necessary service.

To cut himself shaving was another matter. To start the morning with a fresh clean tingle which might dispel his oncoming anxieties, he succeeded in desecrating himself. The morning shave was a rite of behavioral stimulation which set the pattern for that day, to erase the daily turmoil and the grouchiness of the evening before with its carryover into startling nightmares of his sleeping hours. He knew it was too much to ask of a small act of morning ablution, but he had to start somewhere if he wished to help himself. When he cut himself shaving he saw failure written in blood. The new humming gadget he held to his face instilled a sense of mechanistic precision which would come to his aid.

His wife called, "Iz, you're late. Harry will be waiting." Israel Steingut never thought of his first name as a graceful embellishment of his person. Having changed his name once, he could do so again if he took the trouble, just as he could change his telephone number, or his checking account. The alteration would be embarrassing and possibly destructive, as his present identification was a reminder, a portion of the hair shirt woven in his childhood.

"Gott," he hissed. He had nicked himself at an edge of skinfold the machine would not navigate. The old German exclamation erupted at times of minor stress, though he long ago lost any trace of accent.

"You made me cut myself," he accused.

Carla Steingut laughed. "Don't you want to see Harry? You'd better get going. Just wipe your face and hurry so I can get to work."

They were married in a civil ceremony two years before. His Aunt Sophie flew in from New York to attend, taking a twelve-mile cab ride to this Iowa town of eight thousand farm souls clustered about its village shopping center and its large, modern county hospital. Aunt Sophie was content with the secular rite, the short speeches of love, devotion, and rational understanding by colleagues of the newlyweds. Rabbis, Aunt Sophie knew, may have studied God's word but too often used the devil's vocabulary. Social progress was her banner, not theology.

Carla's parents, whom she rarely visited, drove in from Illinois. They were unhappy, their lean furrowed faces hung like wrinkled black drapes. Their beautiful, tall, only child, driven to mass every Sunday at the sacrifice of valuable sleep, the girl they put through nursing school by hiring out for spare time ploughing, was to marry this short German Jew who looked through them with squinty eyes as if they were cattle. Twenty years was an impractical age difference in viable partners, and they held an overriding suspicion that this stocky interloper pushing fifty had plenty of brains but no reproducing capacity. Reproduction on the farm was vital. Life was a farm, plant and grow, mate and multiply.

Carla made certain her husband was calmed after what he called an unsuccessful, nearly brutal shaving experience. She straightened the bedspread, ran her hand lovingly over the colonial maple dresser, and paused at the overhanging mirror. Everyone thought she was attractive, especially for a small rural community, but that did not impress her. Matters of the mind interested her, for which she read the *New Yorker* and the Sunday *New York Times* which she found stacked in the public library. She wanted to know what happened in other states and other cultures, but she did not delve into analytical or philosophical articles. The news, the strains and joys of ordinary living, rural or urban, were the focus of her interest. She recognized the superiority of Israel's intellect but in no way was she cowed by it. There were brainy people and stupid ones, all with their own brands of strangling weakness. Israel had his, and she would work on it. As for herself, she knew she had the rare quality of easy enjoyment. Her hospital work, a movie, shopping, a walk, each offered relaxed gratification which she could enlarge to a low-pitched thrill if she thought about it.

As she bounced out of the house, the rhythm of her buttocks subdued by her nurse's uniform, she glanced at the new coat of white latex she had given their two-story frame house. How comforting to be able to place a down payment on a home and not have to worry about it.

Israel was a good provider. He was also a worry and a challenge for her. Intellectual acumen made him no less dependent upon her, a condition she accepted and secretly enjoyed. When he had a trying day at surgery she would emphasize that he was entitled to a bad result, that he was not God. It was she who pushed him to learn to relax, to accept the grace of a walk in the sun, or the stimulation of a driving rain on his face. She had long thought of having a child, busying herself at home, but there was time for such indulgence. Israel was not yet prepared for disruption of his schedule, and she had to exorcize the wart of worry which could consume him if it grew unchecked. She encouraged him to spend more time with free souls like Harry Pearl.

Israel walked slowly down the porch steps, grunted at a patch of lawn turned yellow by an early cold spell, and buttoned his leather jacket against a stiff breeze. The sun danced in and out. Sheets of gray clouds pushed through brighter cumulus layers. As he walked he stumbled on the uneven cement pavement pads that led to the end of the street on which he lived. Climbing a low meshed-wire fence, he entered Harry Pearl's fields. The corn was mostly down, though large patches of dried stalks dotted the three-hundred-and-sixty-acre property. From behind the modern ranch-style home he approached; distant barks and growls could be heard.

Townspeople called Pearl "crazy Harry." He was an eccentric in the midst of their rural culture, an alluvial deposit whose nonconformity to their sweet land they now accepted. Settling on a farm after the Korean war, Harry promulgated further shock upon the bewildered, taciturn townsfolk by bringing in an Oriental housekeeper. She was sixteen and exceedingly appreciative of her new home, so much so that Harry spent eighteen months in the county court house fighting charges of illicit sex with a minor. When he was jailed for six days because of the clumsy maneuvers of an alcoholic local attorney, Harry thought of it as an adventure. Village residents brought him cookies, hamburgers, and panfried steaks with corn fritters. He was their wounded animal behind bars, the monkey to whom they tossed peanuts.

No one expected Harry Pearl to pull his weight as a tiller of the soil. The mother earth of Iowa did not appear to contribute to his daily sustenance. He flew to Minneapolis or Chicago to return with valises loaded with bagels, lox, frozen quiche, and smoked whitefish, not the sort of tastes and smells to harmonize with cow pies tracked into the living room. After his cleaning girl and flesh warmer left him, presumably for a job in a packing plant, Harry tended his farm and home with diligence. He was an astute farmer, a student of the agricultural pamphlets and journals furnished by the state, and he learned to keep house adequately. For the drudge work—laundry, beating rugs, an occasional sumptuous meal—there were several large-breasted widows in the neighborhood who were glad to help. Sturdy, with waists like trunks and thick solid arms, they all had ulterior motives. Harry was quick to capitalize on their unrestrained desires. Like a salesman touting securities, he had the pitch and the stocky muscular frame to complement an aggressive approach. He received what he needed and managed to ward off the rest. The severity of the ladies' passions made them forget Harry was foreign to Iowa, a misplaced Jewish farmer who was sufficiently adaptable to be considered an amiable fringe member of the community.

Harry waited for Israel with arms extended, to gather in the bounty of camaraderie he expected from a visitor.

"Harry! Why did you want me to come? This is my day off, and I have more important things to do than see your dogs."

"But you *did* come," said Harry. "You could have told me if you didn't want to visit. It's just like you to say you don't want to do something, and then you do it. Maybe it's indecision, or maybe you enjoy fighting with yourself."

"I don't like dogs."

"They are God's creatures. If you don't like the expression, call them children of nature. Tell me, Iz, what beats nature?"

Harry Pearl had acquired six mostly-Husky dogs, not yet fully grown, from a lady friend who raised dogs as a hobby. This was her gratitude for favors received, one dog per favor. It was Harry's intention to train the animals for winter racing. Who knows, maybe in Alaska. Now they were harnessed to a small wooden box-like cart, with wheels he had salvaged from discarded children's toys.

"Sit in the box, Iz, hold the reigns, and say 'mush.'" Israel promptly refused.

"Alright, then I'll show you how it's done." Harry gingerly sat himself down in the cart, legs dangling over the sides. "Mush" became "Giddyap," then "run, you bastards," finally a jumble of lewd imprecations. Nothing happened. Harry smiled at his dogs and they appeared to grin back.

"I had them pulling before you came," he said to Israel. "It looks as if they want you. Get in. Try to make them pull."

Israel was steadfast in refusal. His demeanor was that of a professor who perceived a student error so ludicrous it was beneath his dignity to correct it. The dogs yelped and growled, grew ugly as they waited for some sign of leadership. The two in front, dark, powerful Huskies with bright, intelligent eyes, turned on each other, the one biting at the other's ear. Harry unwedged himself from his seat in the cart and separated the scrappers.

"Iz, this is important to me. One of these dogs is a leader, and I've got to know which one. You don't have to sit in the cart. Stand up front, hold their collars, and back up slowly with them when I get into the cart."

A gust of wind bit at Israel's face, through the clammy sweat which overcame him. Shaken by a simple request from a friend, he wondered why he felt a symptom of early shock. It was a trigger mechanism, an unexpected residue of past reactions. Adventure was a fearful stranger to him. There were horrors he vaguely recalled as a child in Germany, the severity of reactions to them, the stresses of immediate decisions with possible fatal consequences. Nearly buried in brooding darkness was the time he failed to respond to a necessity of the moment, the time his mother was killed.

Israel ran to the head of the yelping pack and commanded Harry. "Get in the cart, and when I say 'go' you yell!"

Harry scurried to obey. He shouted and Israel pulled. The dogs stood as one. With ears pricked they tuned in waves from eons of brutality and determination, reached out to the form tugging at them. Little cart wheels ground over the crusted, stalk-strewn earth. Israel could smell the breath of the dog on his right. The lead dog, red-eyed, slobbering, tense, pulled more than he should. Dr. Israel Steingut attempted to correct his course, disregarding the rest of the team. He fixed on the lead dog's eyes. Man and animal responded to each other, jerk and haul, howl and jerk, the man muttering to himself, the dog grunting between rhythmic efforts.

Progress was slow for a few feet, then the cart catapulted forward at a smooth, rapid pace for twenty yards. Israel ran backward. His foot caught on a stubble of harvested corn. He stumbled and fell. His fear was to be trampled by a horde of salivating mutts and a cart with a madman in it. It did not happen. His fear dissipated. He laughed, until he looked into the moist mouth of the lead dog hovering over his head. Bared yellow teeth darted at his throat, but Harry Pearl's cautionary scream, with Israel's innate propensity for self preservation, caused the doctor to jerk his head to the side. His right ear was nipped, and the dog had had enough. He could easily have fulfilled his natural bent and ripped open the throat of this man who assumed mastery over the pack.

That evening he told Carla how his ear was bitten by a dog. She was concerned. "Was it a deep bite?" she asked.

"No, he nicked me. I was lucky. The dog wasn't full-grown and I moved away in time."

"Perhaps you should get a rabies shot."

Israel was sullen. "Harry said he had them vaccinated."

"Well then, if there's nothing to worry about, it's a big joke; you playing Izzie of the Yukon on the grass with happy Harry Pearl." She walked to the armchair on which he slouched, sat on one side and turned her body in a graceful half twist. She patted his cheek.

"You always get into trouble with dogs. Perhaps the animal senses your fear. Are you afraid of them?"

Israel turned his head from her. Carla was twenty years his junior, and she looked it, dressed in close-fitting jeans and a coral blouse. She had reached the limits of her capabilities as a nurse, and deemed it her privilege to ease his moods with simplistic analyses. His voice was low at first, nearly a monotone.

"To you, everything is funny. Of course it was a trivial incident, though I could have had my neck ripped open. I don't know why I was so upset, but there are reasons you make no effort to understand. I actually was enjoying myself. We got the damned cart going, and that husky was *mine* working for *me*. I might have made it all the way. There was a sense of freedom; no obstruction. I had the beast working for me. Then I fell. I lost control. It's always 'nearly' with me. When am I going to go all the way, not nearly?"

Carla's feet were spread, her hands on her hips. She pursed her lips, the chastising mother-figure, the liberated mother of the seventies, quiche and baked Idahoes for dinner and a whirl in the discos at night. His moods of self-chastisement would not be tolerated. Worry feeds on itself with insatiable appetite. This she knew with certainty. Causes, reason, logic, were not her concern, and she was not about to be drawn into a confrontation of wits or a subtle explication of his chronic problems.

"I don't understand you," she said. "It's mountains out of molehills again. Sure you had a lousy childhood. So what! Lots of people grew up with misery. Somewhere, somehow, they find the strength to break out of it." She softened, purred, "Iz, I'm on your side. Let's wait till something big comes along. Then you can worry!"

Israel's hands reached to her shoulders. He squeezed gently, a signal, a recognition of the part she played in his life; acquiescence to the effectiveness of the berating he needed. Climbing the stairway to the attic bedroom, he would sleep alone tonight. The third step creaked. It would be fixed when he had time, but he had said that for months. He undressed, removed his undershirt and left his shorts on. He was sensitive to the binding pressure of pajamas. He could not sleep in clothes, except for his shorts, fearing his genitals might rub on the sheets.

Old, crusted thoughts whirled about him, brittle thoughts which crumbled when he sought to fit them into some sense of unity. He was not asleep, could not sleep. The image of a dog, a German dog, appeared before him, its head rising and falling on a bed of leaves, rhythmic with the shutter action of his eyelids as he tried to doze. Dogs were to be loved, to return love; their eyes spoke as eloquently as any human tongue. Only a few could not tune into the pitch of nature's resonance, and Israel felt he was one of them.

Chapter 2

HE REMEMBERED WHEN he graduated from medical school and completed his residency at a hospital in the capital of New York State. Having had two years of surgical training in addition to a rotating internship which exposed him to multiple specialties, he decided to enter general practice; and since he was judged competent by his peers, he could perform ordinary surgery, the appendixes and hernias that came his way. He told himself he would be broad in outlook, diversified, non-elitist. Funds were limited, but sufficient for a modest start. For his office he chose a busy street with a long line of industrial plants on one side, with one-story frame dwellings of workers opposite. Here he could minister to industrial accident emergencies and could care for the families of blue-collar workers. It would be a practice replete with ideals, to stand beside the struggling poor and to satisfy his yearning to use his skills.

One run-down, drab gray frame house displayed a vacancy sign for its ground floor. Wafer-sized pieces of old paint dotted the cracked cement steps leading to its wood porch. There was no rail or banister, which would make entrance difficult for the frail and elderly, or for those with crutches. However, Israel considered that most of his work would be with the young, whose chief injuries would be in hands and wrists, parts exposed to the presses and tooling machines grinding away across the road.

The three rooms available would be ample to display his willingness and expertise before a needy public. A large front room would be his waiting room; behind it were two smaller square spaces, one for the examining room, the other to be furnished with a bed and arm chair. Kitchen and bath were closet-size, partitioned off corners of the waiting room. No provisions were made for business office, secretary, storage of files — all would be provided in due time once that first flow of patients formed a nucleus which would spread the word that the new doctor on the street would make every effort for them, would place his head and heart, his consummate skill and standards at their disposal. The business part of medicine was abhorrent to him. Madison Avenue techniques to entice clients, walnut panels and cordovan leather chairs, beaming secretaries who implied busy, busy, a good man is hard to get — these had no part in Dr. Steingut's message to his brethren. His style would be that of a sermon on the mount, simple truths adroitly put, honest appraisals impacting with the cold logic of Newtonian physics.

Israel moved on a bright Sunday afternoon, when his neighbors, or patients-to-be, had eaten their holiday dinners and were taking their usual week-end strolls. The air was clear of smoke and grime. Men wore suits. Wives swathed themselves in bright gingham patterns, a diminutive Easter parade. The moving men Israel hired were hospital technicians with a rented pick-up for spare time jobs. The words "You buy, We'll try" were stenciled on the side of the truck, above "Deliveries — Furniture, Foods, Fuel." As the portage of used paraphernalia commenced, a throng of onlookers lined the entrance to the new doctor's office. An iron-framed bed with a thick lumpy mattress, a cocoa-colored arm chair with large faded stains on its seat, old examination and treatment tables were unloaded. Six new straight-backed wood chairs for the waiting room radiated a hope of sparkle and freshness, quickly dashed by the delivery of three tarnished brass lamps and a series of cardboard boxes tied with clothesline.

Dr. Steingut stuck a stack of cards with name and office hours in a corner of a front window sill. Three advertisements permitted by the county medical society were placed in a local newspaper. The doctor waited. It appeared that important news traveled slowly. For an entire week Israel was the sole occupant of his waiting room. There was no income, and the mail consisted of bills interspersed with brochures with explicit instructions on how to become rich via bank savings plans, insurance programs, and oil drilling ventures. The church around the corner sent "save thy soul" pamphlets.

Israel's soul was appallingly threadbare. Rejuvenescence could come only by way of a sick or injured patient who could make a cash payment. On the eighth day, doomsday, apocalypse, when pangs of revelation whispered "give up, get a salaried job," Israel heard a familiar crackling sound on his front steps. It was the loose chunk of cement which rattled when the mailman came, though this was long after delivery time. Now the clatter was welcomed. A man entered. It could be determined by cursory inspection that he was a bum. Unshaven, unkempt hair with copious dandruff fallen onto a soiled plaid sports jacket; a fringe of padding poked out of a tear in the armpit; a bare big toe peeked from a sodden shoe that had once been committed to honest labor. From his torn sleeves, sooted hands with irregularly chewed nails protruded for Dr. Steingut's inspection, like a prayer for help from one who had long since lost touch with the spiritual world.

The bum's voice was tremulous. His limbs shook in alcoholic frustration. He said, "Can you take care of this? I went to the hospital but they didn't seem to want to get to me." He paused, and added, "I will pay you."

Israel thought, "Please don't lie. The whole world is lying to me. You're a bum, but you're my first patient. Let not my first patient deceive me." He said, "Let's have a look." There was little to do medically. It was one of those cases which looked deceptively alarming. He had cut the palm of his hand in a bar. Encrusted blood which had seeped over his fingers proved too ugly for his sensibility. He had little beauty to show, and could not bear its diminution. The hand was washed, sewn and bandaged, quickly and professionally, with an accompaniment of reassurance from Israel which echoed his gratitude for this his initial patient.

"I can't pay you much," the man said. He repeated the statement. Then, without further inquiry into aftercare, he slapped a twenty dollar bill on the examining table, and weaved out with the air of a drunk resolved to advertise his dignity.

Steingut shouted, "That's too much," but his patient did not turn back. To Israel this was indication, proof, that starting his practice here and now was the right decision. Volume would build up gradually, now that the word was out. Besides, thought Israel, who could guess this unfortunate creature could pay a bill? Adversity, poverty, were but outer garments....

A few desperate souls graced the waiting room thereafter. Not enough to make expenses. Insufficient to test the facts, theories, and techniques crammed into himself after years of study. Stuffed with intellectual tid-bits like a goose with nowhere to go but the chopping block. He had seen medical offices which were hives of activity, where appointments were doled out only after the bill was paid. He would hold on, give it time. There was always the consolation that the little he had done, the dozen or so patients he had seen the past month, had done well. The abstract meaning of the word "reputation," bandied about at every medical gathering, was now more solid to Israel. Reputation, that was what he must develop. Like a fine violin, he required maturation to broadcast his tune.

A good reputation may be undeserved, and a poor one may attach itself to the innocent like a wart. Israel was in neither category. He felt he was in a vacuum into which a gentle breeze occasionally intruded. What he did not realize was the attitude of the poor toward their doctors. Expensive furniture, fashionable dress, cheerful secretaries may invite envy, but it is envy encased in respect. Somewhere in every patient hides the sentiment, "he must be successful if I am to trust myself to him; I don't know enough to judge success in depth; I can only determine it by his person, in his waiting room; give me half the chance to earn what he does and I will look as he does; as no doubt I will someday when I make my bundle!" Israel's ruminations in the realm of reputation embraced sincerity, skill, and perseverance. He failed to include flair, dazzle, and old-style salesmanship.

The final downfall of his venture into private practice had nothing to do with human failure. Two doors away lived a dog, large, long-haired, and slavering. The beast was always hungry. Ribs showed beneath stretched skin, fangs ready to eat anything dead or alive. Every afternoon, at one o'clock, when Israel's office was officially opened to welcome newcomers, the dog loped to Dr. Steingut's front steps, deposited a huge beef bone, and proceeded to gnaw at it furiously. When Israel tried to chase him with shouts and foot-stomping, there followed a spirited leap of two masses of flesh, one forward and one back. The gnawing continued for a half hour, and the splintered bone was left for Israel to remove, an act long delayed by the fear of the intruder lurking nearby.

Persistent, repetitive insults must be stopped or accepted. Israel could not deter the aggressor. Essence of camphor, drops of foul tasting medicine, insect sprays, were deposited on his steps. But he had to quit such distractions as he had to choose between their deterrent effects on the dog and his prospective patients. In a moment of enlightened decision, Israel chose acceptance of his lot. He would not look out of his windows after one o'clock. The scene was blocked from his consciousness.

When he resolved to sell his furniture and look for a salaried job, he had one consolation: A transgression of nature had driven him away, and no scientific skill or power on earth could conquer a cataclysm of nature. His defeat was not his fault. Mysterious forces hung in the air, and if they chose Israel Steingut to fall upon, it made no sense to fight too hard; there is a phase of exhaustion from which one cannot return. His strength lay in permitting his stamina to disintegrate in decreasing increments, so there was always a minimum left to call upon. Israel could let his spring unwind to the last turn, but there had always been sufficient tension to recoup his resilience.

Chapter 3

CARLA DROVE TWELVE miles to her hospital on narrow roads with poorly marked white lines, past flat acres of corn and beans, a sea of harvested fields here and there broken by groveling pigs or a herd of black Angus cattle. Peace. Tranquility. Boredom. Vigorous scenes, urban activity, frenetic action irritated her. Her dreams of adventure were quiet ones, pleasant, of suave, masculine men, restaurants with crystal chandeliers, uniformed doormen admitting jovial patrons to dignified gambling establishments. Often she had to cut short her reveries before she fell from their soaring clouds. She had learned to make peace with what she had; a meaningful job, a safe and comfortable home, the table vegetables she grew, and for aesthetic appreciation some of the most luxurious roses in the county; and yes, a husband. He had obvious faults, but on the whole he, too, was a safe and comfortable factor on her list for living well in Iowa.

When she had reached sixteen she decided to skip college. Standing about middle of her high school class in grades, she knew she would do best in practical matters. Nursing would be her career.

"Daddy," she said, "I want to go to County Hospital for the fall term in nursing school."

Her father was tired and irritated after a wrestling match with a sow that was about to bite the hind end off one of its litter.

"You're a bushel of surprises," he said. "Where in heaven's name did you get that idea?"

"I told you about my plans a month ago, and I've thought of it for longer than that."

"I don't have the time to listen to chit-chat. You are a handsome young woman and there are plenty of boys, farm boys. You might give them some attention. Maybe not now, but soon, you will be married and raise a family."

"Is it the money, Dad? I've saved enough for a year."

"It's not that." He looked at her as if he wished to make a serious point. "You are different from the women in the family. At least I think so. Nursing's fine, a help, but there are other ways of helping. I need help. Mother needs help; and we know you are dependable. The best you can do for your family is to stay on the farm. Later, God willing, you'll have your own place and your own chores to do."

It was twilight, and Carla heard the reverberation of animal groans. A beagle in the next field bayed. Ever returning crickets she knew from infancy sang to her through the shadows. She imagined their voices soothing yet commanding, a constant call to a bolder future. She promised, "You know I won't run off when you need me, Dad. I will do what I want, however. I will help you, but as you say, I am different from other women in the family."

She worked on the farm, in a dry goods store, sold kitchen gadgets, baby-sat in town. When she graduated, her father and mother, faces scrubbed shiny, in new clothes, were proud of their daughter's matriculation into nursing school. Daddy left her that afternoon with a scrap of parting encouragement.

"I'm happy you got through high school. I expected you would. If you don't make it on your own you can come home to the farm. We will have something for you to do, and you might even like it. The world out there is cruel, so don't expect too much."

The road she drove to the hospital widened to a small stretch of four-lane highway with a grassy median strip and a pretentious display of busy traffic. This was a small town, with its hospital sitting on a quiet fringe of land which posed as a suburb. She thought of her father's double-edged good wishes, wanted to speed ahead and bang down on the brakes to stop. Instead, obeying posted hospital rules, she slowed to the required ten miles per hour and parked a few steps from the hospital entrance. Parking was never a problem. If it were really busy here, she thought, there still would be no problem. A five-acre tract of unused farm land lay across the curbing which edged the parking lot.

The hospital was sumptuously appointed for a two-hundred-and-fifty bed institution. Wide tile-floored halls were amply heated or air conditioned, with an ambience of country quiet which belied the pain and suffering residing behind thick walnut doors of spacious single rooms. Only in the emergency room, where she was presently assigned, was there an indication of pressured activity.

Several men and women, rough-hewn farm types, and one gentlemanly looking patient with tie and jacket sat on magenta-cushioned chairs with chrome legs. A cart exposed in one of the cubicles which bordered the room, curtains open, was surrounded by nurses and doctors. The apparent cardiac failure under treatment had raised his head and shoulders, frantically gulping in air which was far too rarified to lighten the plum-colored skin of his face and neck. Veins stood out on his arms, full and tense, bloated as strung-out sausages. Carla pulled off her suede jacket and rushed to help with an oxygen mask. She quickly readied a nasal tube for insertion, checked the machine beside the cart, and twisted various knobs to assure the fitness and capacity of the device should this heart require electrical stimulation.

As the situation stabilized, intravenous medication running, oxygen entering cells almost too sluggish to accept it, the patient's head capitulated, fell back onto its flat pillowed resting place. His cheeks lightened. Breath sounds were less raucous, still rapid but in and out with pleasing rhythm. Everyone about the cart relaxed. Tensed shoulders dropped. Grim tightened lips loosened. One resident who had been particularly unstrung laughed nervously as the damp pallor about his nose disappeared.

He said to Carla, "I don't know what it is, but these cardiacs get to me. I've seen hundreds, but it makes no difference." There was a tinge of accent in his meticulously pronounced phrases, slightly Hispanic, the accent of education affordable by the wealthy of Central or South America.

Carla nodded in understanding. "I know. I get the same feeling. With me its mostly at surgery."

He continued. "Since I am a medical resident, I don't see much surgery. There is more action around some of these heart cases than you find at the operating table."

"I don't know about that," Carla said as she lingered over past experiences when she wished her hands and feet could fly in opposite directions to untangle the confusion of rapid-fire orders from an irate surgeon. "I suppose it's upsetting if you can't get used to it. How long have you been here, doctor?"

They stood in a quiet corner. Emergency-room turmoil had cooled to a normal slow pace. Shaded lights subdued the atmosphere of the room, more like a library, with carts to lie on while reading. The emergency quarters were pleasant, unlike the big-city casualty room where stillness meant disaster.

The resident she had spoken to seemed a relaxed type, not one of those who demanded violent action in the casualty rooms. At lunch on the cafeteria line she saw him four or five places behind her. She surprised herself as she heaped her tray with two portions of Salisbury steak, a mound of mashed potatoes with a puddle of gravy in its center, boiled green beans, and two corn muffins. She placed her tray on a table beside a glassed wall overlooking the lawn, and turned her profile partly toward the serving line. When he had picked up his food he walked to her table.

"May I sit with you, Señorita?" he whispered into her ear. He guessed she might be married, but there was no harm in friendship. He knew women here were complimented by a romantic touch. Had he made the remark in New York or Chicago he might have been brushed off. Carla suffered from more decorum, or inhibition, than to let him know she understood his intent and tone, his subtle parries designed to entice her into a sexually weighted sparring match.

She responded, "Take a chair and sit." She giggled. There was so much food on her tray (and food must not be wasted) that she had less opportunity to talk than he.

He relaxed. His conversation was facile and Carla was a good listener.

The farm in Argentina on which he was born was nothing more than a great expanse of scrub and grass upon which his family raised bulls. The hope of course, was that Luís Perrigo, with whom she now sat beside a cornfield in Iowa, would be a matador. He tried, but his description of his tender feelings for animals, humanity—especially women—soon convinced his mother he was slated for a gentler role.

Carla interrupted, "Is that why you don't like surgery? I've seen pictures where bullfighters stick the animal in the neck. I don't think I care for that myself."

"You have discovered the reason, exactly," he said. "You are very perceptive."

After he had recited a litany of adventure in three continents and five states, she said, "My God, when did you settle down and learn medicine?"

He stood for a moment; lean, tall, jet black hair, brown eyes gleaming.

"I worked hard. I was a conscientious student."

"What did you do after medical school?"

"I worked in a psychiatric hospital and hated every minute of it."

"Are you going home to practice in Argentina?"

"Many times have I thought of it. Believe me, there is much opportunity for someone with my experience. But no. For the present I shall complete my training and practice in a town that needs me."

Carla knew that he must be older than she, perhaps in his mid-thirties, though he appeared younger, dashingly boyish were it not for the suave, cool rigidity he projected. Balancing what he said against what he was, a resident in an unapproved program of a small hospital, she guessed there were difficulties he had not touched upon.

"Why don't you go back to Argentina?" she asked.

"Because this country is training me so I wish to repay it by using my skills here."

"You could use your skills in some needy rural area in Argentina," she said demurely.

"There is no money there," he responded abruptly. "I could starve.

Besides, I did not get along with my family, my mother and father."

"Ha!" Carla thought. " so that's it. Even if he is telling half the truth, it's nice to know his problems relate to money and family like most American men, or men everywhere."

The lunch over, they separated, he to make rounds with one of the staff physicians, she to cover the emergency room. It was a dull afternoon, a few cuts, a sore throat, the usual knee and ankle sprains; dull, if excitement is the goal. Carla required no such perverse stimulation. To comfort the unglamorous patients of her daily routine was sufficient reward. Leaving the hospital that afternoon she hummed a bouncy refrain from a new record she had heard as she wheeled a patient into his room.

> Don't stew baby cause I'll fry your hide,
> Relax baby and I'll make the bread,
> Stay nice baby, I'll keep you cookin'
> You got one job, baby, to stay good lookin'

It was a ditty which she would ordinarily discard. Now it lifted her spirit. Rather it was in tune with her spirit, a surprising effect considering her distaste for the blaring crass music she heard during the day. At home with Israel it was Mozart or Brahms, Haydn when she wanted to doze. Though he did not object to a romantic refrain when he wanted to make love, he never could accept the pounding beat of rock music. Sometimes, she thought, wild piercing music, repetitive and loud, would be good for them to hear; basic, like breaking hardscrabble soil with a pickaxe.

The lyric was sung to Israel that evening as she prepared supper. He snorted, coughed, spat out the morsel of roast beef he had snatched to taste.

"Why bother to remember such a silly, vulgar song?" he asked.

"It's amusing. You should enjoy it. After all, it's about a man putting a woman in her place, isn't it?"

"It's coarse. The same message can be conveyed in a genteel way."

She caressed him. "Israel, try not to analyse to death what doesn't matter. You're gentle, and good to me. You don't push me around, or I would have hollered. Maybe you should step on me just a little, to show me who is boss."

Israel melted into a broad grin. He agreed that a man should project his superiority, but he was aware of an element of risk in doing so. She would not recline and beg to be kicked. She would fight back with the prodigious strengths she possessed, to protect her womanhood. Not much could displease her, for at rock bottom she was a survivor, just as he was in his pseudo-neurotic way. Her burdens were eased out of her consciousness with laughter, whereas he whined till the devils that beset him were exorcised. Both got through their foggy days though they utilized different paths.

Normally, when they coped with cheerlessness or were locked in argument Carla's ingenuous skills bridged the gap between them. Her subtle weapons were repression of sharp points of discussion, light-heartedness touching on facile humor; and if heavy artillery had to be directed toward their energies, seductive tickling of Israel's arms and neck was the signal for a pow-wow, lying down, in bed.

She held his hand and led him up the short flight of painted steps to their bedroom. Both floated about the room as they undressed, anticipating more than they knew would happen. Past experience had accustomed them to a mundane perspective toward sex, though they had read the books, seen the pictures, and were familiar with the possibilities. An element of blandness dulled their activity. There was little petting, stroking, massaging, foreplay. In their daily activities they had seen all the cavities and projections of the body ad nauseum, in exhilarating displays of perfection, in doddering decrepitude, in health and sickness, brown bulbous vaginal warts and flame-red penises too angry to let urine through a swollen exit. As both were fortunate to own healthy organs, they agreed not to waste time with them. No preparatory piddling moves were necessary, no meaningless stoking of fires. Get to work. Attack the project at hand quickly, at the acme of its intensity.

Israel was unclothed, lying down, yet Carla remained standing in her slip.

"The sheets are soft and smooth," he said.

"Not yet," said Carla. "Come, stand up and hold me."

Israel had noted this act of procrastination once before, after they had attended the Chicago Symphony and drained a bottle of wine sent to a cool hotel room one steamy summer night.

"Is anything the matter?" Israel asked.

"No, but I don't want to go at it like some animal on the farm." She amazed herself by her reply. Israel could become accustomed to sex prolonged, or shot out of a cannon, whichever pleased her. In all his enterprises he enjoyed the pithy center of accomplishment, the immediate visible result, whether it was the gleam of leather after he polished his shoes, or the removal of a segment of gangrenous gut from its otherwise healthy environs.

She too accepted her coital pleasure somewhat truncated and unadorned. Graceful and alluring without flaunting her gifts, a woman who could pose for a modernized version of the Kama Sutra, she despised the lewd staring, the buttock tapping, the unsubtle solicitations which were a daily accompaniment of life in and out of the hospital. Stolid and secure enough to enjoy her physical prowess, she eschewed the erotic padding ascribed to a femme fatale. Practicality was her motto, even in the pursuit of pleasure. Indeed, down-to-earth methods were best, without unnecessary frills to dilute the goal sought.

Israel was coy. "You are different, a changed woman." Then, more seriously, "Hell, Carla, I'm getting too old for boyish preliminaries. I thought you were satisfied. You were always the one who couldn't wait. Me, I could have waited, if you wanted it that way."

Carla agreed, though she remained silent. Tonight, however, she pictured the pampas, leather-legged horsemen shouting orders in mellifluous Spanish, a tall gentleman with a honeyed voice kissing her hand. She was in the midst of a shifting field of moods which progressed from languor, to quiver, to uncontrolled eruption.

Carla removed her slip. They were in close embrace, all shame gone, forgetting what had been, immersed only in the present. It was as if they were old hands at the gentle, seductive appurtenances for making love. Israel pulled her to the edge of the bed, sat for a time, then reclined with her. Both struggled for control within themselves, prolonged the intensity of their reactions to that end of desperate passion which could be rewarded with sublime success, or with premature failure. Israel's turgid flesh, wet-tipped in the pain of frustrated craving, probed for its resting place, frantically groped for envelopment. This love, this playing about the edges of love, might have been the rebirth of their relationship.

The phone rang. Israel's thigh muscles tensed for a moment and relaxed, went limp. He grasped the end of his penis to contain a token of ejaculation. As Carla groaned and sat up, he raised the receiver. There had been but one ring, and the caller must have thought the doctor diligent, resting with the phone at his side while burdened with the agony the conscientious physician must suffer for the grief of his patients. Israel might have waited for two, three, or four rings, or left the phone unanswered. Impossible. Years of reflex stirring, ring to ear and hand to phone, were not to be erased by the far less frequent reflex of hand to skin to brain to penis. Had he made an effort and waited before answering there would be time to think, "should I or shouldn't I?" Of course it all would have ended with "I should," though choice of work over pleasure would be delayed by indecision.

"Is this Mrs. Vorcek?" He knew it was by the whine.

"I hate to bother you this time of night, good doctor, but I am in trouble." She always addressed him as "good doctor" as if to immediately subjugate any hostility he might develop against her. "My leg is killing me."

"Did you use warm packs and elevation as I instructed?" Israel asked.

"Last time it did not work. I happen to know that only a shot will work."

"You shouldn't be getting shots, Mrs. Vorcek. It's a simple spasm, and we've been through this half a dozen times."

"Good doctor, would you want me to suffer all night?" Only Israel could have understood her through the crescendo of sighing whimpers.

Israel muttered to Carla, his hand over the receiver, "She asks if I want her to suffer. She really should suffer. Doesn't do a damn thing I tell her."

"I will be there soon, Mrs. Vorcek. Try to relax." The whine disappeared. She said, "Thank you." She had won her skirmish.

Carla sat naked on the bed, her slender ankles firmly pressed against bed rails, elbows on thighs and head cupped in her hands. "Why, oh why do you have to go? I wouldn't mind, but that one is a crock. She knows how to take the whip to you whenever she feels the urge."

"Had I turned her down I would not sleep afterwards, nor do anything else."

"Israel, she is sixty years old, with arteriosclerosis. She does yoga all day, which you told her not to do. She gets cramps when she imagines herself a ballet dancer and stands on her toes for an hour. I would get worse pains than she does. You're entitled to your rest, enjoyment. You owe it to me. Besides, wouldn't she get relief from hot packs and elevation?"

"Sure," said Israel, "but she won't. I can't let her suffer."

"Then you will give her a shot, and another, and more after that. You will get her hooked."

Israel laughed as he dressed. "It's my little secret, Carla. I give her a diluted dose of a non-narcotic. Sometimes I use plain saline. What she craves is attention."

As Israel went down the stairs, black leather bag in hand, Carla shouted, "Why in hell can't you save some of that attention for me!"

She reclined with a sheet over her and tried to doze. Her hands were at her breasts. Intermittently she swept at her nipples with an index finger. Her breasts became mounds, hills dotting a vast expanse of land. Turning, she felt her nipples pressed on the sheet, hills of breasts on a field that stretched to the horizon, a rough field of Iowa corn. She slept. When Israel returned and lay down beside her, she rolled away from him without waking.

Chapter 4

CARLA DROVE TO work next morning a free soul. Never had she considered she was shackled to her past, to her parents, the farm, to Israel. Now freedom was more complete in that it was coupled with a reaching-out to experiment, a tingle of longing. The sensation was not unpleasant as there were no pressures to relieve. She thought she must project herself into her future, into her surroundings and the green fields about her, into the hospital where adventure must surely be waiting ready to spring upon her, or she upon it. The stiff wind that hit her face through the open car window carried a hint of danger with its bite. Good. Danger and fun. What a young woman has to seek and wrestle with once in her life. She had carried on her lithe shoulders the saints of primness and prudery to ward off young devils. Now the devil wore an engaging smile. As she drove into the hospital's parking area it was not until she turned off the radio that she first noticed she was tapping her toes and smacking her thighs together to accompany the song she had just heard.

Luís Ferrigo did not have to seek out Carla in the cafeteria. She seated herself at his table, where he now ate rapidly, not with the dainty casual motions of a Latin American gentleman, but with the gusto of a peasant whose meals were not always this bountiful.

Carla thought, "He's himself now." She sat down without prelimary remarks, stared at him a moment as if to telegraph her forthright disposition, and ate lunch with as much gusto as he.

Luís tipped his cup to drain its last dregs. "I want you to forget our last meeting. When I left you I realized I was childish, a fool. You are intelligent and cannot be taken in by a show of sophistication. I don't know why I do such things. Perhaps it is because I had nothing in Argentina. Beans on the table. Toilet outdoors. Dirt on my hands, always dirty hands. I got through medical school only because a rich relative took me in hand and pushed me. I wanted you to know."

Carla was suspicious of his poignant confession. Was it another line thrown at her? Or a reverse shock treatment to topple the barriers she might erect against him? The thought was dismissed; she was not accustomed to dissect an idea which might end in her own frustration.

Israel did that, and no good came of it. Sudden impressions, face values, were her best gauge of truth and beauty.

"Luís, forget it. Playing games may be okay for a while, but it soon shows. Besides, there may be more truth than you know in what you thought was phony." She had attended early sessions of a great books course and was so disgruntled with debates over what was real and unreal that she knew there could never be any finality to such argument. She knew a problem existed, though no one appeared to have solved it.

As Luís left her he said, "I would like you to visit my apartment."

Carla cooked a dinner for Israel which was planned as fastidiously as a French chef trying for another star on his Michelin rating. She made moussaka. When he was steeped in gloom, when he was manic with elation which would soon drop precipitously as an anchor, a finely prepared dish of Greek food could settle him. The Greeks know how to live, he said. Moussaka and wine was a ploy with which she could manage him. She approached his mood through his stomach rather than his intellect, and she found it amusing.

The portion of food before him was browned and deliciously moist. She had worked hard, sent for ingredients, fussed in a frenzy of inspiration. Israel speared a corner of crusted meat with his fork, rolled it about on his tongue, and grinned. It was a fixed grin, as though frozen on a plaster sculpture, gone only after he sipped his wine. Carla watched him; he was a baby tasting his first spoonful of ice cream.

Then he threw his fork on the table. His lower lip drooped. "I forgot something. I am sorry, truly sorry."

"What did you forget?"

"Mr. Kramer, the hernia operation I did yesterday, is running a temperature. The floor nurse called me about it this afternoon and I completely forgot to check it out."

"How much of a temperature?"

"About one hundred and one."

"But Israel," she said, "a temp of 101, or even 102, isn't unusual this soon after surgery. Even I know that. Was there anything else important about the case?"

"No, just the temp."

"It will be gone by tomorrow. If not, that's the time to do something active. To push antibiotics now is too early. God, it's only the first post-op day."

"You don't have to coach me in handling surgical cases. I know all that, but I couldn't eat if I did not see him."

"None of the other surgeons would see him at this stage."

"They are not as conscientious as I." He stood with jacket buttoned about to open the door when he turned back to the table and still standing, nibbled a loose segment of moussaka. It was his parting apology for her unrewarded effort. "I can't help it," he mumbled as he left.

Carla gripped the table. Of course he could help it. All he had to do was acquaint himself with his strengths, rid himself of doubts which made him run like a rabbit at the slightest sound. She lifted the cover of the ceramic serving dish, placed an oversized portion of the lamb and pasta on her dish and ate with abandon. The remainder, elegant, savory beyond her culinary expectations, she tossed into the garbage. She left a note for Israel that she was going out for a few hours, that he could have a salad and yesterday's cold roast beef when he returned. Carla dressed, taking pains with the application of lipstick and powder, new brands which promised on their labels an iridescent allure for the exotic woman.

Luís lived on the upper floor of a two-story stucco house converted to small apartments. Massive trees on the street shaded old, neatly painted houses. When Carla climbed a flight of nylon carpeted stairs, Luís awaited her at a partly opened door with extended arms. She grasped his hand hesitantly. The living room was eye-catching. A small bright Oriental rug was bordered with voluminous floor pillows, an orange striped armchair, a cream sofa, two large pre-Columbian figures, male and female with obviously exaggerated anatomical parts, graced the far corner of the room. Carla particularly noted the curved foot-long projection that hung from the abdomen of the male sculpture and wondered whether Luís was a devotee of the arts, or a pimp with aesthetic longings.

He said, "It isn't what you think... It's a Mexican reproduction of an antique. What you see is a third foot which acts as a tripod to steady the figure. You can see the other figure, the lady, has a separate base and is quite stable."

Luís poured himself a glass of créme de menthe as Carla sat on the sofa sipping white wine. He sat on an oversized pillow at her feet, in a blue smoking jacket punctuated with black dots, recalling to her a *Playboy* photo of a Hugh Hefner advertisement.

"Are you unhappy?" he asked.

"Why, what do you mean?"

"When you called and said you would come to my apartment, I thought something must have driven you to it. That is not the best way. I would rather have you happy."

"Don't worry about the state of my mental health. I came because I felt like it, though I've never done anything like this before."

"I assume your husband would object if he knew, unless he is an understanding European."

"I don't intend that Israel know; and if he did I never found his objection persistent."

"Israel? He's a Jew?"

"Yes, of a sort."

"We have quite a few in our South American cities. They are said to be clever, and strong willed, but it really isn't so. They won't fight for their rights, I mean fight."

Familiar with the general cross-currents of American racial and religious slurs, Carla was surprised at their apparent international pervasiveness. The individual was the message for her, his or her personal qualities, and not obtuse rumors or sly innuendo. She had always walked away from gossip. To defend Israel, however, was inappropriate at the moment. She had come of her own free will, in close contact with a near stranger who would no doubt take her to bed, which she was willing to accept, just once.

An hour passed filled with banter of art and cars (Luís was partial to Ferrari engines), with interjections by Carla of hospital, crop failure, or women's lib. Her glass of white wine was replenished twice. She was not heady, or tired, but pleasantly buoyant. If ever she had suffered from restrictive social covenants, they had dissolved away. If the vigor and audacity of rejuvenated womanhood were to be asserted, this was the time. She expected he would reach forward from his position on the floor and touch her ankle, but contact occurred only when he inadvertently toppled forward and brushed her leg with his elbow. He hurriedly said "Pardon me, I didn't mean to." As the conversation droned on she felt herself a teacher with a respectful student at her feet. Carla was uncomfortable with this image, more so during a one-shot fling where tenure was not an objective.

"Are you gay?" She spoke as if she were asking for the time.

He tossed his head back and roared with laughter. "Never, never have I been suspected of that. No. I love women."

"Then what about me?" She was as artless as a rejected hooker.

His ears reddened as he spoke, "In my country men do not jump on a woman. We do not want to frighten her. We are civilized, not so temperamental as you think." His voice quavered. He grew more excited and sardonic. He spoke sharply. "You call us Latin lovers, as if we went about pinching bottoms and pulling women down to rape them. We are not like that at all. We are gentlemen."

Carla was cognizant of fright in men, explosive men who attempted to make a sham of their defensiveness. She knew he was not gay. Just too scared when a good looking woman puts her cards on the table. She said, "Luís, be quiet!" She helped him from the floor, and when he was upright she embraced him and kissed his forehead. Lips parted, head held immobile, she waited. No reaction, no attack, no move on his part, no quick tricky passes to her breasts or thighs.

"Christ," she thought. "Iz couldn't be this backward."

Luís tried to explain. He was sorry. This meeting was to have been a novel adventure for him. His childhood had been saturated with sexual myths. Beware the woman who is too direct, they are prostitutes. Surely medical training should have liberated him. Carla listened and understood, but was not touched. If he needed a psychiatrist she could not substitute for one. She had her own problems.

In her car she shifted into reverse, then quickly forward to correct her mistake. The crust of composure with which she warded off disappointment had been pierced. An unfamiliar element of shame, unknown since childhood, gnawed at her. Her freedom, her immunity from self-punishment were threatened. What to tell Israel posed a problem of unusual dimensions, as she had never felt she had to mull over thoughts, concepts, or experiences before unloading them before her husband. The answer was simple. If her evening's activity might irritate him, she would withhold it. If it appeared he would glean more insight into her longings, she would recount step by step how, why, and wherefore, and allow their combined judgements to fuse to an understanding.

As she drove through vibrating shadows of hanging branches, her imagination took over. She might enter her home, suffused with its odor of Greek cooking, to find Israel ruddy-faced, standing in defiance waving his arms.

He might say, "I had cold roast beef, cold and nearly spoiled, while you gorged on a delicious meal before going out to enjoy yourself. Where did you go tonight?"

She might reply, "Out, just out."

He could press on, "The explanation is a poor one and no excuse for the truth. Out, without qualification, is an admission of having done something you wish to hide."

"I'm sorry, Israel," she might offer, "but I thought you knew me better."

"Then you have done nothing you're ashamed of?"

"Of course not. I was lonely and dissatisfied, also unsatisfied. You must realize you have used me as your personal doormat."

"I interfered with you! I stepped on you!" he would say, obviously denying such insinuations.

"Not exactly. You haven't the guts to step on anyone. It's what you don't do that makes me furious."

In her fanciful confrontation she watches Israel throw over a lamp, rage, approach her with ferocious hostility. "You have been with another man. I can tell it in your oh so sweet face."

"Yes, I have been with someone, but nothing happened. I hoped it would. I tried to make it happen."

Twisted with jealousy, activated by frustration in the invasion of his home fires and the defilement of his promised faithful wife, Israel might kick her shin with the bulbous toe of the army surplus shoe he wore when he walked in the fields.

As she dropped to the floor he might say, "Did you lie down for him meekly, willingly, or did he pull you down?"

Having suffered enough indignity, she imagined she would rise and reach for a steel tennis racquet propped in the corner of the room, wave it over his head in menacing gestures of enraged self-righteousness and proclaim, "Once more, you bastard, and I'll blast you till your bones show. Yes, I went down on a soft couch with him, but nothing happened. You won't believe it, but all I got out of it was a feel here and there. That's something you should understand because it's all I get out of you. Everything you want comes before me. Maybe you care for me, but you push me aside whenever the mood strikes you. And I mean mood. Your damn weakness, your insecurity — oh I realize there are reasons for it, but you make no attempt to overcome them. I nearly got screwed tonight, and it would have served you right."

Carla shook her head free of images, of fantasy. Once at home she was herself again, collected and imperturbable as her father would be after locking the cattle safely in the barn before an expectant storm. Her imagination had worn thin. She faced the truth in a corner of the sofa, Israel with head down, staring at the rug, seeking inspiration or solace from its brightly woven figures.

He said meekly, "I am sorry about tonight, about leaving abruptly."

"Did you have your supper?"

"Yes, the roast beef. It was good of you to leave it for me."

"You didn't miss having moussaka?"

"I thought you finished it." After a pause, "I am so sorry, Carla, about leaving when I knew you wanted us to enjoy an evening together. I didn't have to go. My fears overpowered me again. I drove to the hospital like a madman, as if Mr. Kramer would die if I did not see him; as if only I could care for him. When I got there the night nurse was actually amazed because I made the trip, but I didn't put much faith in her judgment. Mr. Kramer was in a chair sipping fruit juice, happy I visited so he could tell me how marvelous he felt. Do you know what I did? I was angry because he felt so well and proceeded to tell him he had no business frightening his doctor."

Carla was fortified by his morose dependence on her, the acceptance of which she sensed to be her own weakness, which she dared not presently expose. She soothed herself by thinking she loved this stupid-smart husband, this jig-saw puzzle she had not yet put together.

Carla said, "Israel my dear, this is the first time I have heard you admit you are a mixed up bundle of nervous energy. Admission is half the battle. You are a good doctor, so good to your patients you might tear yourself apart for them. I don't know where you get the idea you are calloused if you don't jump at every nurse's report. You haven't learned to pick and choose. Sometimes you will be wrong, but that's part of the game. Confidence is what you must develop, or you will be no good to anyone."

Israel stood, his large dark eyes luminescent with tears. "I want to be good to you," he said. She embraced him as she smoothed his hair and brushed the moisture from his lids. In unison they approached the stairs, climbed, held each other tightly to the bedroom. They lay down, overawed by the deep affection which surmounts personal frailties. They made love that night, with passion.

Before they fell asleep Israel muttered to himself in the clarity of vision that precedes loss of consciousness, "No confidence. My great fault. I am upset by little nothings. I tell myself I can't help it, but I can if I can reach the cause." He saw in his memory the figure of a woman on a German farmhouse floor, bleeding. His mother it was, and she called out his boyhood name, Helmut. "I wanted her to get up but she could not and I did not help her. If I couldn't help my mother how can I help myself?" He fell asleep, screamed twice in the night, turned until the covers fell beside the bed.

Next morning he awoke bleary-eyed and drained by fatigue. He recalled Carla's indulgence in love and felt invigorated. Carla bounced about the kitchen like a school girl after her first prom. As she sliced the whole wheat health bread she bought for Israel, she thought of Luís of the pampas. The fake! Israel's impediments were real in view of a shockingly miserable childhood, but beneath it all he was all man. If only she could make him display his wealth of affection more often, for his well-being rather than for hers; if she could induce explosions of virility from self-flagellant moods she could consider their relationship successful.

Chapter 5

THE ELEGANT INVITATION, with its terse German sentences, was printed on parchment paper with flowered borders,

DR. AND MRS. STEINGUT
would be honored by your presence
to commemorate the birth
of their first-born son,
HELMUT STEINGUT
né July 6, 1933.

The address was printed on a separate, smaller card with a tiny street map for the benefit of strangers. Herr Dr. Werner Steingut never dreamed his son would some day be called Israel. In fact, he would have objected to such an appellation in his immediate family, as he was third generation German with a social life and general medical practice comprised of gentiles and a sprinkling of Jews who were at least second generation. He did not deny his Jewishness. He would point with pride to the vigor of his heritage, its scholarly leanings coupled with a relentless struggle for survival, should the issue arise in discussion. For him the Jewish stand at Masada was the epitome of heroism which refuted the slur he heard that it was an act of mass stupidity prompted by religious fanaticism. Yet he believed in a solid German name for his son, such as Helmut. One with biblical connotations, such as Israel, was too foreign, too reminiscent of Jewish ghettos and peddlers, of old men with beards playing with the knotted fringes of their prayer shawls while praying in dark corners.

Half a mile away lived a group of relatively poor Jews with whom the Steingut family had little connection. A few were Orthodox, some retained those accents which could not disguise Polish and Lithuanian origins. As a doctor, Werner did not discriminate. He had built a reputation for treating diseases of the ear, nose, and throat though he welcomed the broad afflictions which were part of general practice. Jews and gentiles sat in his waiting room where an occasional skull cap topped the head of a bearded man who studied his Hebrew Bible while awaiting examination.

During the High Holy Days, with or without his wife Isolde, Dr.

Steingut cleansed his soul at synagogue. Hebrew recitations and sermons did not interest him, as he was too analytical to subject himself to theological admonishments and predictions which he felt forced faith upon him. Yet his pride was sustained by such services. He was no descendent of Teutonic knights heavily armed on powerful horses, with finely crafted sabres, but he did come from a people who knew how to stand and fight without a display of bravado and gaudy paraphernalia. The penultimate victory lay in absorbing punishment from a superior adversary and confounding him by rising again. Once a year, sometimes twice, when he visited the synagogue, he was convinced of the persistence of the historical strength of his forebears.

On several occasions in recent months Dr. Steingut forgot his assessment of the risen Jew come back for another beating. There were rumblings in the city; young rowdies at political meetings who preached social change for the masses, the glory and wealth that belonged to the German of essence, of purity; and the hammer blows to be levelled against non-Aryan malefactors, worms at the core of the beautiful fruit that was Germany. The day of Teutonic prowess was to relive. Cut and kill for noblesse oblige. Dr. Steingut was convinced these political upstarts deserved to be struck down, slapped across their haranguing political mouths which promised terror and violence. His theological idealism was unlike that of his patient with the skull cap, oblivious to incipient inferno and shielded by the Bible.

To be half Jewish in those early days of political turmoil was more confusing than to be zealously entrenched in racial or religious beliefs. Isolde, Werner's wife, was born in Germany of Hungarian parents, her father Christian and her mother Jewish. As the spouse of a physician of local reputation, physically distinguished by his tall, muscular frame, she took care to play the role of a loving, sedate, and subservient wife. In public. At home she displayed an adroitness and temperament which fit the description by erstwhile friends of "that redheaded Hungarian flirt." On their Sunday afternoon walk after a lunch of cold meats and potato salad, they were the picture of a happy, well-to-do German couple with a black-eyed baby between them, complacent in their productivity and largesse.

Isolde was not concerned with politics, especially the Jewish question, as no religious pressures were placed upon her by Dr. Steingut. When they were married she identified as a Jewess, since her mother was of the faith, and she entered into the spirit of an occasional Jewish holiday as if it were a social occasion. The maid helped her prepare the meal with good wine and brandy and she thrived on spirited conversation of fashion and travel. To little Helmut she imparted bits of many cultures; a rousing Hungarian refrain, or a gyrating *zigue-*

ner dance executed half-nude and intently watched by her son, as well as by herself in the bedroom mirror.

Helmut was a happy baby. He was not breast fed, as his mother insisted she must keep her lithe figure as a constant reminder to her husband to be careful of his prized possession so much younger than he. The child's speech and understanding were remarkable, and he vaguely remembered in later years those days of doubt and confusion. One afternoon he lay asleep, exhausted by a morning of play, in a bedroom adjoining his parents. Werner had disappeared to attend a medical society meeting he never missed. The boy's legs ached and he awakened but did not cry. Through the partly opened door, as through a scrim of hazed memory, he recalled two forms closely pressed together, as he often was pressed to his mother. Their speech was whispered and accompanied by soft voices. Soon he could see only bare legs at the end of the bed. Toes cramped, ankles suddenly straightened rigidly, then bent again, feet intertwined like ropes on his pull toys. Noises stopped, legs relaxed, and Helmut fell asleep. At the time he had two distinct impressions, that his mother was in the next room executing an unfamiliar dance, and that some sort of playfulness was taking place, from which he was excluded. Soon he forgot faces, names, actions, left only with an embittered sense of non-participation.

Isolde needed her harmless interludes, as she termed them. Her present lover was a young, blond, mildly pot-bellied German who was Werner's accountant. Sweet and discreet, he constantly referred to his fruitful marriage and two lovely children who did so well with their music. These affairs had occurred infrequently, though they were encouraged by Dr. Steingut's oppressive primness and rigidity. "And why not," she told herself in her pert Hungarian manner, "would it be better if I fought with my husband and made everyone unhappy? I cannot solve the problem, as I do not know how to define it. If I broached the subject to Werner, he would not even try to understand."

Werner was no sexual babe-in-the-woods. He fancied his much-admired wife was the *hausfrau* type whose only ambition was to make a good home for her family. Yet she was erotic, and he enjoyed the thought. There were suspicions, but he could not sustain them with facts, only imaginitive wonderings about her head of red hair entwined with the pallid locks of some burly young Teuton. He shuddered, couldn't wait to come home to see for himself that she was there with his baby. His mind was orderly, investigative, and he would conjure up simple devices to keep her honest.

"Did you go out today?... Where?... What did you do?... Whom did you see?" All asked with a benign smile to show his sole concern was an interest in his wife's well-being. She would answer without hesitation, and he was generally placed at ease. Sometimes a tremor in her voice would set his fantasy in motion, but he would not make an issue of his true reason for inquiry. Instead, he would sharpen his tone to emphasize routine complaints she knew too well — the roast was too highly spiced, butter was warm and soft, beer left on the table uncapped, and the starch in his shirt collars irritated his neck. Werner did not consider Helmut, who listened with a child's fascination as he registered the outbursts as well as his aversion to his father.

Helmut was content in the presence of his mother. She was not the one who insisted that a four-year-old boy use his knife and fork properly, or eat pudding with a spoon when he could shove it into his mouth easily with his fingers. Nor did she insist that children were little adults. His father maintained it never was too early to instill ideals and ambitions, the winning combination which made for morality and high station when full-grown. Later, when Helmut saw his father in situations which required sharp decisions with possible serious consequences, he grew to respect him. After his outbursts, even Papa appeared satisfied, and the boy's fears ended. There was a residue of strength in his father which imparted to Helmut confidence in the basic soft-heartedness of his eruptions.

One day two Jews visited the Steingut home after the doctor's office hours. Both were dressed in average business attire, suit and topcoat, but on raising their hats, skull caps were seen nestled toward the backs of their heads. The elder, tall and thin-faced with a short black beard and spectacles, could have been a merchant or banker, except for the threadbare edges of his coat and trousers. The younger was his son, clean shaven but with long sideburns.

"Dr. Steingut," said the older man, Aaron, a leader in the local synagogue, "we come to warn you."

"I am pleased to see you," said Werner, "but I know what you are going to say. Warnings are the handmaidens of threats, and I am not one to be subjected to threats."

The younger man interceded, "Father and I have not been your patients, as we recently came from Berlin. We appreciate that you are not interested in the synagogue, but our members have been meeting and we wish to tell you that there are rumors."

"Not just rumors," said Aaron. "It's a series of events which are repetitive and progressive, as we have seen elsewhere."

"Elsewhere is not here and then is not now," replied Werner. "I appreciate your interest, but you show fear, which is exactly what they can capitalize on. Fear opens the door to them. We must resist their entrance."

"This is not possible," said Aaron, and turning to his son, he said, "Emanuel, show him."

The young man removed his coat and lifted his shirt from the rear of his trousers. On his right flank a crooked cross was crudely outlined by round pea-size scars, perhaps forty spots which obviously were old ulcerations.

Aaron said, "Emanuel prayed in Hebrew as they threatened emasculation. They wanted him to stop praying and to sing their song. He would not, so they did this with lighted cigarettes."

Isolde walked in with Helmut as Emanuel rushed to tuck his shirt into his trousers.

"No, don't," said Werner, "don't be embarrassed. I want my little boy to see this." Dr. Steingut guided his son to the exposed back with its sculptured skin, ran his fingers over the mutilated area. Helmut asked why the man grew skin blisters.

Werner said, "You had a bee sting once. It's as if this young man were bitten by many bees, except that people did it to him." Helmut recalled the most painful event he had ever suffered. His face contorted.

"Do you know what we should do about this, Helmut? If bees did it, or people, we should put them in cages, or kill them if necessary." Helmut readily agreed to a simple, logical solution.

"You do not understand," said Aaron. "There is no way you can stand up to them. We have information the terror is only beginning, and since you represent a link between the Jewish and Christian communities they will make an example of you. You are a symbol of harmony between two religions. You must leave." He spoke with emphasis.

"And why do you come to warn me, as you too are in danger should your assumptions be correct?"

"Because," said Aaron, "we know what is happening and you do not. At least you are not sufficiently aware to protect yourself. We will do what we can, get out if we can, hide if we must. We will plan, though we may not be successful. You have been good to our people and we all felt you should not be punished for it."

Werner rose and brushed a thick lock of hair from his forehead. A long thin white scar glinted in the lamplight, a neat but incomplete residue of a scalper's art. "I received this from a sabre in the war, and I have the medal that goes with it." His face reddened. "If I must fight, I will. You should leave, save yourselves, as you have not been trained to do otherwise. Some Jews should resist, take revenge. Revenge, do you hear? In that I am more a Jew than you."

Helmut stood erect as his father. Of the bits and pieces of conversation, he understood one with certainty, that if anyone harmed his father there would be terrible retribution. He understood the spirit and meaning of his father, though he did not know the word "revenge."

Friends of the Steinguts were leaving, by train, auto, and a few by plane. A clandestine, painful exodus was taking place, with hasty trips to emigration offices, the sale of clothes and furniture, secret meetings with jewelers and financial consultants who were confreres. Werner was stubborn but not stupid, and it dawned upon him to provide for his family's safety, a temporary arrangement until the gangsters in brown shirts were dealt the lethal blow that was inevitable. The worst that could happen in a city where every brick and board were saturated with the enlightenment of the greatest poets, scientists, and progressive statesmen in the world, could be some local discomfort any city might undergo in times of political unruliness. The country, the rural areas, they would be quiet. Farmers were not easily uprooted in their thinking, if they bothered to think. To the urbanite the state was fatherland; to the farmer it was mother earth.

When Werner heard of beatings in the Jewish community he was incensed, as he knew men like Aaron provoked no one. When he walked the streets he looked over his shoulder. He avoided groups of teenagers, experienced a strange sensation of wariness when he spied a brown-shirted figure in the distance. Anxiety festered within him, but he rationalized. "They are stupid and cowardly," he said. As he was the only Jew in his immediate neighborhood he found no direct evidence to indicate he could be personally threatened.

The office was usually jammed on Tuesday afternoon, but that day he noted only two people in his waiting room, one with the excruciating knee pain of arthritis, another with sore throat and high fever. They had to come. He examined his schedule of the past three weeks and saw that his patient load had declined precipitously. The turmoil of daily routine had reached an ominous depth of quietude.

The doorbell clanged repeatedly. A baby-faced boy of sixteen rushed in and sputtered in a rush of almost unintelligible phrases.

"They have taken my father!"

"Who is 'they'?"

"The brown shirts," he stammered. "They broke down the door and dragged him away."

Dr. Steingut used his professional air of assurance. "Why would they do that? What reason did they give?"

"I don't know. Father had been to a meeting. All the men at the meeting were taken."

Werner's heart skipped several beats of its normal rhythm. He assessed it as an inconsequential phase of excitement. The boy was

Catholic. How was it possible that he, a Jew was passed over, when another of a faith none too friendly to his own was pounced upon? He felt fright, more than fright, terror. He heard the thud of a pulse in his head. If the wolves attacked a Catholic, how much more delectable would be the body of a Jew?

"What can I do?" asked Werner. "What is it you want?"

"Mother could not come. She thinks the house is watched. We need money to try to get father. Mother says we could go to the authorities with money and they will let him go."

Werner's immediate thought was, "It couldn't be that bad. I am not a banker for the Catholic community. The boy was not sent to other parishioners. He comes to me, like noblemen of the middle ages reached out to Jewish money lenders."

He knew the boy and his family. The father was a teller in a small branch bank, he made a living, not wealthy, honest, yes, he was honest. Jolted from his reverie, Werner ran upstairs, and without explanation to Isolde, took ten bills from a wallet in the dresser drawer, bounded down the steps and gave them to the boy.

"Let me know what happens," he said as he ushered him to the door with an arm about his shoulders.

He never saw the family again, though he heard they had closed their apartment and left to visit a relative fifty miles away.

Plans had to be formulated and perfected. No longer was Dr. Steingut immune from the probability of noxious surprises. True, beatings and abductions were serious matters, but few were affected as far as he permitted himself to know. To analyze political events rationally, to take into account the good sense of the mass of German people was to conclude that his fellow Jews were possessed by hysteria. However, to disregard all eventualities would be an affliction of blind pride. An instinctual need for preparedness, to be ready to flee, to fade from the eyes of the enemy so they may be smitten from behind — these were Dr. Steingut's speculations.

He arranged to visit the home of a stout middle-aged patient whose family Werner had treated for ten years. Hans Kroner was a grateful soul, with an easy sense of joviality which expressed genuine admiration for his doctor, though he never was subservient. Rather his creed encompassed a strong measure of independence, in politics as in personal relationships. When Werner entered the small frame house in a poor section of town (Hans was a foreman in a tool plant notorious for its meager wages) he suffered the shame of an inexperienced beggar come to ask for unearned favors. Now the mighty have fallen, he muttered.

Mr. Kroner expressed surprise at his doctor's visit, an apparent social call free from the anxieties of professional attendance. He brought out wine and cheese as they sat alone in the poorly lit and sparsely furnished living room.

"I shall come to the point," Werner started. "You no doubt have heard of certain indiscretions, attacks, against Catholics and Jews. It is probably nothing, but I want my wife and son to be safe."

Hans pushed aside the wine bottle and bent over the small table, their faces almost touched. He was no longer a light-hearted fat man. He was imposing, commanding.

"Dr. Steingut, I wondered when you would come to your senses. Sir, you have been an idiot. I am but a poor working man, one of many, and we all know we can be seriously threatened. Like it or not, you are one of us. Some of us have been killed. That boy who came to your office — I sent him, not his mother. I could not afford to be mixed up in the affair, as I could be next for the chopping block. That you chose to come to me is a stroke of luck, as most of your patients would turn you in."

Werner buried his head in his palms. "I didn't know."

"Now," said Hans, "what can I do?"

"If my wife and son can stay at your cousin's farm they should be safe."

"Perhaps safe for them, not for us. They look everywhere for men of our group."

"I shall remain here."

"What!" Hans exclaimed derisively.

"I don't think they will touch me, as a doctor."

"Don't count on it. The services of a tool maker are valued more than those of a doctor."

"Perhaps I will go later. I cannot leave my practice like a thief runs from the police."

Hans did not argue. He cautioned Werner to go unseen by anyone near his home, and promised he would arrange for Isolde and Helmut to board at his cousin's farm, some seventy-five miles distant. As Werner searched the street outside the door, Hans felt more secure than he had for months. What about the myth of the smart Jew? Or were they too smart to be practical? If there were men like Dr. Steingut, those fascists with horse blinders on their eyes would be so busy chasing Jews they would forget about Catholics.

Sunday was gray. Huge dull clouds sleepwalked their way across the sun. It was a day conducive to introspection. Werner had reached conclusions, turned the core of himself inside out to confront waves of doubt. He called Isolde and Helmut into his study.

"In a few days you will leave for a farm where you will remain. It will be temporary, a safety measure. Hans Kroner's cousin lives there, and I will come when I can tidy up the practice and close this place. Time should pass quickly, as the troubles will burn themselves out, but this action is necessary."

Isolde readily agreed. She was not as assured of her safety as was Werner. Her views were split. She knew she could pass physically as Aryan, thus removing herself from the arena of terror; yet it was possible the half of her that was Jewish might be taken into account. There was no reason why she and Helmut should be embroiled in crazy political and racial quarrels.

Werner spoke to Helmut, "Son, you are a small boy, but I believe you will understand me. No matter what happens you must stay strong. You must not be afraid. Don't let anyone hurt you, and if they do, you have my permission to hurt them. In school you may have heard of turning the other cheek. No one does that today. Do not allow anybody to hit you twice." Helmut was soon to be seven. He pursed his lips, as if he was being coached for a fight with a street rowdy.

Again Tuesday, and the waiting room was empty. One appointment had been scheduled, a booming voiced hairy-chested workman who delivered barrels of beer. For years Werner had performed tonsillectomies in his office under local anesthesia, on patients with a low pain threshold coupled with disdain for hospitals. Removal of tonsils was not a medical event for Dr. Steingut, who had operated in his quarters successfully and repeatedly, but this could be his last surgical endeavor for an unforseeable time. He had done nothing that day and felt insecure. To Werner his lone patient was precious, represented reality tenuously suspended in a rarified atmosphere, supported by threads which could part at any moment. His son Helmut must touch reality, smell it and taste it, he often said. The boy was young, but time, these times, would not be gracious to him.

"Son," he told him, "you are going to watch me perform a tonsillectomy."

"What is that, Papa?" asked Helmut, upbeat, the child adventurer.

"The tonsils are two lumps in the back of the throat. I showed them to you in the mirror when yours were sore. If they are diseased they must be removed. It will not be pleasant, but I want you to watch. Expect some blood. It is not as bad as it looks."

The patient had several double brandies before reaching the doctor so that he had to lean back well in his chair to keep from oozing over the side. Scalpels with straight and curved blades, a gripping forceps with a circular wire loop, were placed in the center of a small table on a white linen drape. Cotton pledgets, syringes and needles, and a vial of clear medication were lined up behind gleaming metal instruments. To Helmut they appeared an array of toy soldiers. The patient grinned, a grin of bravado marinated in alcohol. His attitude soon changed.

As Dr. Steingut cajoled the massive mouth to open with encouraging platitudes and deft squeezes of nose and cheeks, it was obvious that all of the brandy was insufficient. Werner gently injected local anesthesia about both tonsils after swabbing the throat with a cocaine solution.

Dr. Steingut took the instrument with wire loop in one hand, and the long gripping forceps in the other. A padded wad between the teeth would prevent a sudden muscular snap which could sever a finger. The patient grunted, tried to stand. Werner pushed him back into the chair, squeezed his chin to transmit a message that masterful control of the surgeon is not to be refuted. The forceps was thrust through the wire loop and the tonsil grasped and drawn forward. The loop was settled about the base of the tonsil. There was no sound in the room. The patient was resigned. He was not in pain. When the loop tightened and the tonsil cut at its base, squirts of blood backed into his throat, oozed to the sides of his lips.

Helmut was startled by two arms raised high, huge fists clenching and unclenching. Intermittent explosions of gags, and blood-tinged spit shattered the boy's serenity. From the opened throat rasped muffled evocations, "*Gott, Gott,*" accompanied by pendulum movements of legs, a fantasy bicyclist pedalling uphill. The boy put a hand to his own throat, to the sides of his mouth, to wipe off the trickle he imagined flowing over his cheeks.

Werner spoke to Helmut. "Remember, it looks worse than it is. Soon it will be over. Hold on to the table if you must." Helmut stepped toward the table, but as he approached the display of gleaming instruments, now a disheveled battleground wetted with blood and saliva, he sank to his knees. Attempting to stand, he could not, till he grasped a corner of the instrument stand.

The operation completed, surgical appliances were cleaned and stored in their glass cabinet. The waiting room was empty. Werner was contented, happy yet sober. He had done his job well, including a lesson he had long planned to teach his son. Helmut rested on a couch in the living room; receding sunlight played on the gray field of his face. As Isolde walked in from the street Werner placed a cold cloth on the child's forehead and offered him a sip of hot coffee.

"Werner," she said, "you have been operating."

"And I watched," Helmut interjected weakly.

She turned to her husband. "What is the matter with you, allowing a boy to watch an operation! Does it do something for you, make you feel superior? Look at him. Just look at him!"

Before Werner could fumble his reply, Helmut sat up and said, "I watched it, Mother, and it made me feel bad. But I am glad I saw it. Next time will be better." He spoke in a tremulous voice, as if his assurance of a more courageous future was questionable.

Preparations for the departure of Isolde and Helmut were performed in orderly fashion. Rail and bus schedules were investigated so that tickets could be purchased just before leaving, giving no advanced notice to anyone who might be interested. Simple clothes suited to farm life were bought, and firm broad-toed shoes for walking on dirt and rocks. Luggage consisted of a packed box with a wood handle tied on for Helmut to carry, whereas a medium-sized suitcase, tough and light, was Isolde's baggage. Mother and son danced about the living room with the packages. The boy took high, exaggerated steps, groaned in jest at times, then burst into song. They were two clowns cavorting on the edge of grief.

Thursday was to be the day of departure for what was called a sojourn on the farm. Two days before, at dusk, voices rumbled in the street. It was a time of evening when the only noise ever heard was the chirping of birds, or, before a holiday, raucous song of a gravel-throated drunkard. Now, the volume, the timbre of sound, was different. Excited shouts, angry curses, emanated from a crowd of neighbors in shirt sleeves, smoking jackets, women in aprons, some with hair curlers, all milling about in mass confusion. Werner hurriedly put on his jacket, went into the street without a tie.

Faces looked south, where approximately three blocks away smoke trails could be traced to sooted flames from oil soaked rags held high on sticks. Crisp crackling, then garbled cheers, broke above the mumbled cries of onlookers. Two dozen men, followed by hundreds of supporters, women and teenaged youths included, were smashing windows of stores and homes. Hammers, rocks, truncheons, thick leather boots adorning brawny legs, were pounded at any structure which would give way. Here and there, a wild circle of whirling flesh kicked and fist-hammered a prostrate hulk of a man whose crescendo of screams soon muted to groans, to animal grunts, to nothing.

Werner walked back to his home, his teeth grinding uncontrollably. He bit the edge of his tongue, but the swelling and burn hurt only for an instant. He dragged himself through the door and closed it, saw his wife and child, stared at them to relate a story without speaking. They sat as he entered the bathroom, its door left partly open. Helmut watched his father kneel to the toilet and vomit. The beating and kicking, the groaning outside did not need explanation. Its cause, its horror, its total effect was translated for him by his father's retching. Helmut knew too well the discomfort of gags and vomit, but he could not imagine his father knowing. This papa he looked to was anguished, distraught, not the sort of rock to lean on with certainty. Helmut's alignment with his father was being twisted, gnawed by the elder's reduction through grief. The boy, too, was unsettled. If his father was vulnerable, how much more so was he.

Dr. Steingut rarely took sleeping pills or pain medication. Exercise and a warm tub or ice packs on an injured part were Werner's standby for minor difficulties. This night he was too weakened for a warm bath or a brisk walk. He swallowed a barbiturate capsule and poured brandy into a wine glass. Acquainted with the danger of combinations of drugs and alcohol it was apparent he regarded the liquor he held as insufficient to do harm, since he had taken only one capsule.

He thought, "What if I took a full glass of this stuff after a dozen capsules?" He quickly calculated the effect of the imaginary dose of medication and wondered if he would survive. Disgust overwhelmed him. His meanderings were obscene. He drank what he had poured and enjoyed it. Perhaps he ought to do this more often. Later, in fitful spasms of sleep, he saw and smelled the toilet bowl and heard Helmut emit gasps of astonishment.

Without restful sleep, sustained by nips of brandy and an occasional bite of sausage as he passed the refrigerator, Werner's mood was undergoing a process of withdrawal and replacement. He thought of himself as the subject of an exchange transfusion. Instead of blood withdrawn and substituted with life-giving elements, he was losing poise and objectivity, shedding great quantities of the love and humanity with which his profession was supposed to be permeated. The replacements which rejuvenated his tenacity were shock waves of hate and rage. His face reddened, temples throbbed, not with pain but with the pulsed beat of sledgehammer blows on thick glass. As the glass shattered, he cursed.

The day before she was to leave for the farm, Isolde tried to reason with him. Events would engulf him, could not be contained, she said. No one could help him but himself. There was a time to hold his head high and protest, and a time to flee. He must come with his family. Meanwhile she begged that he rest and regain his strength. Perhaps another physician would prescribe medication to settle him down.

"Are you so stupid, so impervious to what I have seen that you should disregard it?" he asked. "Do not dare judge me to be irrational!

I am sane, normal, my head is clear. I want revenge. I could kill for it. That is exactly what I mean. Kill. Everybody does it. Killing is today's sanity." His eyes were suffused and unblinking. Vigorous movements of limbs and body emphasized his eccentric declamation.

Then his frame relaxed, and grinning broadly he ran off in his shirt sleeves. Isolde could not restrain him as he bolted through the door, speeding south with arms over his head shrieking, "I am sane. I am the sane one. God lead me to them. Help me, God. An eye for an eye." It was the only prayer Dr. Steingut had uttered since childhood. Ironically his heaven-directed petitions became more clamorous as he approached the homes of the Orthodox Jews who had undergone the bulk of the brutality he had seen. If they could not have their prayers answered, Werner could not expect more response than the faithful. Or was he in this moment closer to the true faith, awash in agony without a trace of reason to deter him?

A tall, thin brown-shirted youth, swarthy with powerful square shoulders, stood in Werner's path. Surprise and astonishment delayed the young man's reactions. Before he could raise his truncheon, Werner struck his fist into the throat. Somewhere from the youth's upper chest a sharp crackle could be heard; a drawn out gurgle followed. The brown figure slumped to the ground.

Helmut and Isolde were breathless as they reached the scene. They took Werner by the arms, and guided him home past a throng of citizens gathered at a distance without the will to interfere. Some looked on in resignation, as if insanity in the streets were commonplace. To others the drama was a tragedy perpetrated by a demented actor before an audience in the throes of catharsis.

Isolde knew that retribution would come. Two policemen arrived, partly blocking from view a middle-aged man of military bearing with a ribboned medallion hooked on his brown shirt. The police were polite but insistent. Isolde was assured her husband would not be harmed, though he had sent a well known youth leader to the hospital. Werner's status as a physician, and of course his obvious mental disability, would be in his favor. The brown shirt said nothing, but as Dr. Steingut was ushered out by the police, he was immediately turned over to the beribboned militarist. A hammy fist grasped Werner like a vise fastened on a board. Werner felt no pain. He stiffened, his face and chin raised with pride as if he welcomed retribution. About to be punished for his hubris, his arrogance after an insolent attack on a standard bearer of the fatherland, Werner looked upon his chastisement as a rare privilege.

It was midnight before Isolde, confused to distraction, had to mobilize herself to answer a knock at the door. Her visitors were Aaron and a friend. Waiting till the streets were clear before they could walk out, they had travelled at a great risk.

Aaron said, "Please try not to worry. The man was hurt, but it was nothing. Besides, Dr. Steingut is highly respected."

"Where is he?" asked Isolde.

"We don't know. We made inquiries, but no one has seen him."

"Would he be at the police station?"

"He is not there. He has been taken away."

"I want to see him now."

"It's no use," said Aaron. "These matters take time. He is probably in another town. They will question him, and then we shall see."

"What do you mean? I should be able to talk to him." She was indignant.

"The law is different now. The old routines are gone. When we find out where he is held we shall take the necessary steps, pay if we must."

"Then I shall stay here till he returns," said Isolde.

Aaron turned forceful, pointed an index finger at her. "That is the one thing you must not do. We are thinking of you and the boy. Werner forgot himself, was foolish to seek out trouble. You must be more politic. Leave as you planned, as you can only make matters worse by staying. You and the boy may be next, so you must leave. We will let you know whatever happens."

Isolde looked toward Helmut's bedroom. She felt strangely heroic. Werner, the provider, who arranged their daily lives was no longer present. She had never been weak. Against repression she had shown spirit, and Werner's austerity had been thwarted with cunning. These were the virtues she had to uncloset and polish for the duties which faced her. To protect her son's life and hers was more than a duty. It was a demand of nature, like breathing.

That night she awakened Helmut and took him to Aaron's home, which she considered a safe haven for a few days. In the early afternoon of the following day Isolde and her son left, accompanied by a young Jewish boy of seventeen. Six feet tall, blue-eyed with platinum blonde hair, he could be a striking recruit for the Wehrmacht were it not for his circumcision and the star of David he insisted on wearing against his skin. He carried their packages, talked freely of mountains and valleys, skiing and soccer, the loose chatter of any young vacationer.

Johann Kurtzbaum was Aaron's nephew, with both parents alive and well in Warsaw where they owned a small jewelry store. When he arrived to visit his uncle Aaron, he rented a tiny room on a busy thoroughfare, noisy but central to theater, opera, and the technical school to which he had gained admittance. As a seemingly bright young Teuton, and with the fervor with which he pursued mastery over tools, dyes, lathes, and other mechanical devices, no one dreamt of questioning his origins. Local school authorities, aware of their country's future needs, decided he was one of the glowing sparks to be plucked from the ashes of a dormant fatherland.

In Poland, Johann was bored with the Hebrew school he attended as a youth. He chose to stay in Germany when he sought freedom to experience, to enjoy the ebullience and overt expressions of democratic German ideals, to linger in the bubbly, carefree ambience of beer hall crowds. What might have been his road to hedonism was diverted. When Aaron laughed at his far-flung musings and subjected him to the eccentric principles of Hasidic culture, Johann was hooked. "I found it," he would say, "absolute freedom and the devil with the world of worry." Johann was the ideal Jewish guerrilla courier, a Jew of the spirit rather than of the synagogue, who was unscathed by the historical tales of persecution and tortures said to bind his people.

Helmut became attached to his young guide. A buoyant and jaunty attitude were so foreign to the boy that he was at first instinctively suspicious and quiet. Later he, too, was won over to an exchange of light-hearted banter. He stopped to inspect toy trains in a window display, broke away to cross the street in traffic to await the slower travellers, laughed at his mother's remonstrations. His round dark eyes tilted up to Johann, to wonder whether his black hair would ever turn blond. How different was this man from his father, whose concerns centered about the proper use of knife and fork, about wiping a chin moistened by a speck of ice cream, about keeping the voice subdued because it might expose what the listener has no business to know.

Isolde too found relief from the madness that enveloped her. The possibility had dawned upon her that she might never see her husband. Previously she had performed her duties at home, engaged in an occasional escapade, as if these were the sum total of the life she had to confront. In a sense she had escaped, not only from political and social pressures, but from her own ties of restraint. Johann transmitted his effervescence to her, so that she could reach out toward new diversions on her own terms, with Werner in custody and no doubt under stress. Guilt did not thrive in the presence of Johann. She said to herself, "I must remember this young man's attitude. Everyone should emulate him, doing what he can to help without tearing himself apart. For myself I have a right to be happy, though I must do whatever is possible for my family."

Johann took them into a café at the railroad station. At a secluded table he spread a map which delineated each step of the trip they must take. The train would carry them to a village forty miles away, where they would board a bus which would let them off at a crossroads three miles from the farm that was to be their home till further notice. The last few miles were to be covered on foot. They could hire a taxi, but the less attention they attracted in the village the less likely they were to be challenged. Should they meet soldiers or other uniformed personnel, they simply were to exchange greetings and act as if they were residents who had left for the day. Isolation, non-communication, was imperative. Military men were under strict orders to avoid fraternization with townsfolk for they were part of secret anti-aircraft emplacements which dotted the countryside.

As the train rolled out, Johann casually glanced back toward his charges now in flight. There was no hand waving. That was an order; only a wistful smile between acquaintances parting with the presumption they might never see each other. To Helmut the separation meant loss of a companion who was not competitive, or ambitious, or anxious. Isolde gratefully recalled the young man's adroitness and expertise in aiding their departure. He could solve a problem step by step, complete a laborious task with an assured guise of nonchalance. She explained to Helmut as well as she could the dynamics of a man like Johann; the boy fell asleep as he absorbed her analysis.

Train and bus ride progressed smoothly. A few questions had to be asked — where would the bus stop, could a ticket be purchased within the vehicle, was this the bus that passed the crossroad? Pleasure-bound travellers of late August had had their fill of mountains, streams, and oceans so that traffic out of the cities was light. Luggage could be handled easily, without jostling by impetuous throngs rushing back to the routine of autumn. Rapid fire, fleeting visions of birch and walnut trees, foaming valley streams at the fringe of baby mountains, the lull of manured farmlands specked with herds of cattle, imparted an hypnotic effect which erased all memory of violence. An illusion of tranquility was presented and accepted through the lens of nature's benevolence.

They were the only two passengers in the bus, and when getting off the driver pointed out a corner where they could hire a taxi if no one called for them. The driver was thanked, and as he sped off the woman and boy turned away from the stand. Isolde studied her map. Shortly they found themselves on a narrow paved road, unmarked and lonely. Trees thinned out progressively till they passed open planted acreages of beans and corn, here and there a vegetable patch beside a brightly painted farmhouse. It was dusk. There were no lights. The road surface changed to gravel, then to dirt, slim and rutted, a fitting adjunct to the dilapidated farms with peeling paint and loosened shingles. Isolde recalled that Werner spoke of the unity of truth and beauty in the countryside. She now knew this to be poetic fantasy. The mesmerized state of ease she had enjoyed on the train and bus had disappeared. She examined the reality before her, and it was ugly.

Helmut had no difficulty carrying the box beneath his arm or on his head, until they walked up a long, steep hill. Pebbles lodged in his shoes, so that he had to stop to clear them from beneath his toes. As he sat beside the road to remove his shoes for the third time, a small party walked down the hill towards them. The strangers were in the midst of a rousing song, but stopped singing abruptly as they approached the tired couple. There were four of them, men in uniform, two behind two, progressing in step with a sharp marching cadence. When the group had passed Helmut and Isolde by some fifty feet, in silence except for the thrust of jackboots on hard dirt, a man in the rear broke ranks as he yelled to his compatriots, "Stop the silliness. It's only a woman and a boy. We needn't parade by the book for them."

The soldier ran back to Isolde, tipped his hat and politely said, "I am Corporal Axel Gans. This is a rough hill to climb and you look tired. Let me help you, at least to the top of the rise." Certain his offer would be accepted; he shouted to his friends to go ahead, he would join them soon. Isolde, grimy and careworn, did not respond. With fatherly encouragement the soldier lifted Helmut to his feet and accompanied them with his long arm hooked about the box.

"Are you going far?" he asked. They probably could not hire a cab, he thought, for there was no other explanation for what such an attractive woman and well-bred boy were doing in this poor excuse for German countryside.

Isolde decided to talk. It was more natural, safer than a chill of silence from which he could have suspicions. She removed her hat and brushed back her hair. Dim light played softly about her head, caught the sculptured features of her nose and lips as she looked toward her helper. "My name is Isolde, and this is my son Helmut. We are visiting relatives up this road. It is a red farmhouse with white window trim, about a half mile further on." She had been meticulously coached, though she guessed at the distance.

"Of course! I know the place. It stands out because it's kept up well. You would think the farmers in these parts would paint their houses once in a while."

Isolde said, "It is not good farmland and they have difficulty making ends meet." The assessment did not require complex logic, yet she was excited by her response. She was learning to face reality.

Whether she spoke truth or falsehood was secondary, for their safety and sustenance were at stake. Isolde did not lack experience with disarming half-truths. A glance at her son was a reminder she would cheat, lie, maim if necessary.

At the top of the hill Isolde told Axel she no longer needed help. She thanked him and nodded to Helmut to express his gratitude.

"Thank you, sir." the boy said. "Do you live near here? I should like to see you again."

"Yes," replied Axel, "if you call it living. We are stationed about two miles that way." He pointed west into the fields. Then to Isolde, "And I would like to visit you, now that I know where you are staying."

Isolde had made a perfunctory examination of his character. Tall, lean, powerful sloped shoulders, nose smooth-bridged and slightly elongated, black shell rim glasses — altogether a man who could be athletic if he wished, but who leaned toward more scholarly and gentler pursuits. She said, "It would be nice for you to visit with us, but I think you had better wait. I am sure we shall meet someday. You see, my relative has been seriously ill, and it will be some time before we can invite visitors." She was pleased with the plausible ring to her hasty excuse.

As Axel reached out to touch Isolde's shoulder in a perfunctory gesture which proclaimed they were at the threshold of friendship, Helmut saw a long thick scar above his wrist. Reminded of Aaron's son, the boy asked, "Was it burned?"

"No, no. Someday I shall tell you how I got it, but not now." He turned to wave as he ran downhill towards the others.

After a half mile of trudging, the color of a house precisely described to her gleamed in the half-light. The building sat on a solid, well-groomed plot in the midst of unkempt property, with an enormous black enamelled pump handle for well water. The outhouse was at the back, its cover barely visible from the road; chickens on a straw bed in a diminutive hen house, one perched on the sill of a cracked window. Several pigs fenced within an enclave beside a vegetable patch. Beyond the garden of peas, beans, and potatoes, a group of cows huddled in the near corner of the field. Across the road on either side of the house, as far as could be seen, were stretches of trees, some fallen, a few awkwardly tall and majestic amongst many which were dwarfed, with scabby bark.

They left the road to walk the narrow gravel footpath leading to the door. A buxom woman of about fifty with a gingham dress to her ankles and a man's cap on her head came from behind the house. She knew who her visitors were.

The woman spoke to Isolde, "I am Anna Grunstein. Your case

and that of your husband's is familiar to me. You may stay here. Hardly anyone comes by, so you are comparatively safe."

"Thank you," said Isolde, at the edge of tears. "Does anyone else live here?"

"I am alone. My husband died of consumption three years ago."

"I'm sorry. It must be difficult for you."

"Nothing has changed," said Anna. "When a man is sick for ten years his woman must work. I do it all, and it is all mine." She swept her hand outward in a wide arc as if to bless her acreage.

Listening to this oak of a woman in peasant dress and silly cap tilted back on her head, Isolde recognized disturbing similarities which bound the two. Both had lost their husbands. One had already overcome the stress of scraping and foraging for livelihood; the other was yet to confront her new status. Both were cast into a cauldron of insecurity, where slyness and secrecy were to be shared and integrated for mutual security.

Anna was a private, lonely, woman, but when she spoke she made a definitive point and expected an answer. She was the captain of her ship and tolerated no foolishness.

"Have you heard from your husband?" she asked.

"Not yet. I think it will blow over soon and he will come to take us back."

Anna was curt. "Perhaps you believe I know nothing, living here. Not true. I listen to the radio, visit the village twice weekly to read papers, and am generally well informed by my cousin who lives near you. I wish to say, young lady, you will probably be here a long time. Your husband may very well not come to take you away. You must prepare yourself, become hardened. There will be a war; all signs point to it. The soldiers stationed in the fields are not play-acting." She had not spoken at such length for months, but she had to start her guests, her boarders, on firm footing. "Now come inside."

Helmut was lifted onto a thickly padded chair by Anna. "It will make him feel like a man!" was her explanation. The decor of the central room furthered a sense of isolation and safety. A rectangular oak table and sturdy wood seats were placed near a fireplace with nondescript china figures on the mantle, a small oval grass rug sat on one side of the long room dimly lit by a green shaded lamp hung from the ceiling. Helmut was frightened by the starkness of his surroundings. He was not accustomed to the containment of semi-darkness, unless it was bedtime in his own home with his father and mother present for support.

Anna liked the boy. With no children and too many chores to think of involving herself with another man, she had accomodated to a sparse, childless existence. She was not religious nor was she a sexual prude. She had remained faithful to her husband because she had no opportunity to be otherwise.

Sensitive to Helmut's insecurity, Anna proffered the most direct psychologic approach she knew to solve a problem. She fed him sausage, black bread, thinly-sliced potatoes and shredded cabbage. Helmut's appetite was paltry, that of an anxious boy in a haunted house. The sausage revived this spirit. Nothing at home had tasted as zestful. Isolde ate too, in small portions daintily conveyed to the mouth, and she had to interrupt Helmut's gluttony. The boy might find it difficult enough to sleep in a strange bed, she warned, without the added effects of a meal worthy of a lumberjack.

Next morning they were awakened at seven, with the sun already peering beneath the partly-drawn window shades. The oak floors were cool to their bare feet. Anna, who had been up over an hour, prepared breakfast, after which she set an agenda of duties and plans. Isolde was to help with indoor cleaning and cooking, plus small farm chores which she would learn. Helmut would feed the chickens, gather eggs, and help Anna. One hour in the morning and two in the afternoon were to be set aside for Helmut's schooling with no excuses or procrastination. Her insistence on detail was an ominous sign to Isolde, who reasoned that this regimen meant a lengthy stay.

Isolde Steingut's metamorphosis was that of a beautiful woman of the upper-middle-class tossed into the milieu of struggle-for-survival on a dirt farm. Anna eased the transformation by doing the heavy work. Labor did not entirely ease Isolde's anxiety, for she was constantly alert to any news of her husband. After several months and persistent confirmation that Werner could not be located, she no longer was fretful. In time, Werner's whereabouts became a moot question which surfaced when there was little to do. Gradually, her husband and her urban memories became distant, ephemeral as a childhood dream. She would examine the thickened palms of her hands, check her weather-beaten but still attractive face in the mirror, and pat the firm abdominal and thigh muscles she had developed. On balance she was pleased. A newer and more gratifying structure of life was being formed. She felt a strange, feline litheness. Agility and power previously unknown to her seeped from her firmed flesh.

When the boy asked about his father, Isolde casually steered him in other directions. It dawned on him that he would not see his father again. The boy struggled within a vortex of increasing turbulence, and no one smoothed his path of exit. His mother was indulgent and protective, but that was all. He felt body to body contact with her, not heart to heart. Often, confusion whether he liked or hated his mother set in, and he would show his vacillation by putting things off. One of Anna's prescribed jobs would be left unfinished; or he would leave a smelly chore incomplete.

"Mama, when is Papa coming to see us?" He asked more to open himself to his mother than to seek a definitive answer he knew would not be forthcoming.

"Don't bother your little head over it, dearest. Just remember never to tell strangers about father, or where we lived. We may hear soon, or not for a long time, so try to think of other things while you wait."

Helmut persisted, "Is Papa sick, or dead?"

"Don't be a foolish boy. You must forget. We are safe and that is all that matters."

"Is Papa safe?"

Isolde laughed, "Helmut, you are a tease. A boy your age must play, and work, and grow to be strong. You are doing all that, so be satisfied. Come, dear, I'll get a warm bath ready so you will sleep well."

January winds blew across the fields. Bare trees stood as skeletal sentinels guarding a vista of crystalline snow cover. More time was spent indoors. Helmut threw logs on the fire and watched the flames revive, flickering yellow spectres which spoke to him, "what will you do today, and tomorrow, and the day after?" The fire left the boy wrapped in sterile warmth, inevitably to cool as its sparks sputtered and died.

Isolde would attempt to cheer him. "Do you remember Aunt Sophie?" Helmut was too young to recall.

She continued, "Now *there* was a character. Happy, and a fighter. When she believed in something she went all the way, no matter what others thought. She loved adventure. She took chances. When she was fed up with her stubborn father, and your father, and when her husband died, she went to America to start a new life. Someday, maybe, you will meet her."

One evening, after a bounteous supper prepared by Isolde, Helmut wished to do something special for his mother. He offered to close up the hen house door for her. The air was cold and still. A reflective glare from snow pierced the shadows. Irregular patches of light showed through the timber. Helmut saw a standing figure propped against a tree, watching the house. The glint of eyeglasses and the flash of broad sloped shoulders was unmistakeable.

In the house, he was excited. "Mother, there was a man standing outside. Did you know a man was watching the house?"

"What if someone was looking this way? People pass by, and they have a right to look where they want as long as they don't bother us."

Helmut was stunned. In the vast ghostliness of the early night he had spied someone who did not belong there, and he was told it did not deserve inquiry. Then he remembered. The one he saw was the soldier who helped carry their packages when they climbed the hill.

"Mama, I know who it was. I saw the man who helped us climb the hill."

"Yes dear, I believe you are correct."

"Did you see him too?"

"No, but I am certain it was he."

Helmut had developed an analytical mind for one so young. It was a trait sufficiently mature to assure him his mother lied. She had seen the lurking figure several times. Once they had moved toward each other, but he did not come close, not then. As a soldier he was under orders to keep his distance from civilians. Like the boy, he wanted to be close to this attractive woman who moved so smoothly over slippery rocks and holes of unploughed winter ground.

That night Helmut lay in bed with eyes closed to thin slits through which he could watch his mother. She thought he was asleep. Completely undressed, she watched herself before a long, cracked mirror over the dresser. As she stood back for a larger view she ran her hands over her waist. Her fingers groped downward, slowly, over a suppleness of wide hips and muscular thighs, backwards to the softness and symmetry of her buttocks. Sighing, she drew in her abdomen to admire its firm concavity. As she climbed into bed beside Helmut he thought Aunt Sophie would never parade in front of a mirror. Aunt Sophie, he had heard, stood on thick legs with a protruding stomach.

Chapter 6

HELMUT WAS OLDER than twelve when he escaped from Germany to live with Aunt Sophie in the Lower East Side of Manhattan. Though religion was not an issue, she was convinced the youngster had to struggle to understand the dignity of his past. She changed the boy's name from Helmut to Israel; he did not object. With that appellation he could not forget his roots. Israel was precocious in the sciences, so his Aunt steered him toward medicine. He was like most pre-medical students who, when asked why they wished to enter medicine would reply that they wanted to help their fellow-man. Such convictions lacked the empathy implied in such high-minded goals.

On first meeting Carla he had already been through two attempts at private practice, the last interrupted by Vietnam. Now in his forties, he felt he would be secure in a defense plant, a tractor works which manufactured military gear. On the medical staff of an industrial organization Israel had time to look about him, to reflect. The aura was restful, perhaps bucolic. In the midst of frenetic plant activity he saw no destruction, no challenge. A well-equipped community hospital presented the opportunity to become a house surgeon with a private practice. Carla had graduated from nursing school here and was a respected staff nurse.

"Iz," said Mike Hearn, a young staff internist, "I want you to look at one of our nurses." Israel was the serious type, much older than the men and women who recently completed training and used such hospital positions as stepping stones to juicy clinic appointments or remunerative partnerships. When a nurse became ill she looked for a mature and earnest physician. Carla chose Dr. Steingut.

"What's wrong with her?" asked Israel.

"It could be the usual appendix, but there is a red herring. She has lots of tenderness in the right place, but no nausea, no vomiting, no cramps; and even her blood count is okay."

"Any v.d.?" Israel was thorough.

"Not this one. She's clean; at least that's the reputation she has around here."

Israel conjectured that clean "around here" was not necessarily clean everywhere; probably one of those women who manage to keep their names out of the hospital rumor mill, spending their evenings in roadhouses and motels. She could have a blocked tube, usually infected, or an ovary strangled in old adhesions, or an odd type of early pregnancy. Israel's diagnostic wheels turned, loaded with wariness and suspicion, though he had not seen his patient.

He and Mike walked down a long corridor and turned into the emergency room. Carla was under a sheet in a corner room, still in her uniform. Dr. Hearn left after a cursory introduction, with Israel beside the cart in the company of the head nurse. Marie Garland was a wrinkled gnome of a woman who penetrated Israel with an aggressive stare which emphasized her role as guardian of all the virginity that was and ever had been in this hospital.

Israel went through his routine, family history, medical past, onset of symptoms, relationship of time to change of pain. Carla hid beneath the sheet. He left for last what really could cause her ailment.

"Did you ever have venereal disease?" His head turned as if to address the wall.

She was casual. "I never had it, and I don't intend to get it." The head nurse's wrinkles puckered as she smiled. Her girls were good, or else.

"Are you pregnant?" Israel continued.

"Not guilty," answered Carla.

"How do you know?" Israel was quickly interrupted by Miss Garland. She took a step closer to him, interposed herself between doctor and patient. Israel wavered. He had to proceed with the examination. If wrong in his diagnosis, every doctor, nurse, and technician in the place would put him at the bottom of their lists. Pelvic and rectal examinations on a colleague were a minor embarrassment, and Miss Garland's critical eye deterred him. She was mother, critic, and *gauleiter* in the surveillance of treatment of her nurses.

Israel stuttered, "I must do pelvic and rectal examinations."

Carla was authoritative. "Miss Garland, could you please step to the other side of the curtain? And don't worry about me." She threw off the sheet, dragged down her panties and wiggled them off her legs as, with spread thighs, she preempted Dr. Steingut's request for the necessary position.

"You may find this difficult," she said.

"Why?"

"I am a virgin."

Israel's eyes widened, part disbelief, part astonishment. He approached her gently and spread the vulva with well-lubricated fingers. His finger could not easily enter the genital orifice. The hymen was intact. Carla did not move or resist. "Aha!" he thought. "It does appear she has remained intact all these years, but I doubt it; so attractive; not even a wince on handling her genitals. Perhaps she is one of those women who stretches but doesn't rupture." Israel's cynicism diminished at the sound of Miss Garland's artificially induced coughing spell as if she had guessed what happened from the other side of the curtain.

The rectal examination was easily performed, and more productive. As Israel pushed into the pelvis the full length of his finger, he palpated a mass on the right.

"You've got it, doctor," Carla said, "that's where the pain comes from."

Dr. Steingut considered her exclamation an excellent sign. His patient was a normal, reactive individual, with a high pain threshold. Perhaps like an automaton she could be repaired with pliers and screwdriver.

The diagnosis was now more definitive; an unusual type of appendix, where the inflamed organ rolled into a ball and hid beneath a segment of bowel. Walled off by adhesions, its toxins imprisoned, it was deceptively benign in its intact state. Thus the clinical picture had been confused for awhile. At any moment the mass could burst its compartment into the pelvis and abdomen, spewing aggressive organisms far afield.

He told Carla what he had found, turning at times to address Miss Garland, who was surprisingly agreeable.

"We will do another blood count, and probably will operate soon," said Israel.

"Right now if you can," replied Carla without a hint of question or fear.

Dr. Hearn was informed, blood tests were ordered, and instructions given to the surgical supervisors to make ready the operating suite. Hearn called back. "Don't bother with the blood count. You will have to go in whether or not it goes up." Israel agreed, but thought he had better make sure.

"Sure of what?" said Mike. "Iz, even if the blood count is normal my opinion is that you must operate."

The second blood count supported the diagnosis. A proliferation of white cells indicated infection, a healthy body response to a virulent enemy. Israel was relieved. The technicalities of surgery might be a distant concern, but the decision to operate was a barrier he had to hurdle. Procrastination would have been more a natural tendency for Israel — watchful waiting, serial white cell counts, reexamination. This is the way he would tackle problems outside his profession, repairs in his home, making a purchase. As a surgeon he had to force himself to make decisions. His vacillating nature was overcome only by reflexes imprinted by years of training.

The surgery progressed smoothly except for one fearful moment. Mike Hearn assisted, an uncommon task for an internist who took pride in the cerebral approach rather than the mechanical of his surgical colleagues. As the bowel was displaced with careful dissection, cutting minute bits of tissues, advancing with delicate precision, the anguish of the moment lay in an attempt to expose the abscess without its premature rupture.

"Hold this," Israel said to his assistant after placing the prongs of a retractor beneath the mass. Dr. Hearn grasped the instrument slowly and deliberately, a sign he was aware of the danger of a sudden jerk or wavering tension on the bowel he held aside. A minute or so of unvaried retraction was necessary to free the last adhesive shred. Dr. Hearn did well for thirty seconds, when his hand quivered. Imperceptible at first, the movement enlarged to a sway of alarming proportions.

Israel was sharp. "Let go of the retractor!" Dr. Hearn did so.

"What's wrong, Mike? I have to have a steady hand here or I'll bust it open."

"I know, I know. Let me give my arm a rest." He laughed nervously. "What can you expect of an internist?"

The process resumed, careful cuts, spread, lifts, wipes, a few moments of activity and then a rest, halting in deference to Mike's manual poise. With the last deft easement of the final layers of tissue, the offending organ was removed. Those who observed, surgeons, nurses, Miss Garland, showed that deceleration of tension which can be detected in an operating room. Eyes ranged freely now, neck muscles untensed, arms and facial lines hung loose. An imaginary wire which had tightened about Israel's brow disappeared. He helped shift the anesthetized form from the table to a cart and followed its progress to the recovery room.

Still asleep, Carla lay in bed neatly tucked under a glistening white sheet. Her head and an upper arm were exposed. Israel turned for a final inspection before leaving her room. Her breathing was regular, serene, and the contour of her exposed shoulder was the sole visual sign of vibrancy dormant beneath the covers. What a mess it might have been, thought Israel, if Mike's unsteadiness had made him rupture the damn abscess. She was lucky. A beautiful girl with drains and pus coming from her belly would have been an ugly embarrassment.

He was puzzled by Mike's actions. The fact that, as an internist, he did not usually assist in surgery was no reason for such pronounced tremulousness. Such gross movements were often seen in neurological diseases. But Dr. Hearn had no other symptoms. Nor was he fatigued.

Drugs? Alcohol? He had not seen Mike drink, nor did he ever detect an odor on his breath other than the fruitiness of the jelly beans he chewed, to feed the flagging spirit, as Mike would say. Next time, thought Israel, stay away from an internist when an assistant is required. Stick with the professional blood-lovers. They were not as intellectual, downright boring with their gush of stupid jokes, simpletons some of them, but they held instruments and staunched bleeders with the speed and deftness of unfeeling robots.

Carla recovered from surgery like most healthy midwestern farm girls. She progressed rapidly, with no fuss about gas pains, wound discomfort, constipation, or urinary difficulty. That she was not a pampered princess was soon apparent to Israel, or he would have had multiple night calls regarding a tweak here, a pull there, the tightness is killing me doctor, please give me something, not by mouth, it's too slow, how about a shot, doctor. It was a joy to operate on one like Carla, thought Israel. These country folk were stalwart, basic, hard as earth after a dry spell. Or they were bovine, emotionless machines, who lived by Bible-belt admonishments. Israel chided himself on his black and white partitions of human nature.

Dr. Steingut made two daily visits to all post-operative patients unless severe complaints necessitated more constant attendance. For Carla, he popped into the room four or five times a day, whenever he passed her door. In the morning he was very professional, austere, looked at her wound, inquired about daily functions, gave instructions in sitting, standing, walking. As the afternoon wore on, having wrestled with a plethora of problems, he would fall into the chair beside her bed and sigh the relieved moan of a prizefighter at the close of the last round. The blush returned to her cheeks. Straight-brushed hair on her slim, strong neck highlighted the curves of her trunk. She stood so he could palpate her abdomen. It did not matter to Carla that there was no attending nurse in the room. She removed her pajama top and lowered the bottoms till the tie string lay across her pubis. "Now you can examine me properly," she said.

Israel was chagrined. If a nurse had walked in and found her recently incised colleague sporting her belly and full-rounded breasts unashamedly, who would be blamed for the immodest pageant? Israel, of course. Nurses must have some sort of code, he conjectured. They don't interrupt each other unless they perceive a hidden sign, hear a voice that implies help, or receive instructions to watch out for a penile profiteer of a doctor who stalks the halls in search of consolation. It was obvious that Carla was at ease in his presence, even liked him.

Before Carla replaced her pajama top she faced the wall mirror and smoothed her pelvis and chest with her palms. Israel was stunned.

He had seen such motions as a young boy. These hips, too, were wide, the waist narrow and firm, but there was a difference in Carla's stroking of her body. Israel detected no vanity. She was a happy, thankful creature, who reassured herself by touch that she was whole.

Carla could have left the hospital on the third or fourth postoperative day, but she did not go until the seventh. Normally, Israel discharged his patients as early as safety permitted; he was violently opposed to holding patients for convenience, keeping beds filled till the next paying customer presented his body. Carla lived alone in a small apartment and would have had to climb two flights of stairs to reach it. That was enough to convince Israel his patient needed several extra days of care. Though Carla insisted she could take care of herself, Israel remained adamant. It was the first time Israel welched on his principles, stretched standards which he otherwise would not bend or dilute. These were the admonitions of his father, and Carla was the preamble to his emancipation.

Israel visited her apartment often, initially in late afternoons after office hours, later in the evening when out on a call. He would trudge up the stairs, sit and chat. Soon the visits were prearranged, embellished with light dinners she insisted on cooking for him. One evening she surprised him with a platter of bagels, cream cheese, and smoked salmon. Carla got these strange items from a friend coming from Chicago.

"What is this?" asked Israel.

"It's good Jewish food. I thought you would miss it."

"I know about the food, but how did you know?"

"That you are Jewish? Of course, I know. I am familiar with what happened in Germany. The trouble with you doctors is you take nurses for fools. Besides, your name is Israel."

"It's a good biblical name. Anyone in the bible belt could call himself Israel without raising an eyebrow."

"Not with dark hair, big brown eyes, and a nose like yours," she replied.

"I remember Jews who looked like Swedes."

"If there are any, they don't come to the midwest; and they are not so serious as you."

"You're right." He said it to appease her, though he recalled walking to a train with blond Johann Kurtzbaum carrying his package. He stared into a corner of the room.

"Did I say anything wrong?" she asked.

"No, no. Old memories came back." He hugged her, an instinctive, momentary gesture, a falling body reaching out for support.

Carla pointed to her abdomen. "Careful with your scar. It's still tender." She flexed at the waist to avoid pressure on her abdomen, wrapped both arms about his neck and forced his head to hers. A few seconds passed before he responded, and when he did he would not disengage. He held her in a strangled embrace.

She broke away from him slowly, without the anxiety or repulse of a resisting woman, as if she cut off the grip of a loving child. Endearment did not flow readily from Carla, but when it did it was inscribed in concrete. She said, "I like you very much, Israel. Now let's eat."

As Israel squeezed the halves of his bagel to compress its sandwiched components, the cream cheese overflowed in lumps which dropped on the table. Boyish, exuberant, he picked up the moist globs with his fingers and put them into his mouth, washed down the food with gulps of the wine he had brought as a gift.

An uninhibited consciousness revived visions of early childhood; memory returned to a subsequent time, when his adolescence and later life fostered suspicion and wariness. In Carla's eyes he suspected a magnetic luminescence, an eerie pulsation, cooling yet penetrating. Perhaps she laughed at him, took advantage of his concern over her. Or, like most of the local residents, did she screen out and cast aside all of him except that which could benefit her?

"Now you are worried," she said.

"I looked into your eyes."

"And what did you see?"

"Something I wish I hadn't. I don't know if you could call it coldness, or a steely disposition. Then again it might be stability. You are difficult to figure out. You people are all made with iron covers. I have to burrow to find some softness."

Carla raised her voice. "Don't you believe it."

"I see it every day in my practice," he continued. "The imperturbable patient who tells me to go ahead, do what I have to do, unafraid of the possible complications of which I warn him."

"It's a show, a façade. They were taught to carry on against all odds. The fact is, we, they, whimper inside. How many times have you met a cool cucumber of a patient, a Swede or a German, act as if nothing could budge him, then do a complete turnabout and break to pieces when the going got tough."

It was true, thought Israel. He had forgotten. The worse patients, the most dangerous to treat, were those with a metallic exterior, humorless and unemotional. No complaints. Perfect acquiescence. If all went well they were pillars of disciplined strength. "I trust you, doctor, no matter what comes up." Or, after a smooth convalescence, "You did a wonderful job, as I expected you would." But if the temperature rose or a searing cough had to be investigated, then the cycle of blissful trust would be violently broken. Israel thought, "I wish these people, this woman, would tell me what she truly thinks, and act the way she honestly feels."

As if to intercede in his assessment of her, Carla said, "You don't know me. Given other circumstances I might be a different person, wear my emotions on my sleeve. Everyone has a breaking point."

"Not you." He was certain. "You are too steady. It's ingrained in you." He wished she were drawn to him, but he felt far from omnipotent, what with his limited sexual experience. Israel's need was a rock on which to perch and find shelter.

Carla and Israel became more than good friends. When she was stronger, before returning to work, she said, "Iz, we've been sitting in every night. We should celebrate."

"Of course," he said. "But celebrate what?"

"I had hoped I would not have to spell it out. I am growing healthy and stronger, and you are sitting beside one of your professional conquests. We've learned to know each other. Tell you what! Let's get Mike Hearn with a date and go out for a good time."

"Can't we go out together, by ourselves?"

"We can do that another time. Now, we need company. Mike's a happy guy."

"You mean we need someone to enliven the occasion, can't do it by ourselves?"

"Yes, that's right. There are a few things you need to learn, and the most important is to let yourself go. You need to be unstrung. Mike Hearn will be good company for you."

Older, with wisps of gray hair on his temples, Israel could be taken for the chaperone of these lively, snickering youngsters. However Carla was genuine and mature, and would not engage in juvenile tomfoolery. Age, these days, he thought, should be no barrier against serious relationships. He was strong, looked youthful to himself in the mirror, and thank God he was not afflicted with the tremors Mike Hearn suffered when he assisted at surgery.

Chapter 7

Israel envied Mike Hearn's jovial spirit. The party of four visited Eduardo's restaurant, where the proprietor had sought to transport Chicago's French-Italian cuisine to the hinterland. Dr. Hearn drank several oversized steins of beer for every sip Israel could manage. When Mike went to the bathroom and twisted off the doorknob, it was Carla who gave instructions, called for a screwdriver, and managed to free him.

Israel said to her, "When he gets home he'll put an icebag to his head and collapse like a dead bird."

"All he did was relax and blow off steam."

"Nonsense, Carla, he's an alcoholic," Israel spoke as if he sat in judgment over evil incarnate.

"Don't you ever get tipsy? Or do you always have perfect control?"

"I like to think that."

"Perhaps you face your problems; to resolve them is something else." She paused. "We like each other, and I want to understand you. We can't be dishonest with each other."

Israel did not appreciate fractious women who bored into him. Another voice, another cook in the kitchen, especially that of a woman he considered an affable and reposed companion, made solutions painful. Carla's ideas were never gratuitous. Rather, they rose from the silent darkness of deliberation at the proper moment. He had come to his age basically unchanged, without solutions. Perhaps he needed a dash of spice to change the mix, and he was not averse to experimentation.

During hospital hours Israel found himself watching Dr. Hearn, as if the last vestige of a deteriorating medical morality. Both consulted on difficult cases, and Mike gave intravenous injections, placed needles in chest walls or spines to gather evidence for diagnosis. His work was excellent, though Israel detected a tiny tremor of his hand as he approached the point of needle entry. But as the syringe was driven inward, Mike's final execution was swift and crisp. To Israel, this was a marvellous display of control, though he secretly expected and relished the exposure of frailty.

Dr. Hearn was known to local police and state troopers as that Irishman who was known in all of the taverns and could hold his liquor. If he were stopped for a traffic violation, Mike impressed them as an affable and sensible man of wit and humor. Never was he ticketed, as they were aware of his local medical reputation. For most, he was picked to be family physician. Treat the doctor well and he will see to it you get the best care, they said.

Officer Kevin Mowbray cruised behind an old Ford on a late afternoon in December. He automatically registered certain facts — that the car was well driven, within the speed limit, took turns properly, license plates clean and visible. He was a practitioner of the art of reflex remembrance and recall, the cop who revered the academy's teachings of detailed diligence, which, if adhered to, would be rewarded by promotion.

A patch of ice in a rut caught the right front wheel of the Ford; the car shuddered as Dr. Hearn pounded the brake pedal; with a quivering lunge he jumped the curb and crashed into a hydrant. Officer Mowbray swung wildly to the left but could not avoid creasing the fender of his newly-washed vehicle. As the officer approached his victim, he perceived his catch to be of those smart aleck doctors who felt they were above the law.

"Doc," he said, "too bad this had to happen." He checked registration, license, plates, and inspected the damage. "You'll have to notify your insurance company, and the town will have something to say about damage to the hydrant and my car." Mowbray had been taught to begin in a friendly spirit, to start a case with apparent accommodation and sweetness and turn the screws later when the evidence was gathered.

Mike said, "Damn it, I'll make the highway department fill that rut. I could have been killed!" His verbal resentment had to travel a short distance to Officer Mowbray's face, whereupon the latter sniffed and wrinkled his nose. Evidence which he had not suspected was wafted toward him.

"Have you been drinking?" asked Mowbray.

"Not really what could be called drinking. A little beer."

"It stinks all over the place."

Mike laughed. The young squirt was being funny and he would respond in kind. Three lines into a story of a hard-drinking priest, a tippling rabbi, and an abstinent minister, Officer Mowbray's naturally suspicious nature was acutely aroused.

"I'm taking you to the hospital for blood tests," he said.

"Say, do you know who I am? Every cop in the county knows Dr. Michael Hearn, which name is mine, and furthermore they would not like what you are doing. Why go for blood tests? Here, I can show you anything you like — walk a straight line, write in the most legible penmanship you ever saw, or a prescription. I can write you a prescription in Latin."

Officer Mowbray was more convinced than ever that his decision was correct. He ushered Mike into his car and drove to the emergency entrance of the hospital.

"This is outrageous. You have no regard for the medical profession."

"You're no different from anyone else."

Mowbray truly believed it. Mike's voice rose. Intuition reinforced the presentiment that no good would come of this. His manner turned boisterous, aggressive. He pulled at the officer's sleeve, which was promptly and officiously wrenched away. He flattered, pleaded, lectured on the shame which could permanently blemish the record of an innocent man. Nothing swayed the smug cop.

As Mike was led into an examination cubicle he saw his first and only ray of light. Carla was on duty, having relieved the nurse who had gone to supper. Mowbray quoted the chapter and verse of the state legal code to Carla, and completed his recitation with a firm request for a blood alcohol test.

"Officer, please sit in the waiting room around the bend," Carla said. When he disappeared she said to Mike, "I didn't expect to see you here as a patient, well, almost a patient. What happened?"

"A little car accident. I couldn't help hitting a rut. The goddamn hole should have been filled. This guy, the cop, was right on my tail. He's nuts, Carla; he's got to be Dracula's offspring."

"Couldn't you talk him out of the blood test?"

"He's got blood in his eye, wants to make a federal case of it."

Carla's head moved back in the onslaught of stale beer odor. "God, Mike, that blood test could be higher than we'd like."

Mike placed two mints into his mouth. "I suppose it could, but look at me, I'm perfectly fine," as he attempted to convince her by repeatedly touching the end of his nose with an extended finger tip. On the third attempt he struck his eye.

"Come on," she said, "let's get it over with. If the test shows anything serious, I'll say you were not drunk, that you were in control. The clinical condition is important in these cases."

"If the test doesn't mean that much, I have an idea." He paused. His eyes implored her, begged, a stare of bewildered supplication. He continued, "Let me stick your arm. It won't hurt. We'll give him your blood and he won't know the difference. Carla, I promise it won't hurt."

"Mike, it's not the pain. I couldn't do it."

"Why not? You know me. I'm the kind who won't step on insects. If that bastard gets any evidence at all against me he'll finish me off." He pushed an imaginary dagger into his chest.

"Mike, relax. I'll take the sample from you and nothing will come of it."

"No you won't! Damn it, I gave you an alternative. It's my only chance, and you want to shut the door on me. Everybody wants to shut doors on me. I tell you I won't be shit on by every two-bit jerk who has to show authority."

He pushed Carla against the wall, one hand at her throat, the other holding the syringe. He ripped up her sleeve and plunged the needle into the front of her elbow; but its tip was nowhere near the vein. Carla did not cry out. She bent her leg and propelled the heel of her shoe against his knee cap. Mike slumped to the floor, the syringe safe in his hand. Carla bandaged her punctured arm and helped him up. She laid Mike on the table and bandaged an ice bag about his knee. He moaned, could have fought on, but accepted the perverted solace of the loser.

"Take it," he whispered to Carla, pointing to the great vein exposed at his elbow.

Legal aspects of Dr. Hearn's brush with the law were easily resolved, despite Officer Mowbray's insistence that the crime was worthy of jailing. The blood test was found to be slightly above normal, but in veiw of the doctor's record and glorious testimonials by colleagues, the case was dismissed with a warning. Mike still believed he was the subject of persecution.

He vowed to sue the county for its rut-filled roads, but other events rose to diminish his zeal. The hospital board — a doctor, a nurse, and three members of the community — held an emergency meeting. It appears that they had heard of a drinking doctor on their staff, an issue the public interpreted as a dire threat to the life and limb of trusting souls who entered the institution. To them, each bed was an altar, every doctor a priest or minister, though they overlooked the fact that the latter were permitted a nip or two between sermons.

The physician representing the medical staff on the board had to be the most mature, most experienced practitioner available. Israel was a natural choice. He objected, said he was a friend of the defendant, for this was to be an ex-officio trial of consequence without the clog of legal statutes. "We are all friends of Dr. Hearn," they said, "and you have the training to be impartial." For the moment it was forgotten that the verdict was already in. The lay segment of the board — the minister and two businessmen — had already solidified its opinion. One member was president of a loan company, the other a star salesman of medical insurance. Both maintained they were watchdogs of the public domain and would apply the same standards of integrity expected in their own businesses.

The day before the meeting Israel was undecided as to how he should vote. He spoke to the head nurse, who had a vote. "Dr. Steingut," Miss Garland proclaimed, "I am strict, as you know, but I can forgive. If I could not there wouldn't be a nurse or doctor left in this hospital." Israel examined her quizzically. Sunken skin lines radiated from the corners of her parched lips. Her tongue was coated. She was not old enough for the deepened wrinkles on her neck and forehead. Two finger nails were chewed to skin pulp.

"How will you vote?" asked Israel.

"Not guilty, of course. What I really mean is guilty with extenuating circumstances, but I won't mention that. Dr. Hearn has never made a mistake, as far as I know, and if he does the work and doesn't bother my girls, that's good enough for me."

Israel had expected the opposite of her. He recalled Mike had treated Miss Garland for pneumonia, had been ungrudging when called on to examine a nurse at any hour of the day or night. Still, she would have labelled anything else a dereliction of duty. Perhaps she, too, was a closet drinker, or used to be, but the judgment was too complex with too many unknowns to waste time on conjecture. What mattered was that he might now gather enough votes to lift the stigma from Dr. Hearn. Friendship did not attach itself easily to Israel, and when it did it did not stay long. He always wanted someone close, a bosom pal, whose honest warmth might fill the gaps of his own perplexed life.

Israel sought to persuade the minister, who held the crucial vote. The minister's attitude toward Mike's transgression was equal to the Pope's opinion of a priest with a harem. Yet this was a time for persistence, thought Israel, who felt he was cast by fate to guard the underdog, the misunderstood, the flotsam of a society which pounced upon the defenseless. In moments of introspection he had to reassure himself he was the protector of Mike Hearn and not Israel Steingut.

The opinion of the Rev. Dr. Thaddeus Thornbush was of great concern. He was pastor of the imposing First Presbyterian Church, tall, thin, black hair parted in the middle, the acknowledged master of the gentle sermon which subtly brought his flock to the brink of fire and brimstone. Thaddeus was low-key but effective. Israel and the minister stood outside the hospital beside a brass plaque inscribed to its founder, Judge John Downey — The inscription read: "He lived devoted to Justice, Integrity, and the Healing Arts."

Israel said, "Please, sir, I would like a minute of your time. Dr. Hearn's case is coming up. I feel he should be allowed to hold his position in the hospital."

"I don't think so," said Thornbush.

"We know he drinks, but it's not in excess and doesn't interfere with his work."

"There is always the chance it might."

"As a medical man, I assure you Mike is a safe physician, one you may be proud to have on your staff."

"Son, the issue is temperance," said Thornbush in his most fatherly manner.

Israel prodded on. "Mike gets good results, and they are not dependent on moral virtues."

Reverend Thornbush pursed his lips as if to quote his interpretation of gospel. "A hospital must be guided by the spiritual as well as the scientific."

"Mr. Thornbush, sir, we don't seem to be on the same wave length. I am talking of a man whose reputation may be ruined. His livelihood is at stake."

"Dr. Hearn's problem should be judged in its entirety."

Israel's voice was shrill. "I don't follow you. You mouth some vague ideas which could be debated in a seminary, while I'm worried about a man who has a weakness but hurts no one. Help is what he needs, not a sermon."

The discussants had lost their professionalism. Coarseness encroached on civility.

"Son," said the minister, "how dare you preach to me! I can only hope you mend your ways." He turned abruptly and walked away. Israel's mouth opened. He wanted to shout, "Compassion! Have you ever heard of compassion?" but said nothing as his precious swing vote bounded across the lawn in a veil of self righteousness.

Nor was Carla supportive of Israel's opinion, though she appreciated the ardor with which he pursued his beliefs. When told that Miss Garland displayed such unexpected benevolence toward Dr. Hearn, Carla said, "She's a little off the beam, and unpredictable. You can never tell which way that woman will turn. She might like you for the way your hair is combed, or hate you because of a slip in grammar. No, I couldn't go along with her just because she agrees with you. As for the minister, you shouldn't have spoken to him at all. He's pompous and slippery-tongued. It's a wonder anyone believes him."

"Then why are you against Mike? Is it because he knocked you to the wall when he was desperate? Of course it sounds terrible, but he was distraught, and when he saw how foolish he was he did the right thing."

"Israel, nobody knows about his nutty attack in the emergency room. For a time I didn't care if he went to jail. But I agree, that wasn't Mike Hearn sticking the needle in my arm. He would never do it again. It's the drinking at all hours, during work, that I don't like."

"Now you sound like Thornbush."

She was indignant. "Don't put me in the same pew with that minister. I believe in a second chance, but I don't want to see Mike get to the point where he needs a second chance. I've seen enough alcoholics, and surely Mike is one, to know that they must not escape their own punishment. It will be too late when the booze softens his brain. One good boot now for what he did is just what he needs. It's the only sensible thing to do, and it's not easy."

She made sense, thought Israel, but he was reluctant to admit it. Carla's strength lay in her ability to draw upon her unsuspected store of prudence. How was it that Carla, the practical one, and the minister who skirted the evidence, reached the same conclusion? They dealt from the extreme poles of logic. To disregard Mike's needs so blatantly was a form of mental fascism. Israel rationalized that neither of them could assess the true picture. What was important at this moment was a friend in need, and to hell with the future. Israel had embarked on a strong, new, course, wherein he would not waver from a decision in the matter of Dr. Hearn. To falter would confront him with his past, when, a boy, he failed to take the definitive action that might have saved his mother.

The five defacto judges gathered about a long oak table in a mahogony paneled room. It was the only elegant space a community hospital was permitted, and it exuded the stiff, modern splendor of a banker's lounge. For here the alchemists of business transposed matters of healing into dollars and cents, discussed the purchase of a new respirator, or an orthopedic table, provided tables of charges to pay for equipment. The balance sheet was king, and these knights of the oak table defended their financial proposals with monastic zeal and executive insight.

The case of Mike Hearn engendered little debate. Dourness prevailed. Mike had wanted to be there but the hospital code excluded his presence, a legal twist by which the board saved itself the embarrassment of facing the accused. After a few preliminary matters a vote was called by the banker whether or not Dr. Hearn should be forced to seek employment elsewhere. The request for the decision was an interjection, a glum call which smacked of a foregone conclusion.

The head nurse stood up for Mike Hearn, and there were two immediate votes against him. The insurance agent had not yet been called upon. Israel interceded, "Before further votes are called for I wish to say a few words." The men glared at him. Israel's stocky figure loomed impregnable over the board table, a bird of prey about to disrupt the lethargy of the hen house.

Israel began: "I will not repeat what is already acknowledged to be true, that Dr. Hearn is a competent physician who never shirked his duties. I believe he will not repeat his error. We seem to be panic-stricken over what people will think of a doctor who took a few drinks during a working day. Institutions make mistakes and are forgiven; an individual is not. There are times when it is more important to excuse a man or woman, than to defend an organization."

Israel's voice was tremulous. He gazed down at the dark stain of the oak table as if he were ashamed to continue. Words tumbled out.

"My father was a Jew. He was killed because he refused to be dehumanized. He was cut down by a system, an organization. They did not care about him as a person. There was a code, and there were no exceptions. They were not interested in my father the physician who had given the community more than he got. Dr. Hearn has given this community more than he ever received."

The eyes of the insurance agent were filmy wet within an anguished expression. The least intelligent of the lot, he was most susceptible to impassioned rhetoric, might even be swayed to vote contrary to his colleagues.

Israel pounded the table. "What you intend to do is destroy Dr. Hearn. You should not care what others think of him, or the hospital. This board should be a friend to my friend. Please give Dr. Hearn the opportunity which is his right."

Israel sat and wiped his brow. He tapped his finger on the table, his personal Morse code that he, Israel Steingut, had for once challenged adversity with the counsel of his heart. Surely, he thought, the pipsqueaks on the other side of the table must side with him. Should he win the vote, he determined not to gloat. Victory would be sweet, but he would contain his reactions, revel in the triumph silently, as he reflected that he had not told the complete story. The bit about his father was not deliberate, but pulled out of nowhere, perhaps from a convoluted dream about a stubborn father who got what he deserved. Israel's passion of the moment could have been a great lie.

Upon meeting with Carla in a cafe after the meeting, she was jubilant. He nibbled at his dry toast though he had not eaten since breakfast.

Carla said, "I heard you lost."

"That's correct. You bring it up as if it makes you happy."

"Not at all. Miss Garland told me of your speech. She nearly came to tears, loved it when you spoke of your father. I wish I had been there."

"Do you know what that damn minister did? Before the final vote he asked to speak to the others. I couldn't prevent it. He said I equated them with dictators and Nazis. That did it. The insurance agent was in my pocket, but when he voted against Mike he spat it as if I were the one they were kicking off the staff."

"What did you expect? You can't win when the odds are stacked against you. What's important is that you had your say without holding back. That bunch will squirm for a long time because of you."

"Then you would have voted with me."

"I would not! I still believe Mike has to face the music, for his own good."

Israel finished his toast and ordered the waitress to bring a full lunch. He had revived. Now that the affair was over, he had to admit this woman, this Carla he had learned to love, was right in her curious way. Without study or intensive introspection she had fathomed a certain truth in Mike's problems which he had refused to accept. Basically they were in agreement about Dr. Hearn, but she saw the situation in the light of common sense, when she sought his salvation in immediate punishment, as a child should be punished soon after an act of destruction.

Israel was dismayed that he, Carla, and the hospital board were not earth-shaking events in the fortunes of Dr. Hearn. In one week Mike found a position in a state psychiatric institution as a resident internist. He was happy. "Plenty of cardiac pathology to interest me," he said. "Of course it may be difficult to get good histories and that will challenge my diagnostic skills." This ability to avoid the moroseness, to search for a new job, to accommodate to daily conditions, was a trait Israel wished he had. Beer drinking might be a problem, though not as insurmountable as some he knew.

When Mike was about to drive away on a day of goodbyes, Israel noted there were no six-packs of beer, no jugs of wine stashed in the vehicle. The luggage compartment was filled with books and a bundle of unwashed laundry, and on the back seat lay an oversized tan vinyl suitcase, a Sears Roebuck purchase to celebrate a going and a coming. Mike opened the valise to assure Israel nothing alcoholic was tucked beneath clean shirts and long white doctor's coats. A silent communication between friends was in progress, the doubter mollified by the wayward sinner who managed to convey his own piece of advice. "I've had my fling and enjoyed every minute of it. Now I'm ready to settle down." Israel wondered when he would be able to say that.

In Carla's apartment that evening they drank wine and played Mozart on the stereo. Israel maintained that Carla should be exposed to good music if they were to enjoy common interests. When his glass was emptied and they had eaten she placed a Montovani record on the turntable. Carla listened to her favorite melodies with romantic enchantment. Perhaps it was the wine, or the revelations he had gathered from Mike's departure which made him drift into a limp state of pleasurable acceptance. Unlike Carla, ruminations of love-making took no part in his relaxation. The banality of the simple strains he was subjected to required no effort on his part, nor did they stimulate him. A void opened itself to him, a gaping depression to be filled with conjured images. He tried to revive his father as a solid image to see and touch and converse with. Listening within the silence of his half-dream, refrains came to him in monotone; do not use your fork as a spear, it is disgusting...cut the roast without sliding the plate off the table...do not crouch forward; his mother interrupted, defended him with a kiss and a children's tune sung close to his ear.

Carla stood and slowly removed her clothes. She stepped to the center of the room and turned in simulated dance, moved sinuously to entice her partner from his distant reverie. Naked, her long fingers brushed down over her waist, skirted the width of her pelvis to the sculptured protrusion of her buttocks. Israel was startled. He had been in the past, now the present offered reimbursements as well as terrors. As he held her he was astonished that his passion was undiminished by Montovani's violins.

Chapter 8

ISRAEL STEINGUT, AS the boy Helmut, on a farm in Germany, expanded his endurance and aggravated his frailties. Four years of work and growth had not changed the appearance of the acreage on which he and his mother found refuge. Stark, tedious winters were erased in the triumph of spring. Demands of rural autumns were silenced by December snows. Earth, foliage, and crops were the same; only living flesh changed.

That the war had gone badly and was about to be lost was the topic of conversation in the village six miles from the farm. The talk was more in the nature of animated gossip, without the anguish of cities and other more populous farm areas, where crops were ravaged and broken furniture lay beneath mounds of rubble; where burial parties supplanted tears with dry-eyed shock. The Steinguts were fortunate, thus far, to be at a farm and near a village which were relatively untouched.

Once a stray bomb fell in a field. The hole that was excavated laid open an underground stream which had the impact of an archeological find on the visiting population.

Anna Grunstein looked older and felt weaker, but her wits were sharpened by confrontation. The military soon learned of the lush harvest of her expertise and entered into multiple contractual relationships to purchase her foodstuffs. She benefited by avoiding contact with village authorities who would have confiscated rather than pay, who would have sent a trail of inspector assessors to carry off her goods. She produced, gathered, and delivered while the farm remained isolated. Planning and managing were specialities she could afford to develop, as Helmut and Isolde did the heavy work.

Helmut, now twelve, grew stocky and muscular. The cuteness of his boy's nose was replaced by a respectable proboscis exaggerated by the unprofessional cut of his black hair; but his eyes overshadowed facial extensions, dark and searching as two glistening light beams. Schooling was no problem for the boy. Anna and his mother sent for books by mail, and the village library and bookstore asked no questions when texts were sought during infrequent visits to the village. Transactions were consummated just before closing time, when the streets were empty.

In his first spring on the farm Helmut had planted a tree, a poplar, a thin wisp of branch with a small but compact root system. Anna instructed him how deeply to dig, how to support and nourish its growth. He set the roots into the earth on a lazy day when his mind was empty and he was gripped by an undefined urge. Helmut then had no conscious thoughts of growth, of life, or the effects of seasons. The earth was ready and he was ready, and somehow out of an unstructured swirl of vital forces they were drawn to each other. When the tree had managed to grow a stout little stump Helmut stood beside it and examined his flexed biceps. Now it was a four-year growth, triumphant in the shadow it cast as the sun beat down. Helmut thought of his initial planting, how small it had been, how little he was then.

Mother and son knew that Werner Steingut would not return. Unlike the shock and grief of a body, a casket, a funeral, Helmut's brush with death was a constant stream of torment, aimless in its turbulence. He dreamed he was a shipwrecked sailor in a rowboat holding back huge waves with his oar. He wished the oar were wider so that he might succeed, yet he realized the impossibility of his predicament when he awoke. There were many inaccessible solutions, and they confused him. But there were accomplishments too. The reason he had to live on the farm was plain to him, and he had made the necessary adjustments. Anna's peasant shrewdness and daring beneficence toward her refugee boarders were gratefully acknowledged. His mother the urban beauty now was a willing farm worker who sang when she did chores. Isolde was more than well adjusted, she enjoyed herself in her apparent isolation.

"Mother," he said, "I dreamt of father last night. Do you have those dreams?"

"I used to, but its been so long I don't remember any. You, too, must forget. Your father is not here, and we can work our way without him."

"You always took his absence so well, while I hardly remember what he looked like."

"He was attractive like you. Taller, yes, but you will be better built, like a rock."

"I suppose," said Helmut, "you can feel happy because you did all you could for him. Maybe I didn't do enough."

"You were only a child. There is nothing more anyone could have done."

"I know. Still, I feel if it happened again now, right now, I could have talked to him, held him back. I never had the chance to hold him back." He sobbed.

Isolde was more fortunate. She did not remember her dreams.

There were nights when Helmut watched her twist in bed, writhe, call out a train of strange names which ended with Werner. Yet, she always awoke refreshed and ready for work. She was the kind who made her demons confront each other as she urged them on to destruction. By daylight her battlefield was cleared of debris and the first ray of light was her stimulant injection. The only moments of despair which overcame her were filled with anger toward her enforced isolation, or due to physical mishaps, a sliver in the finger after carting wood, a knee burned by hot soup overflowing its pot. Then she would think of Werner and why that stubborn husband, who was supposed to ensure her comfort, did not get her out of this mess. Besides, life would become more stimulating now. An old acquaintance, someone who might be trusted within their little secret circle, was back. The soldier who had carried their boxes up the hill when they first arrived had returned to his old anti-aircraft unit. Axel Gans had been gone a long, lonely two years.

In his first tour of duty near Anna's farm, Axel lived well as the star foragger of his battalion. He found fresh food, liquor, even chocolate, fare fit for generals and visiting dignitaries. No one knew or cared how he filled the larder. But his commanding officer became anxious, perhaps guilt stricken, over his largesse. He would say, "Axel Gans is a wolf with angel wings, and he needs clipping. When the bombs fall Axel will be a detriment to morale." He had Axel transferred to a unit at the front. When Axel saw the barbed wire, ruts, holes, and unshaven soldiers caked with mud and sweat, he decided he could best serve the fatherland in a less troubled spot. His preference was to return to Anna's farm and her two engaging boarders.

One gruesome afternoon the artillary guns became overheated. Hot steel splattered, sweat and blood mingled on limbs and bodies until it was impossible to tell how much a man had bled. Axel, untouched, knew his fate would be sealed in another battle like this. He picked up a shell fragment in his gloved hand, ripped his trousers in a ragged pattern with his knife and crashed the jagged metal into his leg until he felt it scrape the bone. Tearing the flesh of the initial opening, he watched his wounded muscles part in cooked-meat layers.

For three months he resided in a military hospital, thoroughly enjoyed his multiple surgeries and skin grafts. When he totalled the cost of his venture versus its returns, he concluded that his residual, mild limp was a bargain. A man who could not run quickly could still be sent to the line, especially if he whimpered and begged for discharge. Instead, Axel spoke to the authorities with the persuasive sincerity of half-truths.

"Sir, I am highly trained as an anti-aircraft gunner. This is where one so crippled as I can best help my country. My old unit is hard pressed, and the other men will help me where my weak leg might buckle. Please let me serve, sir, to the best of my ability."

Axel was driven to his old unit in a military vehicle which chugged up the hill he knew so well; threadbare tires dragged through gravel to the crest. He saw the white and red farmhouse, revived the pleasant memories of his first tour of duty, the winter nights when he was supposed to be in barracks but managed to walk away almost at will. Axel recalled when he first saw Isolde. He would walk across snow-encrusted fields, would watch for the farmhouse bedroom shade to be raised, and if he waited long enough, he would see the old lady go by. Then the boy, a nice enough young fellow, would jump on the bed, at times fully dressed. Faces could not be closely examined at this distance in the trees, but Axel could detect that the boy might be crying. The way he hung his head, the languid movements of his limbs, conveyed a quality of sorrow.

As he spied through the window, the young mother would enter the room. Axel thought of his visual activities as a form of personality study, not voyeurism. She was pretty, with an enticing figure, and there was no man about the house. Was the husband a soldier? If so he would be a comrade in arms, with whom sharing should be a fact of military life. Or was her husband dead? Perhaps she was burdened with an illegitimate child. There was no sense in conjecture. Should fruit fall from the tree, smell it, lick it, but wait until it is ripe.

Axel's stoicism was shaken when he first glimpsed the lady naked. For a split second he imagined the snow had melted and velvety grass cushioned his feet. When the window shade was lowered abruptly his toes were cold again. The scene, he recalled, would be repeated, waiting under the trees, the nude body framed in the window, and the shade abruptly pulled down. After several such visual dramas on succeeding nights, the shade remained down.

Axel recalled his thoughts when he had first met Isolde. "If I am a despicable voyeur, which I am not, then she is partly to blame for exposing herself. I shall have to meet her properly, above board, like a man and woman should. It will not be difficult, as I am certain we can find a suitable common ground." As he trudged through the snow back to the barracks he felt he could howl like the wolves that once roamed the forest; he lifted the open end of his glove and pinched his wrist between his teeth, savored the taste of his flesh.

Anna Grunstein brought them together. A roof shingle had fallen. It was his afternoon off and he lay in the grass watching the house. He came at once to make the repair and Anna judged she had snared a pair of powerful shoulders and facile, willing hands. Isolde and Helmut were called out and introduced, and Anna coyly suggested that labor need not go unrewarded. She packed four fresh eggs in a bag with rolls of fluffed paper between them, and presented her gift. Axel helped Anna, and invariably returned to the barracks with gifts. Permission to leave camp was now easy to obtain. He visited the farm often, offered his services in a variety of odd jobs.

"Where did you learn to handle tools so well?" Anna asked.

"For a time I was a mechanic. The army wanted me to work on trucks and tanks, but when I saw the heavy work I told them I hurt my back bending over a motor."

"You didn't actually hurt your back." Anna sniffed his slyness.

"Of course not. I stated the facts in such a way they saw me as a hospital patient rather than a soldier. That is why I came to a quiet spot in an anti-aircraft unit."

His skill with a wrench and hammer were prime examples of manual dexterity. With the knife, however, he was an artist. For two bloody years he had worked in a packing plant, where he had to skin a carcass with deft slashes of a knife. When his foreman saw his smooth, easy movements, the controlled cuts executed gracefully as a ballet performer, he gave Axel difficult trim jobs, where he cleared expensive cuts of beef of excess tissue.

"I will make a toy for your son," he informed Isolde. He cut a block of ash from a log, and with rapid hacking and skiving motions with his knife fashioned the figure of a boy with a projecting lump of wood at its side. Slicing away thin slivers the lump emerged as a briefcase.

"You see," said Axel, "this boy goes to school. Helmut doesn't go to school, but he can look at this and will do just as well. What good is school anyway? He can learn more from you and me."

Isolde complimented him on his artistry. She trembled. He had insinuated himself into their lives, had insinuated his suspicion of who they were and why they were there. There was a dangerous irony in the presentation of a wooden schoolboy when he knew Helmut was not registered as a student in the village. Questions from him were expected, but he already had formulated the answers.

Axel came and went, made toys for Helmut, walked and laughed with Isolde. She chose to forget her predicament and Axel helped her do so.

He recalled one day when Isolde and he were to go for a walk. She rushed into an adjoining room to retrieve a scarf from a dresser drawer. Reaching her hand into a pile of laundered clothes and folded sweaters, a black saucer-shaped piece of cloth fell to the floor. Axel stood at the open door. He stepped in to pick up the fallen material, and as he did so Isolde's teeth clenched shut.

He said, "Why, this is a skull cap, the kind Jews wear when they pray."

"It's a memento. My husband used it to cover his head. He had a thin hair line. He couldn't stand the cold." She spoke in a rush, would have continued, but Axel smiled in amusement. Isolde sensed the incredibility of her explanations. Her lies could only lead to deeper disbelief. She hoped he would be as tolerant as Anna.

"No, my dear," Axel said, "That is a boy's yarmulke, Helmut's of course. I know about these things as I lived near a Jewish neighborhood and had several friends who wore them. It makes no difference to me. Bare heads or covered, it makes no difference to me."

He placed his hands on her shoulders gently so that the menace evaporated. She looked at him with defiance. As he squeezed her arms in reassurance he whispered into her ear, "Do not be afraid. I figured it out long ago. You and the boy. Helmut's nose and eyes are not exactly a poster picture of the Aryan youngster those fools believe will save the country. I don't care where you came from. No one else will find out. It's none of their business."

Isolde cried with convulsive, uncontrollable sobs. He dried her tears, stroked her cheeks. The calloused contact of his fingers were tokens of support for her, unknown since she lived on the farm. Often she had thought how tightly bound she was by silence and subterfuge, that she could become as deformed as the feet of a Chinese girl swathed in bandages. Now the bindings were loosened. She could stretch to full length, rise to her toes and laugh for a while.

Long walks, discussions, romps with Helmut, gifts of wine he brought, or a book he knew she wanted for her son — these engaged Axel and Isolde as the war beat out its destructive rhythms miles away. Life was easy for him, and Isolde felt reasonably safe. Anna Grunstein was skeptical, more careful.

"Axel," she said, "you know about my boarders and me. We are in the midst of a hornet's nest. If you say something, anything, we are all in deep trouble. You too."

"Not me, Anna. I am an innocent bystander. But you needn't worry about me."

Anna put her proposition forward, sharply and deliberately, pointed straight at the gut of the problem. She had not evaded the authorities thus far without cognizance of the wiles of peasants who had protected themselves from overlords for centuries. She said, "Axel, how long have you been coming here?"

"Oh, six months or more."

"And when did you begin to take fresh eggs, and pork, and vegetables back to the barracks?"

"From the very first time I visited, and I won't forget how good you have been."

"Never mind that," she waved away all extraneous conversation. "I have a record of all the food I gave you, and on what days. Do you know what the official penalty is for protecting Jews?" She paused. "By someone in the military?" Pause. "For protection in return for receiving bribes?"

Isolde was not present to see the froth at the corners of his mouth, the reflex grasp for his knife in its sheaths, the sheepish grin. Axel turned through a full circle, to dance his way out of this serious business. He wiped his brow.

In a low, even voice he spoke to Anna, "I am a lot like you. I don't believe all this shit that's thrown out to the stupid public today. I wouldn't tell anyone I know, and you can be sure I like to take good care of my health. In a way, we are insurance against each other. If you are good to me, I will be good to you."

When he walked away Anna was satisfied and relieved. He was another man she had bested, this one more dangerous than most. But he had an obvious weakness himself. He was not the type to do what dishonored Japanese did, stick a knife in the belly. What a nerve saying he was just like her! His honor meant that he could be true to his selfishness. The only way to control a man like that was to put him on the block and let a knife swing over his neck.

Anna instructed Isolde, "I spoke to Axel and we straightened out some problems. You may be perfectly normal with him, though you must tell him as little as possible. He won't say a word about us. I fixed that. Of course, if I were you, I would not get too close to him, if you know what I mean. These men can be controlled if they are not crazy. Trouble is, a pretty lady makes some of them crazy. Then watch out, because they no longer know themselves."

When Axel left for the front, he kissed Isolde and pecked Anna on the cheek. "I'll be back," he promised. He lifted Helmut high, told him to study hard and keep his mouth shut, and turned to Isolde, "If he ever wears the skull cap be sure to pull down the shades." She blushed. She did not want him to leave. His visits brought a threat and reality. But she could not hope to meet another man without undue risk to Helmut and herself. She would await his second coming as she would a Messiah, though the fervor with which she anticipated his return was not pious.

Chapter 9

AT FIVE-THIRTY in the morning, when the farm comes to life, it is difficult to guess the cold, moist night might give way to the warmth of the spring day. Anna awakened Helmut and Isolde early. It was Sunday, and she knew there would be a visitor that morning.

"We will breakfast early," Anna said, "so that we can tidy the house and finish chores on time."

"Time for what?" asked Helmut. Now that he was twelve and doing man's work, he sought explanations from his fellow workers.

"I did not want to tell you until I was sure. Two days ago a military vehicle stopped on the road and a man got out. He just looked at the farm for a bit, went back to his seat, and the driver was off. It was Axel."

Isolde stiffened. She lost her grip on the fork she held, stooped to retrieve it as it rattled to the floor.

Helmut said, "What! Axel Gans? I remember him. He's the one who made the wooden toys I played with when I was a kid."

"Correct," said Anna. "He helped us, about two years ago, and we repaid him with food which he took back to the barracks. I delivered eggs there yesterday and I checked with the lieutenant. It was Axel who looked us over, and I expect he'll show up this morning."

"But does he know, about us?" As man of the household, Helmut was no longer passive in matters of family security.

Isolde responded slowly, "He does know about us, Helmut. He promised to keep it secret. I believe he has kept his promise."

"If he has changed, if he talks," Helmut said emphatically, "we could be picked up. So far people don't know about us, or if they do they don't care. I don't want anything to go wrong now."

Anna was stern. "Finish your breakfast. Nothing has changed. Axel Gans will be just as he was."

At eleven that morning Helmut sat on a log before the house. When the crunch of impacted leaves startled him, he dropped the book he held. He ran forward and halted. Axel Gans approached rapidly, almost at a run. He threw himself at Helmut and hugged him closely. He tried to lift the boy, managed to raise him a few inches but had to let him down. The soldier's brow was furrowed in pain.

"Now we are equal," said Axel. "I no longer can pick you up like a boy."

They walked hand in hand to the house. Isolde welcomed him, turned her cheek for a brotherly greeting. Her lips quivered; she could not contain the foolish lump in her chest. Anna stood her ground, like a general inspecting his ranks, then stepped toward Axel and placed her hands on his arms. It was a pragmatic greeting. Stepping back she looked at him, up, down, up, and said, "You are fit, Mr. Gans, very fit, except for that leg."

"Yes, I am lucky." Axel faced Anna. "And I see you won't be satisfied till I tell you all about it. Alright, later. I'll tell you later." They sat for an early dinner. Axel laughed as Anna sought pardon for a meager repast; he had not seen fresh meat and greens for years.

"Where did you get the food?" exclaimed Axel, who considered himself a forager par excellance, a purveyor of the unobtainable.

"We have our ways," said Anna. "There are shortages, as you know, and there are tricks to overcome them."

He told them where he had been, the desperate fighting, his relief upon suffering his wound, hospital was the next best place to life on the farm, the military reverses of German forces, the war was lost and he did not care. He said, "Nowhere in the past years have I eaten like this. I wish this lousy war would end, one way or the other."

As the afternoon progressed Anna insinuated subtle questions and ambivalent requests, which prodded Axel to talk. Then, in the graceless fashion of an investigative reporter who has her quarry opened up, she asked, "Axel, how did you get your wound?" He was surprised but unflustered.

"I could lie to you, but I won't. I did it to myself with a piece of hot steel, and they bought the story I told them." He turned to Helmut. "You might think I am a coward, but that is not so. I took a risk, could have been shot. What is important is to believe in something, and do what you must to get it; or, just as important, if you hate something or someone, you should have the will to wipe it out, kill if you have to."

Helmut mulled over the statement. He overflowed with fancied revenge. Instead of the will to retaliate, he was left with a chasm of doubt and skepticism which he could not fill. Anna, however, was eminently satisfied with Axel's discourse. She removed her notebook from her pocket, the book in which she entered sales, gifts of food, dates and names, and she wrote slowly and legibly on a clean page what Axel had said about his wound. She repeated it to him to check its accuracy.

"Why do you tell us this story about your leg?" Isolde asked.

Axel was serious. "What you have put down is correct, Anna. I will even sign my name to it. I have thought it over, and I know what I am doing. My secret is yours. You know what is most dangerous to me. You have my confidence and I would like yours. Since you know as much about me as I do of you, you can feel perfectly safe in my presence."

Instinctively Anna perceived she had obtained a kind of insurance, a fairly safe means by which to ride out the war. A situation could arise where he would deny the self infliction of his wound, whereas she could hardly evade a charge of harboring Jews once an investigation was begun. She planned to further implicate Axel.

Unknowingly, Axel solved Anna's dilemma. His work in the anti-aircraft unit consisted of keeping books, arranging leaves of absence and typing rosters. Chided by his buddies for sedentary military duties performed within a schedule as lax as any officer's he would point to his leg and exaggerate his limp.

"How did you get your scars?" they asked, cognizant of Axel's penchant for avoiding irritants.

"It was after I killed over two hundred of the enemy. It had to come sooner or later."

"Come on, Axel," they laughed, "you never saw one of the enemy. If you did, you ran the other way and probably tripped over a rabbit."

However, the men respected his ability to forage rather than his military spirit. He frequently brought food from the farm, and the officer in charge smacked his thick lips over mouth-watering bounties sent by Anna Grunstein. Though they received deliveries in quantity as well as quality, part had to be turned over, with full accounting, to the quartermaster corps in the village. The give and take was satisfactory, but there was a great deal more where those fresh rations were grown and stored. He approached Axel for a deal.

"Corporal, you know the farm across the field where that young widow and boy live?"

"Yes sir," said Axel, wondering whether he was the subject of a fishing expedition regarding the farm's occupants.

"They do well for themselves, don't they?"

"I believe so," Axel agreed, "though I do not ask about their business. I visit the place for wholesome relaxation, like a make-believe family. Sir, if it weren't for the war I believe I would be a hard working family man."

"Who the hell cares about your personal longings! I remember you used to bring back a side of roast pig, a couple dozen eggs. Now you come with dribbles. We want as much as they can spare."

Axel guessed his intention. He spoke like a submissive schoolboy,

"Won't it have to go through the quartermaster corps? They always want their share."

"That's where you come in. You can't do heavy work, so you have to give me your brains. Or wits. Make a deal with that farm woman."

"I can tell Mrs. Grunstein you demand all she can spare. She can't refuse a German officer."

"No, dumbbell. We don't want complaints from her to the authorities. We'll suck her into an arrangement she can't complain about. We'll pay. Not what she would get on the open market, but enough. Tell her we could become very good friends; if not, we could find our own complaints against her, or anyone else for that matter."

Axel progressed to particulars. "How would I keep the accounts for payment?"

"The men will contribute to a fund. Call it the athletic and recreation fund. You know, keep fit for the fatherland and all that crap. You will keep the books."

When Axel described the scheme to Anna, she frowned, a decided external expression of disbelief and moral indignation. Internally she executed flying leaps and somersaults.

She said, "Axel, do you realize what could happen if the quartermaster corps found out?"

He chuckled. "It would be a big stew, with my lieutenant in the pot first, then me and you."

"Well," she said, "it's practically an order, and like you soldiers, I must obey orders."

Her safety insurance was now double-barreled, top level, backed by the hides of officers of the German army. She could easily keep her part of the bargain in the chain of supply, and they had to keep theirs, for there were questions which could be asked, books which could be checked. If they came after Isolde, or Helmut, or herself, she would repay them in kind.

Anna's contractual ingenuity transformed the farm into an enclave of comparative freedom. In this carefree ambience Axel and Isolde grew closer. When he no longer helped with the chores, they walked past exposed fields and gardens into the screened depths of nearby woods. The edge of the forest was orderly, spaced with broad-trunked trees through which sunlight streamed. They sat against an oak beside a patch of moss.

Axel said, "This is the life. You should be happy."

"Momentarily, yes," Isolde replied, "Happiness should include a feeling of permanence, and I haven't had that for years."

He placed his arm across her shoulders and released the top button of his jacket. "Think of the present, the beauty of nature about us, the silence, no one watching; and we are together." He reached inside her sweater but she pulled away from his hand. In the old days, in the city, she also would have discouraged such approaches, but it would have been a coy reminder that slow is best. Those were days when she focused on how to attract men to the chase, how to refuse them to the point of male frustration, then to win them back to passion. Her body was stronger than ever. She would give of herself again, but it would be to a man whose sincerity reflected hers.

She faced Axel. "You have done a great deal for Helmut and me. I like you, but I cannot do what you want."

Axel spoke quickly, as if giving orders. "What about the window shades? When I first saw you, you showed your body at an open window. Now you act like a middle-aged countess, sniffing too long over what you want and might not get."

"I am sorry if it was like that. I am different now. I hoped you would recognize it."

"You Jews are all the same," Axel shouted. "You wheedle us into thinking what you want us to think, then you change your tune."

"Please, Axel. I can't imagine why you feel such hatred. I thought I knew you well; you showed us compassion and tolerance. Now this nastiness."

His voice was dulcet. "Isolde, my dear, forgive me. I, too, have been through hell. I too, have changed, but in a different way, and I should not repeat the language of stupid fools. For a moment I gave in to the foul talk of a soldier's barracks. Please believe me when I tell you it was not I who said those things to you. I was like a boy who hears a dirty word and repeats it in anger without realizing what it means. I respect you too much to hurt you." He kissed her and she accepted the apology of his lips.

Axel Gans had rekindled the persuasive aptitude of his youth. He had made brilliant excuses to a woman of perception, a difficult task when out of practice. At any rate, he would not have enjoyed her on a bed of leaves which probably teemed with ants.

Axel focused Isolde's attention to his right arm. "Do you see this scar?" He raised his sleeve to show a line of raised leathery flesh. "You might be pleased to know how I got it." He told how as a young man he had protected a Jewish friend in a knife attack. Isolde was enraptured, and alarmed. His scars, his limp, the compelling vitality of his deeds, bespoke a violence beneath the façade of pleasantries. She had not discerned the savage nature beneath his timely humor. To blame him totally would be wrong, for she too recalled flashes of vicious hatred, dreams of death inflicted on her assailants. She thought of her son Helmut, scholarly, immersed in tenderness. The boy should know how to fight back.

"Axel," she said, "you are a strong man. I mean it. You have courage. I wish my son could be taught to stand up for himself if he ever needed to."

Axel grinned. "I am no hero. Far from it. The real question is, against whom should you show courage? I became brave to protect myself. There is selfishness in such an attitude, but survival is what counts. Helmut is too much of a gentleman. I would hate to teach him to be courageous for others, with not enough left over to take care of himself."

"You told me you defended a friend you hardly knew. That is not being selfish."

"Ah, yes, I often wondered about that." Axel would not explain further, as he suspected he had abrogated one of his principles when he diluted the concept of self-preservation.

"Maybe I had the courage of a gentle dog who attacks to protect her young," he added. "We don't know why or how we react when we are hurt." Axel echoed his own insecurity.

To tutor a self-educated boy of twelve was a serious matter for Corporal Gans. Axel examined himself, flexed his muscles, drew in his abdomen, and knew immediately he had been handed a mission of macho evangelism. He showed Helmut his scars and described how he received them. The old wounds were the initial chapters of the boy's tutelage. When Helmut relayed his lesson to Anna, she also wished to propose a dictum of learning, one she had found most successful: "Listen well, ask few questions, agree if you must, but don't believe it till you find out for yourself."

Helmut decided to put his teacher to the test. "When those bums attacked your friend, how did you manage to get the knife away after you were cut?"

"Take the knife," said Axel, "hold it as tightly as you can." Helmut grasped the hilt with a hand which had moved rocks, tugged roots, held a straining cow in check. A sharp flick of Axel's hand struck the boy's fingers, his wrist flexed and the knife fell.

"There are little tricks to every trade," said Axel.

Helmut wanted to know why he had to let go, what reason could be given for his enforced weakness. "Never mind," shouted Axel, "just learn how to do it." The boy was impressed. Casual respect for Axel was revived. The glamor of results superceded the logic on which they were based.

Helmut's lessons progressed in earnest. Body-building exercises preceded wrestling, karate, and knife play. Helmut rejected the latter as brutal; too prone to cause an accident. Axel reprimanded, "You don't concentrate. Get the feel of the handle, the balance, and grip hard when you stick it in." Helmut failed to pierce the bark of the tree they used for practice. At supper, Axel said to Helmut, "sharpen that kitchen knife and cut up the chicken." A huge hen graced the platter. The boy had read about joints and ligaments, and carved the bird cleanly and quickly. Axel encouraged him. "You can cut a chicken better than me." But he thought, "He thinks too much, that boy. No animal instinct."

Helmut sensed his mentor's disappointment. The quick kill, the sudden, brutal plunge was repugnant to the boy. Wrestling was an exercise he understood, where holds could be studied and executed within the dynamics of engineering principles. Isolde furnished a daily pitcher of warm milk for the combatants. She watched as they engaged with entangled limbs, rolled on the ground, strained for a controlling position. Each had a hand locked on the other's wrists so that all four limbs were immobilized, when Helmut caught Axel's scarred leg in the bend of his ankle as they tossed for advantage. As Isolde poured her nutrient gift into a glass she demanded they stop and drink, as if the milk of kindness she offered would remind them they were at play, and not in a vicious test of superiority.

Helmut's leverage was evident when he twisted the wounded leg, and with Axel grunting in pain the soldier rolled onto his back. In his confusion and fear that he might land hard Axel loosened his grip for an instant. The boy tore his wrist away, rocked back, and with a jerk pinioned Axel's arm behind his chest. Another tearing pull put Axel on his abdomen with his shoulder and elbow fixed at his rear, and with the knee of a husky twelve-year-old jammed into his neck.

Isolde shouted, "Please, Helmut, don't hurt him. Let him up."

"Nothing doing, Mother." Then he tittered and remarked to Axel with the casual confidence of a victor who could repeat his performance at will, "You know that I could break your shoulder with this position. It's a simple mechanical principle." He released his pressure as Axel spat out a volume of air with a bellow of distress. Isolde complimented Axel on the success of his teaching. In fact, she maintained, they ought to quit altogether and return to the more serious side of living, such as repairing broken hinges, cutting logs, clearing brush, honest work involving all the exercise they would want.

The normal reaction of a victorious boy should be a prolonged period of self satisfaction, perhaps a degree of boastfulness expressed to himself if not to others. He was sixty pounds lighter, short, inexperienced, and he had subdued a man trained to fight. What a thrill to sense that moment of weakness, the fleeting chaos of his opponent, when he had the presence of mind to jump in for the kill! The expression made him uncomfortable. Victory led to anxiety. Axel could have been his father, and having beaten him, Helmut felt he took advantage of an old man.

Helmut said, "Did I hurt your leg? I did not wish to press on the scar."

"No, not much. It stings a little, and I wanted to protect the skin. But I compliment you for finding a weak spot and using it. That is good."

"I apologize," said Helmut.

"For what? Because you beat me? Don't be foolish. I don't mind. Really, I am proud. Remember, I am the teacher." He lied.

Axel suffered nagging doubts that he led two lives which clashed and which he could not control. In the barracks he was really a bookkeeper and a scavenger; he had fallen into a quiet little group, a family, and wondered whether his position vis-á-vis the boy had been undermined. Inadvertantly he was cast into the role of father. The idea had thrust itself on him so suddenly he overstated its significance. Naturally he had tried to be helpful to his friends, but he expected some returns, respect, perhaps a degree of adulation. That was a father's right, wasn't it? So far he had demanded nothing more than a placid relationship. It was time he demanded appreciation, perhaps reverance, even fear.

For the first time he saw Isolde as a source of irritation. Persistently she had refused to sleep with him, though she teased him with kisses and touches. If he became excited she reached into his pants. For this indulgence he was thankful, also satisfied that he was better off than his barracks buddies. Lately, however, she gave the impression he got more than he deserved. She was light hearted, poked fun at their activities; but he could not accept the lack of respect when he was possessed with his image of father figure, commander of the tribe.

She was coy. "Axel, what would you have done if you had not found us? Loneliness would have killed you."

"Oh, I don't know. I have always managed to do well for myself."

"Even you would have had trouble finding friends if it were not for Anna and me."

Axel was petulant. "If you believe you saved me from suicide, forget it. I am my own man and I don't need a woman to tell me how to be happy. To help Helmut was a bigger thrill than anything you did for me."

Unaware of the depth of his anger she chided him. "You had a good time with Helmut, but it seems he's outgrown you. Now you are left with Anna and me, and Anna isn't so nice to look at."

"So," he thought, "she thinks this boy of hers can squeeze me whenever he wants." He was no hen to be cut up and put in her pot. If she wanted to play games, he would oblige.

The following afternoon Axel arrived later than usual. Bookwork at camp had to be completed, and a soldier caught his hand in the breech of an anti-aircraft gun, which required medical appointments, reports, and arrangements for transportation. This, and the dampness of impending rain or sleet which turned his scars into throbbing cords of tissue, nettled him. He approached Helmut from the rear, playfully swung an arm about his throat, and thrust the dull end of his knife hilt into his back. As he released his grasp Helmut glimpsed the knife blade, imagined the worst and screeched. Axel exonerated himself by tickling the boy's ribs.

"My boy, you have to stop daydreaming. If you don't protect yourself, you may never get out of this place."

For two years Helmut had been aware of the tumultuous frustration growing like a tumor when he heard stories of brutality toward Jews. He had repressed urges to kick the barbarians into submission, beat in their faces with rocks. As he developed physically, he sensed another part of him which could not be discovered in the pages of a book. He had learned to muse over and track distant, untouchable stars while he lay on his back. A growing voice whispered to him to get up and confront someone, anyone, to stand and look Goliath in the eye.

"Come on, then," Helmut blustered in impatience, "if you want to teach me, let's get it over with."

Axel launched into the methodical, gory aspects of plunge, rip, and twist. "You only have a few parts to go for — neck, armpit, under the ribs. If you get him for good you can walk away and not have to look back. Always thrust hard, and keep away from bones." In spite of his wounded leg, Axel demonstrated swift approaches from various angles, missed the boy's skin by a terrifying narrow margin. Helmut heard swishes whiz by, was frozen by the glitter of the blade in its expertly executed passes. He was the culprit, capriciously judged and sentenced, standing defenseless before his torturer. When the boy was asked to try this technique of the clean, clear-cut kill, he gyrated and swung with ineffectual awkwardness.

With disgust, as a parting gesture of disparagement against the boy's genteel disposition, Axel lunged at a soft spot below the chin. The blow stopped short in a masterly swing of perfect timing. Slowly, deliberately, he pushed the knife into the skin of the mesmerized body before him. The nick drew a drop of blood. Helmut said nothing, stared. He wondered if there was to be further punishment, or death, whether he would flinch before his demise, or say, "Here I am, ready for whatever you can give." A gush of sweat blinded him and he fell unconscious.

Anna, who had been perched at a window to speculate on the wasteful hours of foolish men, ran out with a cold wet cloth. She patted Helmut's brow and cheeks until he revived.

Axel was all smiles. "It's nothing, nothing. A little slip and a tiny scratch. He will learn form it."

"Learn what? So he can go about sticking whomever he doesn't like?"

"If you treat him like a baby, he will grow up like one. Put a diaper on him, so he can pretend he's your infant son. Wipe his ass for him. I'm sick of the way you treat him, and me. I count for something too. You had no right to pounce on me as if I were a devil come to smell up your synagogue." Then he grinned and stroked Helmut's head, stood and patted Anna's shoulder, as if he had relieved the pressure of a deep abscess which finally had burrowed its way to the surface.

The air of strife cleared in forty-eight hours. That Axel could sulk for so long was an unknown ingredient of his optimistic nature. Isolde shared in his revival. She brought his coat to him and eased it over his arms and shoulders as if he were a victim of arthritis. If his legs were tired, she wished to massage them, but Axel refused. Gradually the bloom of his self esteem returned, so he could talk freely to Helmut and Isolde, but not to Anna. They remained politely distant.

Helmut, too, could adjust to the severity of his life-style when he met two youngsters of his age group. A boy and a girl from a farm closer to the village visited Helmut, and at first their visits were regarded with suspicion and fear. Anna could not guess what unguarded talk, what innocent observation might stimulate an investigation. Soon it became apparent that the new visitors also sought anonymity. They were not Jewish, but the boy's parents had been politically involved against the state and were wandering in parts unknown. The youngster lived with his cousin, Gretchen Rennert, a tall, pigtailed comely girl who relished the thought that she stood at the brink of maturity. Manfred was taller than Helmut, thinner, with sandy hair, green eyes, and a stubby nose which Helmut envied.

Manfred and his cousin Gretchen visited more frequently as their assurance grew that they were with friends. They told of skirmishes and patrols several miles on the other side of the village, of a bridge crumbled by a direct bomb hit, or captured parachutists in another town. All turned to Axel Gans for verification. Were these facts or rumors, and were they as significant as they imagined? Yes, it was all true. He assured them with the empathy of a distant relative in a family crisis, and Anna despised his haphazard comments without trace of genuine concern. If a shell were to crush the house and squash everyone within, he no doubt would be found standing between splintered beams sipping his favorite beer. Those who had struggled to stay alive would be eliminated whereas Axel would remain a healthy survivor.

When the boys ran and kicked a football, Axel joined them. He bubbled with enthusiasm, though he could not maintain the youngsters' pace running and jumping. Manfred knew of his physical difficulty, and expressly chose difficult paths to follow, on rough ground and up rutted hills. Helmut was more sympathetic, but he no longer looked at Axel as the arbiter of morality or physical conditioning. Axel had led the boys over a rough field strewn with boulders and spaced with irregularly placed holes. Patches of snow camouflaged the path's contours. The boys were first to gain the top of a hill, where they sat and watched Axel stumble and curse in a grotesque effort to reach them. He gripped his tortured leg and finally approached the summit, to drag himself up on his belly.

Manfred said, "Do you want an oxygen tank? You look like you made the top of Mount Everest."

Axel gasped, "Was it as bad as that?" When he breathed more easily he turned to Manfred. "Young fellows like you may have speed, but it's for a short haul. Playing is one thing, but if you have to reach a place the hard way, if you have to run for your life, you need more than legs and lungs. I'm talking about common sense, and will, especially the will to go on when it is easier to die."

The boys were silent. Helmut regarded the statement as part of his war experience, most likely the time when Axel wounded himself after choosing on which side of the scales of chance his life lay. A solid leaden cloud moved into position above the hill. Clouds, snow, bleak eerie stillness, were a foreboding. Helmut no longer was in the playful world of romping boys and girls. He was being inducted into a haunted army where cruelty and barbarism were the marks of the victor.

The light moved as they walked down the hill, Axel in front as the boys permitted him the comfort of his own stride. On a flat surface Manfred sped ahead. He raised his eyes to the sky and shrieked garbled cries of jubilation, a paeon to youthful energy. Axel recognized the unrestrained rapture which once was his own, but which over the years had oozed from him.

Manfred looked down on a grayish brown huddled ball of fur lying down in a hole. He reached toward it but it jumped onto the wet grass, immobile. He picked up the young rabbit nearly full grown and inspected its legs, one of which was awkwardly bent and limp.

"Axel, come and see. It's a crippled rabbit."

Axel took the animal from him. "If you put it back it will die, or some animal will kill it."

Helmut interceded. "We can take it home and fix it up. I know how to splint a leg."

"No," said Axel. "Once his limb is like that it will never be normal. Sooner or later it will be curtains for him." Manfred nodded in agreement.

"Ah, Manfred, so you see my point. Good. There is hope for you."

As he spoke he cupped his hand and gently placed it about the animal's head. With a twist and a snap the neck was broken. Its head dangled. The bulky coat of protective winter fur flattened to a snug shroud. Axel pinched the broken foreleg between his thumb and index finger, alternately flexed and straightened it with a post-facto interest in what could cause such injury. As he threw the rabbit into a clump of brush he sighed.

Manfred hid his agitation with misplaced exhilaration. He dashed up the hill and back, threw stones at clouds, at last succumbed to an overpowering torpor which even he realized was a signal to go home and rest.

Helmut stood fixed at what he regarded to be the altar of execution. Silent a few moments, rapidly gulping large draughts of air, he turned to Axel. "I don't think you should have done that. I could have taken the rabbit home."

"So you would have patched it up. Then what? A crippled animal has no life."

"*You* are crippled," said Helmut. The exaggeration affected Axel as if it were solid truth. His face was contorted when he shouted to the boy.

"I suppose you were born to be the smart one. If you used your head you would know I too have a brain. Cut my leg off and I keep going. Whatever happens I can overcome it. Some can make do, some cannot, and if not they end up like the rabbit. I did the damn bunny a favor."

Helmut trudged back in a haze of imaginative wondering, searched for answers with dark images. He saw Axel in a shell hole clutching his torn limb with the agonized desperation of one who has nothing to look to but painful death. The boy hoisted a huge rock over his head and imagined he would smash it against the skull of the wounded soldier. But the rock fell off its mark, well behind his back. Helmut ran to the farm in silence, with fanciful cries for help reverberating into the distant hills. His dream of confusion, which teetered between just punishment and sentimental empathy, was to remain with him. Even when he grew up to be an Iowan would he suffer constant constraint at crossroads of decision.

In the night Helmut tossed fitfully in bed. His erstwhile friend, Axel Gans, was no longer the man who made wood toys to play with. A plane of brutality had surfaced from a structure he thought he knew. Yet Axel was ever so gentle when he caressed the rabbit's head before the final twist; and he was good to the inhabitants of the farm. Helmut wondered which of Axel's traits, positive or negative, would triumph.

Chapter 10

ANNA CONSIDERED IT a stroke of luck to have found a playmate for Helmut. She deliberated over her decision to invite Manfred to the farm with the same seriousness that presaged the acceptance of Isolde and her son. Though added acquaintances weakened the chain of security she had forged, sooner or later Helmut had to meet someone to fill his longing for friendship. If at all possible, it was much safer to choose a comrade with suitable credentials. Manfred Renner's father published a small newspaper of liberal ideology. Renner and his wife fled, and when they left Manfred was placed with his uncle on a distant farm near an isolated village. Anna was apprised of the Renner history and made discreet inquiries to judge the reliability of her information.

The local Renners with whom Manfred was boarded were ordinary farm folk, apolitical and pragmatic, who leaned toward whatever party line insured the greatest profit. They preferred no associations with their brother. Help was scarce; the boy would be useful. Good food was provided, the work was not overtaxing, and he was free to come and go as he pleased. With one proviso—drilled like a novitiate into a secret organization, he never, never was to talk of his parents.

Manfred's cousin, Gretchen, was older by a few months. Brought up on a farm where work overshadowed play, she was subjected to disciplined drills by rigid parents, with careful instruction in the watchfullness a young girl must adopt to ward off boys who pressed too close. She must not sit with legs apart, nor raise the dress; too broad a smile might give a wrong impression. So many parental proscriptions were offered that none took a firm hold. Gretchen's social ethics were assiduously planted and constantly reinforced, but they withered with overfertilization.

Manfred visited the Grunstein farm occasionally at first, then more frequently. He found an attractive opposite in Helmut, who in turn was stimulated by his friend's haphazard, carefree, and at times dangerous presence. Helmut diluted his zest for unrestrained activity with a penchant for caution. He thought carefully, weighed pros and cons, was totally aware of the inertia of spirit he had acquired. Otherwise why would he envy Manfred's refreshing recklessness?

The boys eyed a huge, black walnut tree, a triumph of nature for

Helmut, and a challenge to triumph over for Manfred. Overripe for plucking, there were dozens of fallen nuts under foot, but these were not good enough for Manfred to pick. He singled out a cluster of ripening fruit which dangled on a limb near the top. This was what he wanted and must have. Helmut was awed when he looked upward, as the spot Manfred chose was at least two stories high, perched on the end of a long branch which appeared to be an elongated twig hardly able to sustain itself, no less the weight of a healthy young man. Difficulties were pointed out to Manfred, who looked on reason as the better part of cowardice. He was armored with rashness and overconfidence. Like a mountain climber his ambition was to possess the top because it was there, but he never bothered to plan the ascent.

Manfred slithered his lanky frame up the trunk. Two thirds up he took stock of his situation and paused to look down. The reality of height, the trajectory of walnuts falling in bursts of accelerated speed, were sufficiently impressive to place his bravado in question. Cautiously, trembling, he reached his foot out to engage the limb. His sweating palm slid on the mother trunk, and he hung for an instant by his foot until he could grasp another limb. He shouted, "Help! Help! Helmut! Come up, I need help!" In desperation, as he called for his savior, reason, caution, cowardice were acceptable, even admirable, attributes.

Helmut climbed the tree slowly. His short muscular body was more awkward than that of his lean friend, but he clung and gripped more firmly. Though the ascent seemed to take ages, Helmut was surprised at his sense of security. He helped Manfred back to the trunk, and both were soon secure at the foot of the tree.

"Do you still want the nuts?" Helmut asked.

"What nuts?"

"I'll get them for you." Helmut ran to the house and returned with a garden rake, shaking it as a scientist might shake a test tube which contained a new discovery. He shinnied up the tree to below the branch Manfred held so dear and using the teeth of the rake bent the limb to a semicircle. Nuts picked and pockets filled, Helmut climbed down quickly, and in a surge of unaccustomed bravado he jumped the last five feet with the rake still clutched in his hand. Manfred was inordinately placid. He sat on the grass and played with the walnuts like a child with blocks, moving them about in abstract configurations. When he recovered from the humility which had repressed him, he stood and hurled the nuts one by one into the distance.

Friendship between the boys cooled. They addressed each other without the warmth and conviviality which was the basis of their activity. Helmut's temperament was deeply affected, for he thought of his exploit with amusement. He was fortified by his display of strength and skill which proved his superiority over his constantly bragging companion. Having erupted from an image of a fearful bookworm by an act which combined thought and daring, he tasted the unusual flavor of victory. The discomfort of having humiliated his friend made Helmut wish he had not climbed the tree. Helmut could not accept pleasure at the expense of another, nor did he reason that Manfred had been stupid and unreasonable in his action and reaction. When Helmut tried to sort out and analyze his feelings, he got stuck somewhere between self-punishment and bewilderment.

Axel criticized Helmut. "You shouldn't have helped him. If he gets into trouble, let him find his own way out. If he wants to be a crazy squirrel, he should learn to climb like one."

"But he's my friend," said Helmut.

"You are your only friend, especially when both of you are so stupid."

Calling the boys stupid bound them into a unity of the damned. Any rancor which might have separated them changed to normal adolescent envy, and Manfred was satisfied his counterpart would not criticize him for an asinine performance. Helmut was curiously fulfilled by his friend's penchant for escapades.

Manfred had frequently been to the village, Helmut only rarely, in a circuitous and secretive manner as if he were a spy. That is how he would feel if he walked about with a Star of David hung at his back. Often he thought he would be happier bearing a cross which he need not hide, but he quickly divorced himself of such an impossible idea. Still, the village was there, and he had not explored it. Manfred posed a proposition as intriguing as it was rash. They would somehow go to the village together and check it out, take a chance, as being bored to death was more than a phrase for healthy youngsters affixed to one place as if they were expected to grow roots and leaves.

"Do you have any money?" asked Manfred. "We could go to the movies. The last time I saw the billboard they featured girls in a beauty contest. They were half-dressed, tits sticking out."

"I have some money I've saved, but you're exaggerating. They wouldn't show girls without clothes."

"Not entirely naked. Big blondes with a lot of skin uncovered. It must have been a good show. The soldiers loved it."

Helmut's appreciation of smut had been abysmally dulled. Having seen few women — his mother was the prettiest of all — he was left little opportunity to reflect what a grown boy might do with what he saw.

Lately, however, with Gretchen on the scene, he awoke to her curvaceous features. Helmut's pedantic views of nature were subject to erosion.

The boys left in mid-afternoon after chores. No one knew of their plans. Walking, trotting on dirt roads and across fields, they arrived at the periphery of the village, where familiar farmhouses gave way to widely spaced framed houses, then to several brick edifices with sumptuous lawns, and finally to a bustling main street closely packed with neat two- and three-story tenaments and a row of stores. Though there were few passers-by — this was mid-week — Helmut visualized he was in a crowd, a throng of walking informers whose object was to seek him out.

"Keep your head up," instructed Manfred. "Nobody knows us, and they aren't interested. Lots of strangers come through every day."

Helmut looked forward. His eyes danced side to side. He felt in his pocket for his knife, the one with the long blade, but he had left it home. "It wouldn't do any good," he thought, "not even for Axel, if he were caught in my position." Manfred urged him toward the movie house billboard.

Their anticipation was crushed in disappointment. Signs above the theatre's entrance spelled out in large block letters, Closed for the Duration. Glass panes were cracked into lines radiating from a central point as if hit by shrapnel. Manfred recalled a loudspeaker blaring music on his previous visit. No tunes, no marches, no clapping of hands or ribald shouts enlivened the theater entrance this day. If the general tone of the place was a disappointment, the billboard which was to house the visual titillation of their dreams was a disaster. Large enough for two full-sized figures, paper was peeled or ripped off the pink flesh of one leg. The view was not especially appealing, shoe, ankle, calf, but no knee. Rain-splotched mud spots emulated some morbid rash.

Initially, the other side of the advertisement had shown promise of a more alluring motif. A forehead and part of the nose were visible. Both breasts, which the boys scrutinized as if they were rare stamps, were defaced by torn strips where mounds should have been. No trace of nipple was discernable. Imagination had to supplant reality. Manfred put his finger on a dab of lavender he insisted was part of a crotch. It was the size of a walnut with vertical wrinkles depicted, which Helmut calculated by height, width, and anatomical configuration to be an area somewhere below the navel but nowhere near the genitals. Manfred raised his fist in deep frustration and turned away. Helmut thought he heard a rush of inspiratory breath followed by a stifled sob, like a faucet opened then instantly shut.

Helmut said, "You are right. This place must have been fun. You are lucky to have seen it." Manfred accepted the admission that he was the envy of his comrades.

Helmut wondered why he had come, why he was expected to delight in girls' pictures. Of course they were sexy, but they were artificial. His mother, for example, was not artificial, and though she disturbed him when he saw her naked, he found he could transfer his vision onto another unclothed body, Gretchen's. He used to think of Gretchen as thin and gangly, an elongated strip of glass thinned out under the flame of a Bunsen burner. Now the glass was being blown out into symmetrical bulges. Something was puffing Gretchen into a wonder of vibrant form.

The boys looked into a window filled with books. Manfred wished to move to more interesting areas, but Helmut insisted on entering. Multicolored book jackets presented a clean contrast to the defilement of the movie theater. Here was an open door which breathed life and promise for Helmut. Manfred finally agreed to go in when the proposition was stated that there were pictures to examine, works of art which held nothing back. The proprietor was elderly, with the dashing grey moustache of a vaudevillian turned scholar. Black rimmed glasses perched near the tip of his nose.

He pursed his lips when he recognized Manfred. The Renner family and the boy in their charge were known to him. Mildly chummy, polite from a distance, he posed sterile questions such as "How are things on the farm?" and "Are your aunt and uncle well?" Turning his attention to Helmut, he was even more reluctant to extract any history of a stranger about whom the farmers exchanged whispered rumors. Helmut was inured to the silent approach, had been taught to encourage it. No names, no introductions, no loose prattle about where he lived or where he came from. But he could ask for a book.

Helmut sensed he was in secure territory. "Do you have a volume on the work of Albert Einstein?"

"What!" exclaimed the proprietor as if he were denying a request for pornographic photos.

"Einstein, the great physicist." Suddenly Helmut recalled he could just as well have asked for a volume on the great Jewish physicist. It was an unforgiveable error. The boy stood at attention with lips pressed thin, ready to hold out his arms in acquiescence to a demand for search and seizure.

The proprietor lifted his glasses high on the bridge of his nose. "I never heard of him." He spoke slowly and gently. "You look like a lad who enjoys books. Now here is one I heartily recommend, *A Short History of the Roman Empire*. It doesn't sell well, as there aren't many interested readers of ancient history. Take it. There is no charge. If I don't give it away I will probably have to throw it out."

Helmut sputtered incoherently. The proprietor continued. "Don't say a word. Put it under your arm and walk out of here as if nothing happened. And good reading." As the boys left, the bookseller addressed Manfred. "It is getting late. If you are not supposed to be out at this hour, don't worry about me. No one asks questions, and if they did I would not tell."

The boys ambled through the door dazed, for different reasons: Manfred for the enigmatic exchange he witnessed; Helmut for his discovery of humaneness, kindness in the midst of terror.

"How did he know we weren't supposed to be out?" asked Manfred.

"He didn't know." Helmut walked with renewed energy. Gripping the book firmly he reassured himself its smooth, firm contours were still in his grasp. Not everyone was an enemy. In out of the way places, cellars, crevices, and bookstores, friends lived in a vortex of anticipated despair and shadowy hope.

Most store fronts the boys passed were drab till they paused at a window filled with clothes. Neatly displayed mannikins of a more fashionable era stared back at them with elegant, cold faces atop unnaturally perfect physiques. Some bore evidence of neglect, or futile efforts at renovation, with broken noses and skinned cheeks. Coats and suits hung neatly and unwrinkled, a testimonial to the professional pride of the tradesman who sought to squeeze the ultimate in splendor from the second hand apparel at his disposal. Boys are not devoted to the niceties of couture, but the scarred bodies of mannikins supporting pathetic burdens, magnetized them. The store front was a clarion call to hopelessness. Clearly, they were well-off on a farm where work translated to new growth bursting with color and succulence, not tarnish and ersatz.

Helmut perceived the undercurrent of civilian misery and privation that abounded. He decided it was time to be uplifted, and the only course open to him was to usurp his friend's role as an unpredictable, irrational swashbuckler. He began to run followed by Manfred, wildly, without direction up and down streets, through side alleys and on open roads. Nothing was encountered which might entertain them. No street bands, no tittering girls, or women flaunting their hips, not even a friendly civilian street corner discourse or hostile argument.

A convoy of military vehicles passed through the village. It proceeded slowly, almost leisurely, a tired spectacle of mud-encrusted trucks and half-trucks, some with fenders and doors crushed in, one truck with part of its supercarriage blown away leaving jagged borders of steel and wood framework. In contrast with their machines the men in the vehicles waved and shouted, pointed in the direction they were going as if to say, "We're headed that way, won't you come along?" Having returned from an active front they were headed for rest and any recreation still available. They were not the image of a winning team.

A small vehicle at the end of the convoy pulled away from the rear of the column and took a sharp left turn to halt Manfred and Helmut. The deliberate route the car took was as frightening to the boys as an impending hammer blow; they awaited the final crush which would mash them onto the cement walk. A soldier vaulted out of the vehicle and limped toward them. It was Axel.

"I drove all over looking for you. Where have you been?"

"We went for a walk, " said Helmut, promptly supported by Manfred. "Only a walk."

Axel pointed to the rear of his car and they jumped in.

"Now I must drive you back, then go to the base. It's too much. Sitting in my car makes my leg hurt. If I can't sleep tonight I know who is to blame." He rolled his hands as if he were wringing out laundry, to simulate how he would like to exact punishment.

"We are sorry," said Helmut.

"Tell it to Anna and your mother. They are worried sick over you. Who knows what trouble two crazy kids can get into wandering around here? I tell you, if you got caught it would be no picnic. I was about to ask for you at the police station, which I did not want to do. The two of you could be on your way to God knows where by now."

Manfred was exuberant. "But we had a great time."

"What! In this little stinking town? You don't know what a good time is. Wait! Just wait till Anna gets hold of you!"

Axel's prediction of physical retribution did not materialize, though Anna and Isolde had spent an afternoon of terror and misgiving until the boys returned. Manfred was sent home and Axel returned to the barracks. Helmut and the two women ate in silence. The dishes cleared, Anna addressed Helmut beside the wood fire.

"I hope you know what you boys did."

"We were wrong. We should not have run away."

"I wouldn't refer to it as running away" said Isolde. "You had every intention to return. Let us say it was an escapade."

"More than an escapade," Anna said. "They left us behind without thinking of their responsibility to us."

Helmut grew defensive. "Manfred thought it would be fun and I agreed. We never see anyone, I mean strange faces, and we felt it was about time we did."

"Well then, " replied Anna, "you still do not realize what I mean by responsibility. Let me tell you. What if someone in the village had no use for us but never had the will or the chance to speak up? Seeing you wandering about could be just what they need to lodge a complaint, or report, or even gossip. So far they have forgotten why we are here, and you could be a drastic reminder. Each of us depends on the other. If you do something silly we can all be punished for it."

Helmut's face sagged in shame. His boast of carrying a man's burden, the respect he earned with his counsel in family meetings, were diminished if not shattered. Anna emphasized responsibility, which had no relation to the muscular development he could admire in a mirror. The key to being grown up was to think of others; first others, then himself. Somehow he felt cheated. Was he of any importance at all? Should he do everything for Anna and his mother, and nothing for himself, he would attain the height of responsibility. Helmut sensed he was being emptied of all joyous possibility, destined to be crushed permanently by the good deeds he would perform for others.

Isolde was more casual toward his adventure. "I am happy you enjoyed yourself. You deserve it. Perhaps your timing was wrong. If we wait, and not too long, we will all be able to go where we choose."

He kissed her and said, "Mother, I would do anything for you. I love you." When he lay in bed he relived his experience with Manfred. Dozing, he wondered whether he was mature enough to carry out his responsibility to his mother.

Manfred and Gretchen appeared three days later. Helmut took them aside, sat with them on boulders cooled by near freezing temperatures, and lectured them regarding their duties to friends and families. He added that the pressures under which they lived could not last. After a short time, he did not know when, they could relax. Manfred and Gretchen were uninvolved, impatiently listened to the philosophical intrusions on their adolescence.

Manfred said, "We know all about it. Forget the speeches. Just tell us what we must do, especially about Axel."

"What about Axel?" Helmut was suddenly aware Manfred had thought of a very practical issue, one he had not considered.

"He's a soldier, isn't he? He could tell them you are a Jew."

"Never. He wouldn't."

Manfred grinned. He had entered another phase of boyish relationships, a tussle for superiority via parental beratement. "How can you be so sure of Axel? I wonder. Of course he is with your mother most of the day."

"What's wrong about that?" Helmut hoped his would be the last word.

"He goes to bed with her, doesn't he?"

Helmut bounded off the rock. His initial reaction to kick out was restrained. Manfred's insinuation could be true, though he simply had not conjured up images of sex where Isolde was involved. As he walked briskly from Manfred, Gretchen ran to him and took his arm. "Don't listen to him, Helmut. We would be miserable without you and your family. Manfred doesn't think like you. He's big, but he's like a baby." Helmut bathed in the comfort she offered.

Through the winter months the liaison between Helmut and Gretchen developed slowly, as a flower bulb gathers energy in darkness to prepare for the emergence of spring blossoms. Gretchen visited infrequently during the winter, and in March Helmut had not seen her for over a month. She had grown outward. Helmut hummed to himself as she approached him, no longer an awkward girl-child who appeared conscious of the alignment of her thighs with each step. She was straight and smooth-skinned and her feet turned out with the seductive grace of a ballet dancer. A bouncing bulk of shoulder-length hair complemented her gaze of calloused assurance. She knew her attributes, whereas she refused to recognize her weaknesses. She thought she had successfully traversed the last swampy tributary of adolescence.

Helmut saw in her freshness, a new light to expose the niggling disturbances that pursued him. Sexually, he was normally motivated, and he occasionally read a magazine with pictures which reinforced his passion. Earlier, when he watched his mother undress, he would suppress subsequent stirrings, turn away, but lately he took care not to look at her nakedness since he fancied such voyeurism was impure. As he watched Gretchen he was thrilled by her into strange, coarse sensations of what he would do if they were alone. Attack her. Put her on her back. Lie on top of her and reach beneath her clothes. An overpowering blush ended his dream.

Gretchen too had suffered through irksome and puzzling pangs of adolescence. Cousin Manfred was the tall, loose-jointed type who wanted boy-to-boy action. If he bumped into her, or inadvertantly patted her back, it was for some athletic reason. As an energizer of girls' sexual circuits he was of no consequence. The one who made her think she had advanced into womanhood was her father, not that he ever mishandled her in an unfatherly way. The man worked hard and his interest lay in a heavy meal followed by a long session in a rocking chair. He came alive in these very moments of evening repose. His eyes sharpened toward every detail of the room and to whatever could be seen through the window. He was like a nocturnal bird, an owl, awakened by night to seek the rewards and sustenance he had earned.

Most of the sights upon which he feasted were inspected with a casual attention born of familiarity. But Gretchen, a remodeled and evolving figure which crossed his vision, produced a more mercurial effect. She did not know she was being visually dissected until he began to criticize her. If she bent forward he said she showed too much thigh, backwards, and she pushed out her front too prominently for a nice young girl. She was to keep her legs together when sitting. To comb her hair in public was to call attention to herself.

In the beginning she was confused by the horrible revelations which grew out of his rivetted stare; her own papa who was distant yet good to her; not one she could talk to but whom she could depend upon. He gave her in security what he lacked in parental love. She had heard of fathers and daughters in bed together, mothers and sons too. Since she was an optimist, she reached for a benign conclusion. Papa wasn't so bad, no worse than other men who couldn't resist what she had. Patting herself, wiggling before the mirror, reaching to her groin, she determined she was more than a dirt-mover's daughter or mama's kitchen helper. She was irresistible.

Gretchen stood close to Axel. "Fix my hair," she said. "The wind made a mess of me."

He straightened several intertwined strands. "There, I have it in good shape. You are now as cute as ever." Gretchen found no solace in his description. "Cute" was applied to her as a child when she sat on her mother's lap and neighbors punched her bulbous cheeks as they cooed over her well fed look. Bumping into him, pretending not to see where she was going, she held onto Axel with the pretense her ankle was hurt. Though she teetered cautiously as if his loosened grip would cause a fall, Axel was impervious to her pretended disability. He picked her high off the ground and set her down on both feet. She forgot to wince, and he assured her all was well except she failed to look where she was going.

For a few days the momentum of her romantic search was stilled. She had used poor judgment, which had nothing to do with her body. A more fertile field lay within her grasp — Helmut. She had to be cautious. He was timid, introspective, and his responses were cloaked with anxiety. No doubt he would be an easy victim, but she wished to entice him gradually so he would not burn in his own flame. A slow, relentless tease was in order. She decided to invite Helmut to a picnic.

He met her on a misty afternoon near the north edge of the farm, so that a short walk in the woods placed them on a lush patch of low grass. When she flipped open the top of the basket her hands undulated gracefully as if she conducted a symphony. Two immense sandwiches were exposed, expansive cuts of black bread with thick slices of bologna bathed in butter and embellished with a leaf of dark green lettuce. Then a jar of warm milk. The prize of the menu was three mounds of dark brown grain sweetened with syrup and ersatz chocolate.

Helmut ate with difficulty. He had to open his jaws wide to the point of aching. As the edges of the sandwich were politely nibbled, butter oozed onto his fingers. With bites of desperation, as he wished to please his hostess, he consumed whatever she placed in his grasp, wiping his hands periodically on his trousers to avoid the mess slipping from his fingers.

She offered the dessert balls and coquettishly tilted her head with confidence that the dish she made with her own hands would over-whelm any young man's resistance. Helmut's first bite was tasty, not too sweet, with a nutty grain flavor. A sudden pain indicated he had struck a hard shell of grain or the husk of a nut. The offending frag-ments were loosened by reaching into his mouth with twisting move-ments. His gums, sore after several stuck fragments, were washed with gulps of warm milk.

The sheet they sat on had been soaked by wet grass. Clothes clung to their buttocks and thighs like soiled diapers. But they walked home in good spirits, Gretchen pleased with her audacious first venture, Helmut excited by his first date. The food was lousy, he thought, but the initial reaction was an instantaneous one and quickly discarded. Whereas Gretchen thought she had made a successful approach to love, Helmut enjoyed the afternoon because he recalled childhood picnics, where his mother fed him tidbits which dribbled onto his freshly laundered suit. Each youngster was unaware of their effect on each other. Though their goals differed, a slim underlying bond be-tween them awaited some act, some light caress, to unify them.

At supper Anna and Isolde remarked that Helmut ate practically nothing and submerged himself in an air of solitude. Not all unex-pected, they said, as the youngsters were seen hauling away a huge picnic basket. Helmut readied himself to respond to questions regard-ing his health, why he had no appetite, his apparent nausea and un-controlled belching.

Anna said, "You won't starve. We saw the basket. Did she feed you bologna?"

"How did you know?" He had assumed his date was private.

"It's an easy, quick meal and doesn't require much preparation," said Isolde.

"But Gretchen made a dessert, little chocolate covered balls which were tasty."

Anna lectured. "Beware of young ladies who feed you, and if they trouble themselves to make a dessert, it is time to look over your shoulder." She laughed. "That girl likes you and doesn't know exactly what to do about it. She pushes food into you as if giving lumps of sugar to a jumpy horse. You don't want to be tamed yet, do you?"

Helmut left the table, flushed and excited. Gretchen liked him well enough to cook and spend an afternoon with him, like family. Again he failed to look into himself and think positively, to escape the consternation and dread he imagined belonged to the rabbit that Axel killed. Instead of holding his strong qualities to full view, he held back and sniffed from a distance the aroma of maturity. Time to move out and break through his shyness. Time to perform. If Gretchen thought he was a weakling who dragged his ass away from girls, he would show her a different side. What side? He had to think about it.

Helmut was swamped with indecision, but Gretchen would furnish a circumstance for his deliverance. As they ran she complained she tore her blouse on a tree limb. Actually she had reached back and ripped open the top buttons. Helmut was to piece together the torn flaps of her clothes. He stood behind her, pulled at an edge of cloth, laid bare a shoulder. Gretchen sat, as she was taller than he, and expressly because there was no other way he would have an unobstructed view of the delicate mound of her breast. But Helmut afforded himself only a quick glance in front, having judged the back of her shoulder to be more familiar, thus less disturbing territory. He definitely was not an adventurer, yet he was trapped by a strawberry mole the width of a pencil. It had all the attributes of a misplaced, nubile nipple, rosy and blushing with modesty for its eccentric location on a background of creamy skin. Helmut touched the projection, felt its craggy yielding surface which blanched as he pressed. His hand found her shoulder blade, its contours undulating between bone and soft flesh. His pants filled with a stinging bulge, not unpleasant but disappointing, like a taste of delicacy and no more. He moved his body closer to her.

In the touch of a man's hand Gretchen knew her moment of participation had arrived. She drew Helmut's arm forward, placed his fingers on her nipple. He stood petrified, a trunk of immobility, with one hand on her breast, his gaze fixed on her mole, and his penis straining for exit. Action time, the sublime moment, had presented itself to Helmut, but he remained a rock of futility, all weight and hardness with no one to shove him forward. Gretchen was no help. She had used her talents to take her to this moment, but not what to do when she got there. Helmut would not let go, he couldn't, and Gretchen was rooted in unforeseen doubts. He hoped she would say something, do something. In an instant he had been overcome by a vision and a touch.

He might let go of her, calm himself, laugh over the experience which would plunge him back to the cute little boy stage, head hung low, not talking till spoken to, requiring a pat on the cheek and laid to sleep with a good night peck from mother.

Was this to be his permanent outlook, acting when prodded, speaking when spoken to, engaging in escapades only when encouraged by others? Manfred had pushed him where he never would have gone himself. Anna and Isolde corrected and guided him. Axel berated him. But it took Gretchen to expose desire. He ought now to become a leader and take others by the hand. If not, he would grow up cackling to wrinkled old men about images of romance, like Anna spoke of old loves after she drank a glass of cherry brandy. He helped Gretchen up and turned to face her. She sensed his determination and was frightened by it.

"Gretchen, I want you to come with me. I know a place where we will be alone." Helmut had crossed the barrier.

"Where? What for?"

"Come." He appeared the experienced lover reassuring a young virgin.

She followed him into the barn. Helmut guided Gretchen up a ladder to the hayloft, where they lay in a bed of straw. A crack in the roof had let rain in, and the straw smelled of sweet grass mixed with slightly decomposed garbage. Gretchen sniffed at the odor, but Helmut was unaffected. Sitting beside her he pulled down her blouse.

She made no effort to cover her bared chest, though she said, "What are you doing?" She was filled with anxiety but could not reveal her fear in view of the effort she had made to entice a male, any male, into Helmut's position. They stared at each other, unsure of the next move. Helmut hugged her. She professed pain, which so distressed him he pulled away. He could not understand her objection beside his delight, better than running, sweating, eating, far better than receiving a compliment for superior knowledge. Exhilaration rattled his brain and tingled his thighs, swept through him in a current of anticipation to emerge at the swollen ripeness of his penis.

He rushed to remove his pants and place himself between her legs, but she rigidly refused to spread herself. Not fear or virtue or forewarnings of dire consequences kept her locked against his insertion. She did not know what to do, and neither did Helmut. In his rush Helmut forgot the details he had read with intellectual precision. He was satisfied when his genitals brushed her upper thigh. The ejaculation was followed by a sensation of a void, a hole left in his abdomen, a cavern with damp, gloomy walls.

Gretchen dressed in silence. Decidedly she had experienced a surge of sexual thrill, but she was not quite certain what she was supposed to have felt. Watching Helmut stiffen and hold his breath, moist with sweat, then sensing the thrust of a warm stream on her thighs was not what she imagined should happen. But it would do. When she learned more, she reasoned, she would adjust to a partner lying beside her.

Helmut uttered a host of complaints at supper, the roast was not brown enough, gravy too thick, potatoes soggy; but he devoured every morsel he could reach. The milk was nearly sour, chairs too hard, and why didn't they listen to him when he spoke. Anna and Isolde were astounded. From polite obeissance to niggling jibes within twenty-four hours was a sickness, if not physical then mental. After double portions of dessert they caught him spooning potatoes from a pot on the stove. The women discussed his behavior and concluded Helmut showed extreme manifestations of growing pains. They agreed to watch and wait before searching more actively for the cause of a gigantic appetite coupled with a nagging behavior.

Two days passed before Helmut was himself again. Difficult days. Helmut had instinctively avoided questions, "Where were you all afternoon? What made you so hungry? Why do you act as if you are in a dream?" He took the initiative and accused his mother of everything he could think of. But there were afflictions he could not bring into the open. He dreamt he walked with his mother in the early evening when she fell into a pit. Wailing in anguish she disappeared. Helmut called Anna, who lay down on her belly, laughing. In the oncoming darkness he could make out Anna's fat thighs and soiled panties. The dream recurred twice, after which he forgot it, left only with the hazy impression that he and Isolde were drawing apart.

Nearly asleep one evening he saw Axel kiss his mother, and he rubbed his eyes violently to prove this was not a dream. She soothed Axel's back, head, shoulders, buttocks, with fitful massaging motions which were wild and unpatterned as if she were in the throes of unrestrained convulsive seizures. Formerly Helmut would have been muddled and agitated. Now he was relieved by the sight. He felt independent of his mother. What he witnessed engrossed him in a different. new way, as if he watched a friend in an act with comic overtones. Had he been spied on when he lay with Gretchen, it too would have been an hilarious sight for the viewer. He reviewed his escapade with Gretchen, felt a familiar surge into his crotch, waves of heat and expansion, until a discharge delivered him from the onslaught of his imagination. The bed sheet with which he wiped himself was soothingly cold as he fell asleep.

Chapter 11

THAT IT WAS Saturday was easy to remember, as the work load was lighter, and Sunday would be even better. A low pitched boom shook the walls of the farmhouse. The floor danced beneath his feet. Whip-snapping sounds came at him from two directions, one on the heels of the other. He called to his mother and Anna. Two windows were shattered, one at the front, one at the side of the house. All three ran in the direction of the blast.

Less than a mile down the road several people had gathered at the edge of a crater gouged from the edge of a grove of trees. Two ragged tree trunks lay horizontal, their roots peeking into a twenty-foot depth of carbon-spotted earth. Grass borders were charred and irregular patches poured smoke. A truck and two small vehicles screeched to a halt, discharged soldiers with snugged helmuts and rifles in hand. The bomb was a large one, they said, a terrorizing tactic rather than a definitive attack. The lieutenant in charge responded to questions almost gleefully and predicted there would be more bombs dropped to frighten the population.

The episode was a long-awaited testimonial to the end of the langorous days distant from war zones. Comfortable indifference was to become a figment of memory. The farm and village folk were to join a meaner world, where inspectors and political bosses sniffed out their belongings, took what an insatiable war office could consume, and generally invaded the security of isolation they enjoyed. Air raids, paratroopers, and artillary barrages were to be the business of playful generals who would disfigure old maps and strangle villages and their occupants.

Axel threatened gloom. "Hide your food."

Anna lost her composure. "Don't frighten us. We have an airtight arrangement with the barracks. They won't touch us."

Axel was impatient. "Always you have the final say. Everything you depended on before goes out the window. Poof! You will be in the soup if you refuse to accept what is happening. I will tell you what you must do, and if you don't, it is too bad."

Isolde brushed back Axel's hair and he spoke quietly.

"We are now a part of the war. The village is full of authorities, military and political. A nasty bunch. They were busy elsewhere, but we are now in the middle of it and they will come snooping around. Oh, it's not what you think. Right now it's food they want, not Jews, though they will look for that later. In the meantime, they will take every scrap you produce, arrangement or no arrangement."

The restful mood of the village turned to chaos. Villagers who formerly walked at leisure, engaged in local gossip laced with humor, gathered in back rooms for card games and brandy, now hurried to destinations with sullen, worn expressions. A camouflaged limousine brought to the town hall a group of civilians who gave orders which brooked no argument, no why or what if; minute instructions to trained scavengers to requisition every scrap of clothing, food, metal, coal, and wood. Officers and soldiers at the barracks lost their autonomy, trembled, crapped in their tailored pants, Axel said. The villagers no longer dealt with the military, who possessed passable human qualities which allowed them to overlook or engage in barter, graft, and a form of mutually beneficial greed. Super patriotic civilians with enormous power now controlled all personal and business transactions.

Helmut boiled the situation down to good and evil, with evil paramount and good trampled upon and hiding in disgrace. Recalling the book seller, he asked Axel what was to become of him.

"That fool," said Axel, "is gone. They found out about his past, one of those liberal fellows. Everything was dumped in the street, books, fixtures, furniture they couldn't use, smashed and burned. The man was careless. It serves him right, wherever he is, if he's alive."

Helmut opened his mouth to protest, but Isolde cautioned him to be silent.

Anna waited for a black night when a sliver of moon appeared. She, Isolde, and Helmut each carried a bag of potatoes wrapped in double burlap and a sack of flour in wax paper within old bread boxes. Thirty yards behind the house they took turns digging, close to a boulder which would serve as a marker. Shallow swards of grass and roots were elevated before they dug into stony depths of the soil. Anna worked prodigiously with deep thrusts of her spade. She stopped and placed her hand on her chest and would have continued if Helmut had not taken her shovel from her. Isolde dug out smaller segments and Helmut loosened the ground with a pickaxe to enable him to throw out a stream of rocks and loam. The food they brought was packed down and buried, with the excess dirt carried into the woods in boxes and the sod carefully tamped down over their cache. The women turned to go, but Helmut stared at the work area. He had dug a hole large enough to bury himself, a resting place unaffected by noise of bombs or shouts of intruders. Here was food from which hope could spring on demand.

Anna clutched her upper abdomen as they returned. A wisp of moonlight played on her face, screwed into the grimace of a terrorized gargoyle. Helmut asked if he might carry her. She forced a smile and called him a silly boy. As Helmut watched her on the couch with a hot water bottle on her chest, he imagined her pain was a huge rock he held over his head, a weight which wore down his arms until he would collapse. He had to hold on if he were to be of use. Anna asked for a doctor, one old retired doctor who lived amongst his books and cobwebs in a rundown house three miles away. Helmut ran the distance without a stop.

Dr. Lange was an old friend of Anna's, perhaps an old lover, judging from his beatific expression when he saw her. His baggy, spotted pants with buttons missing from his jacket and a frayed tie demonstrated he was poor, or could not take care of himself. As a physician he was not a bell-weather of confidence but he radiated wisdom spiced with jollity. Helmut forgot the doctor's clothes. He fixed his gaze on a combed shock of white hair which vied with the fullness of a snowy moustache. Dr. Lange was a poster ad for the old German *Kultur*, down but not out, secluded like a mole in a burrow awaiting better weather.

"Anna my dear," he said, "you work too hard."

"Doesn't everyone?" she whispered.

"Of course. But there are limits, and we pay a price for going beyond our limits. Your heart muscle is a little strained, and you must rest."

"You rest. There is too much for me to do." Dr. Lange stepped back, looked first at Helmut, then toward Isolde, as if to tell Anna she did not give credit to the two healthy bodies beside him. Anna understood his silent chastisement.

"How long before I can work?"

"A month in bed and two months of relative inactivity afterward." She knew he dealt with more than a strain. Infinitely practical, she acknowledged retreat might be the handmaiden of attack, and sank back in acquiescence. Dr. Lange left digitalis for Anna. "Take it," he said, "it's one of nature's remedies."

Though Dr. Lange visited Anna every other day (the trip was too taxing for daily care), his lively quips of reassurance, changes of medication, the hours in which he recalled gay old times did not cheer his patient. Anna had a distinct awareness, a premonition of what could happen, and she specifically ordered that no consultants were to be brought in. She enjoyed with Dr. Lange a trusting, personal relationship, a commitment to fate. There were to be no interlopers who would demand hospitalization with its accompaniment of official registrations and questionnaires. She was alone in life except for her boarders, friends in need who had supplied her with a final mission. Her death would be an extension of solitude, and not a factor in their exposure to medical and political investigation.

Isolde thought Anna had lost her courage, but Helmut perceived her stubborn will. Her downgrade was gradual but relentless. When she insisted on getting out of bed to inspect the stove, wash a few dishes, Helmut supported her. She leaned on him, which he took to be an ominous sign, as Anna never permitted assistance. At night she slept on three pillows, and in the morning, the bed or couch was exactly as it had been prepared, as if she had hypnotized herself into a state of acceptance against pain and labored breathing.

She died after a long gasp, with her lips contorted in a grimness she could no longer belittle or reject.

The shock of Anna's death posed a problem; what to do with her body. Her neighbors were never close and would not know for months that she was missing. Of paramount concern for Helmut and Isolde was the continuation of their isolation. Dr. Lange would be no problem, as he had been out of practice, removed from society for years, a part of the aged past categorized as the walking dead. Axel would learn the news but it was best not to embroil him at the moment, as he was no longer the paragon of trustworthiness who would lie their way out of official predicaments. Of all people, Gretchen and Manfred became the inadvertant helpers they needed to solve their dilemma.

The Renner youths arrived excited and tense. Gretchen's parents were moving to find work and sustenance. It was not decided whether Manfred would travel with them. Mr. Renner was the ideal accomplice for the burial, as he would not talk for fear of aligning himself with Manfred's father, nor would he be present if questions were asked. When the subject was presented by Gretchen, Mr. Renner agreed after some thought. He had better do it and leave quickly, as he could be associated with Helmut and Isolde. Manfred and Gretchen had come to the farm too often, too secretly, to be considered casual acquaintances of an underground operator with two Jewish boarders.

Anna's remains, wrapped in papers and sheets, tucked under a straw pile in the fruit cellar, began to smell. Helmut wept as he watered the sheets with disinfectants. Finally, after plans were discussed and argued over, Helmut and Mr. Renner carried the body into the forest. At one point, the man wanted to save energy and drag their burden, but Helmut objected. "It's like burying a dead cow," Mr. Renner said, his mind already fixed on this explanation if he were questioned. They laid her deep and covered the site with brush. Isolde, following, blurted out a few lines of the Kaddish, the Hebrew prayer for the dead, a token of a culture she forgot she still owned.

Helmut asked Isolde, "Was that a Hebrew prayer? Was it something they said thousands of years ago?"

"Yes," she answered.

"It's beautiful. Anna would have liked it."

Anna's death was a milestone for Helmut and Isolde. They were travellers on a road which now forked toward unknown destinations. To complicate matters, they were brought face to face with a forgotten fear. A tall, squinting civilian knocked on the door, and with a smile more like a leer proclaimed he was part of a new team brought into the area to check on things, an ambivalent way of giving notice he could turn the place inside out and take what he wanted. He displayed a document in his wallet, and with the charm of a poised cobra asked for their identification. Helmut suffered through his arsenal of violent images, kitchen knives to swing, the axe lying against the wood pile, a wad of cloth soaked in turpentine then lit and thrown. In an instant his thoughts were subdued in a wave of quaking which he hid by standing behind his mother.

"Your papers, please!"

Isolde turned to walk to an old trunk in a corner of the bedroom, but half way there she faced him, "Won't you come in?"

"Of course." The response was given as if he expected the invitation, demanded it.

He sat rigidly, placed his hat on the table, circled the room with practised eyes, paused at each chair, chest of drawers, or cabinet which might contain valuables. Alarmed, Helmut fidgeted. Surely this man must know the worst, with his professional gaze pressing through walls and into dark corners, a meticulous scientist of search. Isolde remained unflustered as she presented a sheaf of papers, all forged. He perused them haphazardly and threw them on the table as if he had gone through a routine which did not interest him.

"Madame, I am acquainted with the productivity of this farm. You live well. You eat well. And you know of course that your country entertains a policy of sharing. It is a humanitarian activity, and we expect everyone to comply." He quickly jotted down a list of what he wanted ready for delivery in forty-eight hours, to be picked up by truck he would dispatch. A professional tax assessor could not have been more proficient after a week's work. Rapid calculations coupled with cold glances with which he blanketed the farm enabled him to assess its worth in grain and livestock, of which he requested half the entire lot. Isolde and Helmut were relieved, since they might have been included as postscripts on the bottom of his list. Upon leaving he said to Isolde, "I did not pay much attention to your papers, Madame. Perhaps another time."

Trucks arrived as promised and were loaded by soldiers who cursed as they worked. The farm took on an uncluttered appearance, surprisingly tidy and emptied of misplaced hay, wood, and mounds of manure. If the seizure of grain, cattle, pigs and chickens were repeated, the grounds would become barren and clean, though nothing would remain to eat, sell, or barter. Isolde maintained an icy calm, which Helmut read as despair. And what if that inspector returned and really examined their papers?

A shallow stream swollen by months of rain ran across fields two miles north of the farm. Water meandered through a deep ravine cut by heavier flows of past decades. Out of this bucolic scene came the sounds of gunshots and machine gun rattles which kicked up curtains of dust on both sides of the ravine. A handful of parachutists, thought to be British, had been dropped and were pinned down on the far side of the stream. Men from Axel's unit as well as a platoon of infantry faced the intruders.

Helmut had crawled to within a few hundred yards of the action. He saw hands raised and guns thrown to the ground, unarmed men clambering down the sides of the ravine, through the stream and up the other side, soaked, exhausted, hands held high in terror. A sharp command rang out, which instantly triggered a cacaphony of rat-tat-tats, little crackling sounds which of themselves were minor breaks in the stillness of the fields, like the delicate crunchings of hundreds of tree twigs after an ice storm. The parachutists who advanced fell, some forward, some backward. Helmut was dazzled by the carnage. He felt inconsequential, a spectator from another world who could do nothing.

He told Isolde he had seen many men killed, and it was like watching tiny figures brought down in a shooting gallery. She could no longer offer him platitudes of motherly encouragement. Violence was too near and could become personal. Isolde said, "As the war gets closer you will feel it more. Watch out you are not part of the shooting. Get as far away from it as you can. But if you must protect yourself, then you will have to."

Helmut understood. He had heard Axel on the same subject, and Anna had mentioned that violence and killing are sometimes the prerogative, the duty of gentle people, even scholars. All he could think of now was an eerie image of violence, where men fell.

Chapter 12

AXEL GANS ACTED as if Anna's death had devastated him. He spoke glowingly of Anna. He drank whatever he could get to his lips, cheap wine from bombed cellars, vile concoctions he exchanged for an egg or a few potatoes. Axel's features changed. The lower lip thickened and drooped as if it were pulled down by sheer weight, exposing yellowed teeth with bits of food embedded along the gums. No longer standing straight, his hunched shoulders complemented the forward sag of his body, which he propelled with an exaggerated limp. His degenerated appearance was due to the ravages of insecurity and the loss of those qualities which he loved in himself. No longer could he plan activities with confidence in his ability to wheedle and lie.

He was once comforted by his status of a father figure. Always single and free-wheeling, unemcumbered by wife and children in his deliberations, Axel thought he had found a situation on the farm where he was a father as well as advisor; not completely, but sufficiently for his needs. Little Helmut, his friend and student, no longer respected him. Isolde appeared too busy and too worried about the future to console him with love. Should the vicious cycle progress, sex no longer would be an issue, as he wondered whether his urge could be aroused by any woman. Lately he could not even arouse himself.

The smooth working arrangements at the barracks had disintegrated. Special deals for barter of food or liquor were shelved. Tough, careful snoopers applied stringent controls against slick tricksters. Axel was stricken by the dangerous instability of his life-style; his nerves were frayed; he could no longer pluck the ripe plum of opportunity. Worse, his clout had so dissipated he might even be returned to the front as an infantryman.

Helmut was disturbed by the emergence of a vicious streak in Axel which was evident in minor confrontations. As he passed the boy, he would shove Helmut violently to the ground. The soldier intimated "stay out of my way if you want to stay healthy!" Isolde, who recognized Axel's unusual moods as the pressure of war, was less alarmed than her son; she had not yet been the recipient of his assault.

When Axel came to the farm he would curtly pass Helmut and Manfred, and enter the house to meet with Isolde. The boys did not know what transpired, but Axel usually spent no more than ten minutes indoors. Evidently these meetings were unproductive, with the soldier left disgruntled and muttering to himself.

Manfred one day confronted Axel. "It looks like you didn't make it with her." The soldier slapped him to the ground and kicked him. Helmut tried to drag off the victim, but he too was beaten.

Isolde worried that Axel might harm the boys, yet she felt herself immune from his outbursts. The man had become boorish, a trait she had known and easily handled in other men. Though she never entertained a thought of marriage to Axel, and was certain this was not his intent, she nevertheless classed him as the type who might become a wife beater, one she had best not incite to argument. Having submitted to sexual completion with him only once, she resolved never to do so again, as she was fearful of pregnancy. In bed together, partly undressed, she took pains to bring him to climax, though she scrupulously guarded against vaginal entry. She felt she gave him relief for which he ought to be grateful. And if he were frustrated by ungrateful sex, that was how it had to be. She and Helmut might be forced to pack and slip away at any hour, sneak off with their boxes to parts unknown, a hellish enough predicament without the burden of pregnancy.

Helmut was enveloped by a cloud of uncertainty about his mother. One night he dreamed he was suspended by ropes, which snapped one by one, until he was held by a single strand, the handiwork of Isolde.

Helmut lay asleep. Trees weighted with ice prongs groaned in the wind. Axel knocked and was ushered in by Isolde, startled by this late night visit. He was frantic as he justified his presence. Soldiers were deserting, enemy units approached, all hell could break loose. Disorder was rampant and roads from the village were filled with fleeing carts, animals, and battered vehicles fortunate enough to contain a few cupfuls of gasoline. He advised that they leave by a route he had mapped through the forest. Should they reach a quiet sector they would rest. If the flow of military action cut them off, they would head for enemy lines. To fall into allied hands would be safer than capture by cadres of enraged German fanatics.

Isolde asked, "Should I wake Helmut and pack now?"

Axel smiled. "No, not that fast. I came to say my last goodbye, and we are entitled to a little privacy."

Isolde noted that he had preened himself, shaved; uniform pressed, shirt and tie cleaned and neatly in place. She had not seen him so fastidiously attired for months. Odd that he should have taken such pains in the midst of turmoil, on the verge of desertion from his unit.

"What will happen to you?" she asked.

"Never mind me. I will do what I must. One thing I know, they will never get me back at the front again."

"Then you will come with us?"

"No. All I can do is tell you where to go."

"Well then, if it's goodbye..." she blurted.

He interrupted her and pushed her onto the couch. "I want one more time together with you, and by God it will be a good one," he snapped.

"Not now, Axel. Please. After what you told me how can you expect me to be...?"

He lifted a bottle of wine from the lower shelf of an oak cabinet, poured a tumbler and drained it. Refilling his glass and another for Isolde, he held it out to her.

"I can't now," she said. "Look at this place. I've got to put it in order to sort out what we can take." Axel forced the glass to her lips. She smiled and shook her head in playful rejection. He held the back of her head and pressed the rim against her mouth until she was forced to swallow. Two gulps and Axel was satisfied.

"You see," he said, "it was not so terrible. Tonight we will make this an evening to remember. Wherever we end up, we should have a supreme moment to remember." He undressed with fumbled movements of uncontrolled agitation.

Isolde flattered him. "You look very handsome tonight. I want to remember you as you are."

"Good, then you appreciate the pains I have taken. Tonight, my dear, it's all the way, all you can give me."

She was accustomed to his innuendos in sexual play and she stripped off her dress and shoes but left her undergarments in place. He pulled them off, impatiently, abruptly. When they lay down she fondled him, stroked his thighs, but he drew away her hands. He forced her legs apart and urged her to open herself to him.

She turned to the side. "No Axel, we've talked it over, it isn't right."

He smashed his fist into her mouth. She screamed a short subdued scream of terror.

"Please Axel, do what you want," she pleaded as she wiped the blood from her mouth. Her thighs were spread for him but she could not control the convulsive movements of her limbs.

"My little Jewess bitch," he shouted, "now you are afraid of what I can do. You've played with me enough. You'll see. I'm good enough for any of your kind."

As he spoke, he ejaculated outside her. He gazed at his flabby organ, the ultimate denouncement of his manhood. He sobbed, "Now everything is gone. I trusted you and look what you've done!" He dipped his fingers in his semen and rubbed them together to emphasize his disappointment.

His assailant was at his mercy. Isolde felt his madness. As she lifted her body and supported her frame on her elbows, she placed one foot on his chest and shoved him to the floor.

At the door Helmut saw the knife flash in the dim light. The blade started low, very low, executed a short swift arc upward and plunged into her vagina. Axel ripped and tore, his arm muscles bulging with effort. Helmut stood mesmerized, a participant in a nightmare of blood and screams and the unintelligible growls of a dog tearing at a rabbit. Helmut lifted the axe which lay against a stack of logs near the stove. Slowly, in the exaggerated fluidity of a sleepwalker he raised the weapon. Too late. Axel struck him at the side of his head with both fists, again and again, until the boy fell unconscious.

The shimmer of lights and shadows played about his head. Gusts of chill breezes swept in through the open door to impart a grotesque swing to the ceiling light. The scene could have been a second phase of a dream he wished to forget, except for the mildly pungent odor that filled the room. To stand was difficult. He approached the silent, mottled figure, spread-eagled and torn, placed his fingers on her split lip and sobbed. Revulsion turned inward as he recalled his ineptitude with the axe. Furtively he peered into corners of the room for help, someone to answer questions, to hear him out. He ran out, then returned to cover Isolde with a blanket. In the brisk night air he was overcome by the impulse to distance himself from the horror. He writhed as if he were a snared fish, but the hook would not disengage.

Where to go. Whom to tell. Only Manfred. When he reached the Renner farm it was dark. Manfred responded to the pounding on the door, half asleep in rumpled clothes. His uncle and aunt had left that day with Gretchen, and Manfred refused their lukewarm invitation to flee with them. Instead he planned to ask Helmut and his mother if he could tag along with them.

"Axel did it. My mother was killed." Helmut sobbed.

Manfred did not ask for particulars. "Come on, I'll go with you."

They walked back slowly, with eons of blank time before them. They planned to bury Isolde where Anna lay buried. Part way there she fell from their hands. They dug the grave where her body dropped. No markings were placed. Nor did they bother to hide the remains beneath a cover of grass. As if to complete the day's work, they uncovered the cache of food Anna had hidden and carried away a sack of potatoes and a container of flour.

The forest was their comrade in loneliness. Deprived of roads, hours, people, it offered an existence which made the past appear an apparition which housed a nightmare. The physical effort of trudging up and down hills laden with sodden leaves, jumping over boulders and streams, grasping supportive branches on precipitous ledges was sufficient to erase remembrance. Only when they had stopped to rest, after the first flush of pride of accomplishment had passed, did they recall their misery. Helmut would burst into tears, though revived by the exigencies of the moment when they had to build a fire, slice potatoes and sausage, and prepare a meal. The necessity to cut wood, wash, prepare a sleeping area, proved effective antidotes against gloom.

The first night they slept beside a rivulet which pounded down from distant hills. Covered with coats and a thin blanket in which Helmut had wrapped his clothes, they were stiffened with cold. Each clutched the other against attacks of shivers, inseparable as new lovers. Their discomfort mobilized them to action. Weakened, they built a fire so they could sleep, and decided to make plans, to think like explorers.

As they were about to doze off, Helmut whispered, "Manfred, this fire can be seen a mile away."

"Who cares?" Manfred whispered back.

"We'd better care. We don't want to get caught." Neither made a move to douse the fire. They slept that night. In the morning each awoke with an awareness that aloneness, unobtrusive wilderness, were of themselves only partial guarantors of their safety.

They slogged toward an open area where the warmth of a pleasant morning pierced the sparse tree cover. It was a happy hour. An embrace of sunshine which contrasted with the night's chill made them reel in the heady enchantment of life worth living. Until they saw a farm in the distance they did not think of plans, safety, food. Approaching slowly, behind bushes and trees, they enjoyed an unmistakeable cacaphony of atonal sounds — chickens, pecking, scratching, and fighting. Before them were fresh meals, which traipsed about aimlessly, scavenged for their needs, unaware that the more they ate and grew the sooner they would be captured and killed, altogether a predicament so similar to the boys' they would have been depressed with despair had they realized it.

"If I catch a chicken," Helmut said, "will you kill it?"

"Sure, I've done it many times. Chickens yell when you cut them, so I'd better wring its neck. Less noise." Manfred wrung his hands to emphasize his Neanderthal instincts.

Helmut crawled unseen to the side of the flimsy fence. Lifting the wire, about to grab a fat brown hen, a small dog appeared from nowhere in the enclosure and ran toward him. His coat sleeve snared on a curl of loose wire. Eyes closed, his face contorted in expectation of a savage bite, he was greeted instead with a moist licking from a tail-wagging mangy spaniel. Helmut freed his arm and adroitly locked his calloused hand about a chicken's neck. As he dragged it under the fence the dog managed to burrow beneath the lower edge of the wire. Manfred was greeted with two gifts, one to kill, one to feed.

Manfred nearly tore off the bird's head, after which Helmut plucked the feathers and roasted the carcass. They cut segments with a pocket knife and fed the dog generous portions of skin and bones. The animal was ravenous as well as suspicious. Three pairs of eyes squinted at each other to guard against attacks upon their territorial imperative.

It was clear to the boys that to survive they would have to skirt the edges of the forest where there was relatively little cover, to forage for food in the open country. No farmer would catch them, with reasonable care. Their danger lay in crossing roads and fields travelled by roving bands of German military, frustrated, irrational soldiers who might fire at the twitter of a bird.

The dog would not leave. Curiously he did not bark, which reinforced the growing impression that he would be a noiseless companion who might even be taught to catch a rabbit. However, as a third member who could supplement their food supply, the dog was a failure. The one and only instance in which a tired old rabbit appeared, they learned the dog could bark, not an ordinary gruff bark but an unrelenting howl as he excitedly reared on his hind legs, but did not give chase. Helmut caught the rabbit, it was so slow, but it was so obviously near death they would not eat it.

For five days the boys travelled toward what they guessed to be the enemy lines. Occasionally, on warm afternoons, they rested to wash the dog, rubbed him with dry dirt to scrape off insects and debris, then dipped him in one of the many streams encountered. With a rag they towelled him dry, and Helmut groomed him with an old pocket comb. They slept next to one another. Stolen turnips, an odd potato, a chicken, and once a pheasant which they smashed with a rock were ample fare. For added warmth they stole a mildewed horse blanket from a barn, and since they thought it would not dry they did not wash it. The dog refused to go near the blanket.

"You see," said Manfred, "that mutt likes perfumed blankets."

"He is more civilized than we are," replied Helmut.

The glow of adventure which subdued his misery was itself becoming a vehicle for boredom and normal yearnings. His wants were simple enough; to walk unafraid, to eat at a table, to face adults who listened while they stood by with constructive criticism. He wanted to fight for his independence from someone he depended on, who would release his hold with reluctance. Since he had lost his father in childhood, he had relied on his mother to foster the fulfillment of maturity. Grief seized him.

Helmut and Manfred stumbled into a long ravine laden with thorn bushes so intertwined they could not avoid scratching their flesh. The dog yelped as his snout brushed a limb. Fifty feet in front, parallel to the ravine, an elongated rise lay across their route. Apparently this was a rill flattened at its height to accomodate walkers and small vehicles, a makeshift road of dirt and gravel. Footsteps, a heavy marching tread, rumbled in the distance; no steady rhythm to the beat, no orderly left, right, but a tired, plodding of jackboots. Probably, they guessed, four or five soldiers had walked away from their battle lines. The dog began a low pitched growl. Perhaps he had once been kicked by such boots, Helmut thought. That the dog could bark loudly was a jolting discovery, as silence was an absolute necessity if they were to choose their captors. Noise at the wrong moment could mean imprisonment or death.

With his tail stiffly extended and his head forward the animal signalled an aggressiveness the boys had not perceived when he romped and played like any farm pet. He was poised to bark and attack, and if not kept still they would be detected.

Helmut cautioned Manfred. "Grab his nose, and if he wants to bark, choke him, whatever it takes to keep him quiet."

"I don't know if I can," said Manfred.

"Why not? You did it with a chicken."

"It's not the same. I'll try."

The heavy-footed tread on the road was more distinct, mingled with voices in a breeze which blew German phrases toward them. The dog struggled to free himself. Manfred sweated as the moist snout slipped from his grasp.

"Choke him," whispered Helmut, "or we're finished. They will shoot at any sound."

Manfred trembled. His hands shook as he attempted to circle the animal's throat. The boots resounded fiercely, like the screaming crowd the night his father was taken away. His mind's eye registered the perfect weapon. Helmut swooped down, gathered the smoothly contoured rock in his palm, and in an arc of violent motion crushed the dog's skull.

Both boys sank beneath the cover of a rambling bush, Helmut over the dog's body as a parent protects a child from falling debris. When the soldiers passed Helmut stood and lifted the animal close to his chest. This was his final inspection, which would imprint itself within him, the killer and his victim, the perpetrator of an egotistical act of self preservation at the expense of love.

"Why didn't you hold on?" He asked Manfred, though already aware of the answer.

"I would have had to choke him," Manfred whispered. "I couldn't do it," he cried, in his first burst of tears. Helmut was startled that he could feel victory as well as grief in the same instant; sadness from the warm body he held and the thrill of accomplishment performed in the face of necessity. Helmut had chosen between love and survival.

After three hours of arduous walking, fatigued and dishevelled, they heard a strange language, unlike the phraseology and expressions Manfred learned at school or Helmut from his mother when they studied English.

Gruff shouts of, "Get your ass moving," and "Fuck off, Pogorney," which they knew to be American but could not translate, were their initial greetings. Two forlorn adolescents encased in grime, with fearful half smiles and with arms raised, walked to a burly sergeant and his squad of unkempt men who squabbled in a most unmilitary manner.

"Jeez, it's a coupla kids." The sergeant lowered his rifle. The boys were searched, plied with chocolate, and removed to division headquarters. Manfred declared his intention to find his parents and was sent to a larger center, though not before both were interviewed by an interpreter and intelligence officer. When the boys parted they shook hands. Tall, skinny Manfred looked down at his stocky friend. It is difficult to show respect while looking down at someone, but Manfred managed it. Droplets of silent tears flushed his eyelids as he bent to hug Helmut.

The American officer at a rear echelon interrogation center was dapper in his sparkling creased uniform and handlebar moustache. Helmut thought he could be a German commander with his rapid-fire questions and stiff posture. In fact he was the only representative image of military discipline Helmut had observed in a week of wandering from compound to compound. Except for short sentences, his shocking German pronounciation and halting delivery detracted from the austerity of his bearing.

"Your father and mother?" the captain asked crisply as if he were asking about a missing pair of shoes.

"Dead."

"Religion?"

"Jewish."

The officer looked upward, appeared to soften his mood. Helmut surmised he sat opposite a friend, a man of tolerance, perhaps Jewish.

"Is that so?" he asked. "How did you stay alive?"

"We hid on a farm, my mother and I. My father disappeared years ago." The officer took notes, jotted abbreviations which would be passed on to statisticians who would compress the lost, living, and dead into appropriate columns.

"That is interesting," he said. "You Jews have a way of surviving. You always leave a hard core, for reseeding." He spoke with a hint of recrimination.

"Your mother?"

"She was murdered."

"You mean she was killed, by a bullet, or shrapnel, or in the gas chamber." He was impatient with exaggerations or presumptions of unproved atrocities.

"No, she was murdered. A German soldier who knew her did it. He used his knife." Helmut was numbed in speech, as if he recited from a text he memorized but could not understand.

"Oh! One of those crimes! Well, it's not in our jurisdiction. Perhaps the civilian authorities will look into it. The problem now is what to do with you."

Helmut had been prepared by his mother for just such an eventuality. She had stuffed into his rear pocket a folded sheet of paper overwrapped with cardboard retrieved from the bottom of a shoe box. It was a document to be cherished, a ticket for survival with evidence of personal identification. "If we are separated," Isolde had told him, "try to get in touch with Aunt Sophie in America. The address is on this paper. There are refugee agencies to help you." Helmut felt for his paper, its cover soft and wrinkled by the penetrated mud and dew of countless resting places. He whipped out the dirty gray sheet with the flourish of an ambassador presenting credentials to a foreign potentate, and read "Sophie Steingut," but could not pronounce Houston Street.

"It's in New York City of United States of America," Helmut said. "She is my aunt and wants me to stay with her."

Chapter 13

SOPHIE STEINGUT PREDATED women's liberation. She never acknowledged motherhood to be a cherished facet of female essence. The adolescent nephew she was to take under her wing would not be a surrogate child, yet she anticipated his arrival with unbounded joy as well as intense interest. He would be a rare project, a challenge, a live-in assignment spewed from the decay of Europe's political mismanagement, ripe for the instillation of egalitarian and humane concepts.

For five months she had sent telegrams and met with representatives of Jewish agencies before she stood dockside awaiting Helmut's arrival. A wan, muscular adolescent walked toward her with a canvas bag over his shoulder. She was not critical of his appearance — a ragged shock of black hair, downy fuzz on his chin, torn khaki pants, a shirt with sleeves to his finger tips, and oversized paratrooper boots. What she did see were the sad, darting black eyes and an air of imperturbability and resignation which were the mark of those who had lost their battle with fate. She categorized him as a youngster gone into early retirement. She wanted to shout to him, "This is not the gas chamber, it is America, not all sweetness and light but with breathing space and a chance to wage the good fight against oppressors and corruptors."

As she approached in her print dress, with piston-action stocky legs and elbows stuck out from her sides, Helmut was mindful of a tank garlanded with flowers rolling toward a throng in a liberated village. He wanted to step aside and run, but she was upon him, took his arm in a diminutive hand which clamped down with a remarkably reassuring squeeze.

Her greeting was abrupt. "You are Helmut Steingut. You know who I am." She spoke in German, but soon found he had a useful command of English. Her arms dropped as she stepped back for further inspection. Then, in the midst of hundreds of hugging, gesticulating families meeting new arrivals, she placed her hands on his cheeks and gently kissed his brow.

"Helmut is not the name for you," she exclaimed. "It is too hard, too German. We will find another."

On leaving the subway through boisterous crowds of the Lower East Side, the boy recounted his experiences. His timid monotone and reticence to dote on painful episodes were gently prodded, though mainly she listened and encouraged. He had to unburden himself at a pace he chose. When Helmut spoke of Anna he paused, stumbled repeatedly in the telling. Aunt Sophie, too, appeared to be a rock with a soft core, dependable, supportive on wobbly terrain, though she would tolerate no foolishness. She too, was old. Would she also die and leave him when he most needed her?

Waves of fright were carried to him by the strangeness of the place, the jostling crowds, fierce colors of a hundred shades of skin, bearded Jews in long coats and black hats; muttering, lonely, hunched men with dry lips, and smells ranging from rancid garbage to meat roasting under a bed of garlic and onions. How different from the country he knew, with its homogeneous strollers in the city or the docile faces of the village. And no comparison with his farm life. Here, people replaced thickly packed tufts of grass. This was another kind of battleground, without guns or shattering explosions, but with no place to hide. His only cheer was the sight of a horse stalled in traffic and sensible enough to use his waiting time for a massive output of manure. Helmut breathed deeply to catch the pungent odor of warm droppings, but all he got was the smell of urine from an elderly man near him. He had smelled it after Anna died. Death was at his side. Quickly he moved ahead to forget, until he met a welcome scent of fresh-baked goods from an Italian storefront.

Sophie made her living tutoring and translating with occasional secretarial jobs. Her apartment was three flights up a scaled-paint hallway, at the back. The bedroom was the size of a large closet, which it actually was, with no windows. Living room and kitchen were in close embrace, together, where she could take three steps to a half-rusted gas stove. Sophie ate well. Food was that which went inside, a building block for body and mind. She guided the boy to a chair and watched him devour a meal.

"No, we cannot tolerate Helmut for your name," Sophie mused. "How would you like Bridgely for a name?" They had taken the subway to view the Brooklyn Bridge at close quarters, as bridges were an attraction Sophie could not resist. They spawned the peoples of various boroughs, arteries which connected those separated by dirty rivers. "People must not be isolated. We should know what is happening on the other side. If there is a tragedy, or celebration, we should share in it." Helmut did not agree with her concept of social grace. What ought to be wasn't, and it was too time-consuming to dote on the future. The present had to do, like the bridge he gazed at, in awe of its structure and function. Its resistance to wind and water by the gentle sway of its supports, like a mother rocking her child to sleep. Only the two great concrete pillars appeared fierce, warlike, and above them, soothing the cement erections, hung the sinking and rising spans of interlocking ironwork. Helmut thought of skeletons of extinct birds hooked end to end so men could walk over their bones.

Bridgley was entirely too fancy for a boy's name, and she did not wish him to be ridiculed. An independent spirit would shuck that off, but Helmut had a long way to travel before he could attain independence. She would instill in him a powerful simplicity, compassion, understanding, and a vision of history. A demon out of her heritage gripped her, a heritage whose rituals she derided as lovely myths.

"Israel! That's the name for you. I know it's Jewish and biblical and common in this neighborhood, but it's like this old bridge. Its been around for a long time, and it stands for something. I don't care about Hebrew scholarship, or ceremony, or religious tales, but all your life you should know you were treated like a slave, like an insane animal, by those who lost all sense of compassion. If I called you Harold, or Robert, you might never remember. Maybe you won't like Israel, but it will be good for you."

One week in America and half his name was amputated. He did not object, as he had no ingrained affinity for any part of his name. If ever he had been taught to align pride with family emblems or appellations, he had lost it to the more urgent demand of survival. Name was of no consequence. To speak, travel, sleep without apprehension, these are the underpinnings of self-esteem. It was enough to wake in the morning and feel himself a whole body, not lacerated or shot through, a body to fill with an appetizing breakfast before its exposure to the day's events.

Aunt Sophie thought she was a good Jew. She revelled in the dramatic turns of Jewish history. Victories over oppressors were qualities to be applied to today's struggles. Paranoid notions that Jews were born to soak up punishment so that good and evil might be sharply delineated, were the products of minds too slothful to counter adversity. The price they paid was self-chastisement through default, since they did not strive to overcome. She did not preach "Let my people go." She said, "Hit them where it hurts."

Israel's acquaintances were undergoing or had passed through the rite of bar mitzvah. In this neighborhood of Old Testament associations he heard fascinating accounts of the maturity rites he was supposed to have taken. His friends prayed their way through adolescence, while he had travelled a route of exasperation, hunger, and terror. To his surprise, it was Sophie who brought up the issue.

She said, "The bar mitzvah ceremony as such means nothing to me. True, it is thousands of years old, but old is not necessarily good. Different tribes killed off each other for longer than that, but we don't advise murder. Besides, the old meaning of the ceremony is lost in fancy catering, expensive presents, and dance bands."

One Friday night Sophie prepared an extravagent meal and invited her friends, a Polish and a Viennese immigrant, and a young woman she had befriended. No one wore skullcaps, though Israel placed a handkerchief on his head as he rose after dinner to give his bar mitzvah speech. He did not know why he had to cover his head, but recalled relatives doing so as a child. In his view it seemed right, as it was one of a few good memories. He spoke with the voice of a young man who had gathered his courage and determination for an evening.

"I have seen what some people can do to others and I don't understand. Friends kill friends, and there are enemies everywhere. I run and save myself, but others do not. They lie there. Sometimes I think it would be better if I did not run. At night I think of running and stopping, running and stopping, but I don't know which to do. In the morning, when I wake up, I hardly know where I am. Then, when I feel better, I want to do something for my old friends. I would like to be able to hurt the people that hurt them. I want the strength to do that. But after I've thought about what I want, I get frightened, afraid that if I try too hard I might fail. Then I don't think of it anymore. What I mean is, I end up without knowing what to do." He paused, "I hope I didn't bore you, but this was on my mind for a long time. Thank you."

The applause was restrained. "Did I do alright?" Israel whispered in an aside to Sophie.

She answered, "For a bar mitzvah it was unusual, which shows you are not ordinary. That is good. The main thing is you are unhappy."

"I feel good about what I said."

"It always feels good to let out your troubles, but I am thinking of the future." She was emphatic. "I hope you will keep in mind there are good times ahead for you, school, what you will become. And fun should not be excluded. It's no sin to laugh."

"I laugh sometimes."

"Do it more often. Think of how lucky you are, the chances you will have. As for living with me, I'm not so bad."

"Of course not." He hugged her broad, squat body.

The young woman raised her glass. "I want to drink a toast." Tumblers were filled. "I wish Israel much happiness. You should go far, Israel, and may you enjoy every step of the way." The boy drained his tumbler and sat down. The room whirled about him. Alone in a room of guests, he was carefree in the midst of care, yet he was the cog about which frivolity revolved.

When his head cleared and they were alone, Sophie said to Israel, "This night must not pass before you have considered your future. Now, what do you want to do?"

"I haven't thought about my future. Couldn't we wait until tomorrow?"

"This is the time," she said. "If we work on it now the decision will stick with you." According to Sophie, the most solid determination was made when facts were fresh.

She said, "I would like to have you study medicine."

"Like father?"

"Yes. Not that a son is bound to his father's career, most aren't, but you have the intelligence, the feeling, to be a good doctor; and you are interested in science."

"I never wanted to be a doctor. Math and physics were my best subjects. History, too. I'm good in that."

"History is out! You can enjoy it by reading. To make a good living as a student of history is another matter. All you could do is teach, and the fate of teachers is in the hands of nitwits who will get rid of you in hard times. You want freedom, don't you? Then forget about teaching."

The argument was effective.

She continued. "And you can use math and physics in medicine. Besides, you can make a good living." Sophie suffered with stomach cramps when she stretched the truth, and now she imagined she was being torn by a swinging chain. To a friend or neighbor she would have given advice that no good work is done without enjoyment, so be what you want. Israel was her packet of flesh and bones responsibility, not exactly her son, but as close as she would ever be to one. He was too vulnerable, too marked by adversity to decide what was best. Never had she considered financial independence to be a factor in career choices, but they were in America, where money was a requirement for self improvement as well as social progress. "He must not wear rags like me," she vowed to herself.

Israel's image of his self-worth was shaped in the confusion of early experiences. He had been subjected to Axel's egotistical delusions and his father's authoritarianism; to the wisdom and adamancy of Anna, and now to the fervor of Aunt Sophie. Somewhere there had to be a middle road, where the ultimate goal was the recognition and acceptance of reality.

He sensed this spirit of relaxed effort in his closest high school friend. Lin Chiu was American born of Chinese immigrant parents.

Both did well in school. After school they worked for a merchant selling socks, gloves, and shirts from an outdoor stand on Orchard Street. Occasionally, they went to a movie, took girls boating in Central Park, and made rare visits to museums. They would talk for hours about a machine featured in *Popular Mechanics*, or the experimental applications of newer forms of energy.

Sports in their school meant calisthenics, basketball, and gymnastics on antiquated equipment. Football was too expensive for the school's budget until Patrick Quinn, a spirited school coach, beat the system. With other gym teachers he formed neighborhood teams, more like disciplined gangs, to play on a grassy plot at the tip of Manhattan Island. Merchants provided old gear. When Coach Quinn spied Israel's musculature and Lin Chiu's speed, he recruited them.

Israel spoke to Sophie about football, and Lin introduced his parents to his new sport.

"My aunt gave in," Israel reported. "She objected to football at first, said I'd get hurt, and that I had to save myself for better things. She's afraid I'll make a lousy doctor if I break my fingers."

"What did you tell her to convince her?"

"Nothing, except that we have rules to follow, and I wouldn't be crippled. I showed her the helmet and shoulder guards and all she could say was how could I get around in a suit of armor."

"My father and mother are different," Lin said. "They want me to play."

"I thought Chinese people don't believe in football."

"So did I. But they have this American thing going. If a guy on the block gets elected dog catcher, they hang out an American flag. I hoped they would say no, I couldn't play, not nice for a smart Chinese boy. Christ, they're more gung ho than Coach Quinn."

Lin was appointed halfback and Israel made guard. They played the Paddy Saints, a crew of tough Irish and Polish boys with a sprinkling of Italians. Lin carried the ball frequently and successfully. Israel was four inches shorter than his opponent guard, but he soon learned his opposite's weakness. If Israel drove low and to the left, the Saints' player invariably tumbled over Israel's back to the right, which opened a path for Lin, quickly recognized as a player who could snake his way through a random series of needle eyes.

Shouts and curses abounded. "Why the hell can't you stop the chink?" or "There he goes again; it's fucking slant eyes." And at times grudging respect like "Hey, yellow belly, you got balls."

Lin's courage had a time to live and a time to die. In a particular vicious play, Lin found himself alone and upright, pushing irrationally against a wall of bodies. Someone grasped his ankle and yanked it. As he fell he heard a snap. He grunted an expletive he had not used since hunger pains when a child. Lin's ankle was a hideous vision of swollen yellow mottled skin. Israel thought his Chinese friend displayed obvious pain, breathed rapidly, and gripped his injured member with an accompanying cry of "Do something. Get me out of here." Just like people who weren't Chinese.

Coach Quinn was ecstatic. "We beat the pants off them. They're tough, real tough, and this is the one I wanted." He cooled somewhat when he saw Lin's long pale foot sticking out of what appeared to be a partly deflated bleached football. "Say, how did you get that?"

Israel and Mr. Quinn carried Lin into the coach's two-door sedan where they crowded him into the back seat and drove him to the hospital. The young doctor in the emergency room had to admit the manner of injury was unusual. "Not much football played here." Stabbings, beatings with heavy weapons, and shootings were so familiar they bored him. Here was an anatomical insult he could attribute to a precise series of adverse body dynamics, just as he had read in the books. The injury was so classic it was bizarre. After he rushed Lin through x-ray he took pleasure in turning the foot in the reverse direction it had been driven, a quick twist and shove to reinstate the natural contours of the limb, which he then encased in plaster.

When Mr. Chiu senior arrived, he made a quick assessment. "It's okay. Lin will play again."

Lin exploded. "I don't want to play. I'm through." The coach looked to Mr. Chiu for an instillation of courage, a pep talk. Between them, the pressure would be such the boy would have to participate. Quinn wanted a call to arms, the fighting spirit, the basic patriotic concept of do it for the team in spite of yourself.

Mr. Chiu turned to Israel. "What do you think about Lin playing football?"

"If he doesn't want to, I don't think he should." Quinn murmured something about Irish and Polack kids who had guts.

Mr. Chiu paused. "I think we should wait. Let him heal and be well. Later, on a day with no pain, he can tell us what he wishes to do. If he says no play, that's what it will be."

Lin never again touched a football. Israel completed the final scheduled game with the vow he would not try out for the sport in college. But Sophie, he thought, was not altogether right. He had to get a taste of what the game was like. But that coach! Selfish, did it all for his own good, hid behind the old idea that he made men out of boys. Israel concluded he alone must shape his development.

Lin and Israel enrolled at the City College of New York on an afternoon when they sweated over lists of science courses they could attend together. Israel asked, "Did your father ever tell you what to do, what you should become?"

"Yes and no," replied Lin. "He laid it out and told me stories about a man who did this, another who did that. Really he gave me all sides of the picture, but in the end he let me choose. He put it on the table, plain. That's what he likes to do. The rest is up to me."

Israel was concerned whether he could think under stress, to control himself in a pressing situation. Patience was of the essence, the will to permit time to shift to one's favor, yet patience could be expanded into lassitude.

Chapter 14

THE THREE-AND-A-HALF years in which Israel completed a Bachelor of Science degree were distinguished by outstanding grades and a series of odd jobs after school and on weekends. Gulp a sandwich before work. Hurry to make the subway ride. Gyrate and pirouette in the macabre dance of the subway riders. Israel maintained his mental equilibrium by rationalizations which eased his predicament. If he passed a playground and watched ball players and frolicking youngsters, he conjured up his future. "When I finish school I'll have plenty of time to play. Let me get through the hard, unexciting work; then I can enjoy myself."

That Israel should enter medical school was a foregone conclusion. Sophie had ordained it, yet his choice of a midwestern university was an unexpected blow to her.

"Why go way out there? You can graduate here and open an office in this neighborhood, close by."

He was repelled by a proposal which placed him under her kind but heavy hand. The struggle to leave New York was lost until he showed her the midwest was less expensive, perhaps the difference between an uninterrupted education and having to stop to earn tuition, an argument which Sophie pondered deeply. One of her rules of progress was, "If you want something, push hard and don't stop." Of course he was right; high time he preened his wings for flight. Having learned to take care of herself, so must he.

Early in his freshman year in medical school in Iowa, Israel met with an obstructive influence which could have proved disastrous — anatomy. This was purported to be a subject of unimaginable difficulty. Once he overcame the odor of formaldehyde, in which the bodies were marinated, he became intrigued with nature's designs and hurdled the block with ease. Leathery muscles, nerves, arteries, entwined themselves in and about bones and organs in frustrating patterns.

The apparent pandemonium of parts, once unravelled, could be traced toward definitive goals and functions. Intricacies of finger movements, shifting ligament tensions, the convolutions of nerves and arteries, all melded to feed the brain and receive from it responsive commands. To Israel the process was a stupendous romance, a unity of function fashioned from a host of disparate and entangled structures. He developed an anatomical love only a surgeon would understand and covet.

The issue which nearly scuttled his medical career was one of blood. Details of morbid anatomy which lay inert and mummified on a dissecting table were not as personalized as a subject who was warm and breathed, who choked and twitched. Israel watched a young woman already anaesthetized, wheeled into the operating room. Attendants shifted the lithe frame onto an imposing table under merging beams of blue-white light. Her lower abdomen was illuminated in a circle of radiance, which divorced this portion of her body from adjacent darkened flesh. She breathed rhythmically under a mask which reminded Israel of a time when the Germans feared gas attacks.

Intense quiet was broken by the click of instruments lined up on a cloth covered table. A mystic aura enveloped the room, the severity of passionate participation in a spiritual observance. Then the surgeon told his favorite story about a priest, a minister, and a rabbi. Laughter beneath surgical masks, giggles from nurses, injected a certain stimulus into the room, a coarse energy which signalled it was the moment to begin surgery.

At the first cut, the initial spurt of blood, Israel gripped a rail at the rear of the operating suite. He was not faint, he did not grasp for support, for he had anticipated and prepared himself for this rite of purification. The blood of his childhood had always pressed upon him, asleep and awake. Dreams of a deep red river to be crossed, a caustic stream his feet must not touch, were revived. Israel knew he had come against a barrier to his medical maturity, which he had to transcend. Blood appalled him, yet he decided to expose himself to all surgery and so immune himself from his past. Perhaps he would make surgery his profession.

The verdict reached could have been born of self punishment for imagined defects, or it could have arisen from the reservoir of toughness which resides in a survivor. Or both. Israel suffered from a schizophrenia of weaknesses and strength, but he relied on the supposition that persistent confrontation of his deficiency would make it disappear; or he would become so accustomed to its onslaught he no longer would be affected.

At the end of his first year Israel travelled home by bus. Open fields and rural villages gave way to complex road systems which led to traffic-infested cities. He was impressed by the graduated crescendo of terrain and population, the placid serenity which inevitably merged into hurried ant hills of activity. Where there were more people, more life, there was more misery. Still, most city dwellers would not change location if given the opportunity. There must be some element of acceptance, some bright new song of contentment which he could not hear.

In New York, Israel planned to visit Lin Chiu who now worked in a Ph.D. program at a prestigious university. Before Israel found where the younger men of the biophysics program were closeted, he was shifted past three receptionists. In the basement, past a cement corridor with sweating walls from boiler room steam, a series of windowless storage cubicles had been transformed by a coat of paint into cheerless laboratories for unknown researchers. Lin worked in a corner room whose walls were lined with stacked cages filled with the patter and twitter of hundreds of white mice. Atop a metal table lay electrical boxes with attached probes, a generator, and coils of insulated wire. A defaced pine desk groaned beneath piles of books and paper. There was barely room for both men to stand together and embrace.

Israel noted Lin's pastel blue laboratory coat. "It's blue," he said. "You should wear white; it's better for your image."

"White is for medical doctors," Lin laughed. "It is too pure and virginal, and we have no pretense here."

Questions and answers flew between them. Family. Friends. Weather. The city, country life, hospital, studies.

"And how is your father?" remarked Israel.

"The same old pop. Gets on my nerves sometimes. He remembers one line from Shakespeare, 'This above all, to thine own self be true,' and he hits me with it every day."

"Not bad," Israel said. "At least he doesn't keep reciting it in Chinese."

Israel was interested in Lin's mice.

"We find," Lin said with enthusiasm, "that an electric current helps bones to heal." Israel did not know. Lin continued, "For example, if we break an animal's bone and keep the fragments apart we can use a current stimulus to induce healing."

Israel asked, "How do you know, given time, those bones wouldn't have healed naturally, without electric currents?"

"Oh," replied Lin, speaking to a novice who should not delve into finer aspects of experimental protocol, "we use controls. Some get the current. Some don't, and we check the differences between them."

Lin displayed an almost imperceptible smile which Israel recalled meant embarrassment or perturbation. He paused, stroked one of the wire coils on the table. "It's a job I've been ordered to push through. We're not worrying about detailed controls at this point."

"But if you start on the wrong foot, whatever you build on could be false," said Israel.

"First we have to stay ahead of others working on the same problem. The university tells me to publish a paper, quick, tie the concepts down in the scientific journals. That way we get to be number one. Later, we can check the experiments properly."

Israel felt he was an intruder, a passing witness to a form of burglary. He knew that once an experimental result is published, it would take monumental criticism to admit the thrust of the work was without foundation. Israel camouflaged his disappointment.

"Let's go to dinner," he suggested casually. "There is a little Greek restaurant I passed near the hospital." They reminisced about girls of the Lower East Side and football. It was a pleasant evening.

Few passengers rode the bus back to Iowa. Again the progression of changing terrain, in reverse, opened to him. He left behind crowds, fumes, multilayered roadways. He squirmed in a quagmire of aborted illusions, even as the lush fields invited him into their expansive horizons. Research had been considered an ideal undertaking. Poor in monetary value but free from the subtle chicanery and role-play required to develop a coterie of patients. His father, Aunt Sophie, what he had seen in Germany, even his genes had infused in him a legacy of ideals which he associated with the true spirit of the good life. But they were mistaken. Lin Chiu taught him that. Ideals were the purveyance of dead saints, and he did not wish to die. Papa Chiu knew the answers, but such solutions were locked in an immutable code, not transferable, and everyone had to find his own key.

Israel was inexorably drawn to surgery as a career. Brutal hours of study, emergencies in the night, enormous layers of facts to be absorbed left him no choice but an existence of work and sleep, a contribution from his body and brain which somehow had to be repaid. Hidden in his consciousness was the supposition that he could always return to old values, but first he must conquer phobias. Blood, for example. When he operated he held his breath as he made the initial incision, then engrossed himself in the mechanical intricacies of the procedure, so that blood could be rationalized as a benign fluid whose flow he could control.

One night the ghost of idealism reappeared to haunt him with its backlash. Israel was on an obstetric service. Should a difficult problem arise he was to call the attending obstetrician, a man of experience and guidance, Dr. S. B. Van Loon. That Van Loon never arrived in time was of no consequence in most cases, as Israel would complete the delivery just as the tardy consultant made a majestic entry to congratulate the new mother and father.

Mrs. Locardo's seventh child was about to make an exit via a route that had been nicely stretched by previous deliveries. Never had she suffered through an obstructed labor, and what should have been push and shove followed by restful sleep, became a nightmare. Her canal opened in grudging opposition. Dr. Van Loon was called. She continued to groan and weaken as the hours passed by and her intermittent silences warned of disaster. A pink trickle moistened her genitals, then a stream, a flood of red which soaked the bed. Israel plunged his fist into the abdominal wall to shut off the flow within the major artery, and with his left hand reached for whatever he could find, a heap of linen towels on the instrument table. One was shoved into the vagina, then another and a third, packed in tightly until the flow of blood receded to a trickle.

Van Loon's ruddy face framed in his freshly brushed goatee, peeked through the glass door of the obstetric suite.

"I got here just in time," he said as they removed their gowns.

"Yes, just in time, " agreed Israel.

"And you did very well." Van Loon always managed to contrive a gracious compliment. He was a consummate optimist, made no reference to particulars, to the delay in arrival of expert assistants. His motto was, "Don't cry before you are cut." Since his results were largely successful, he saw no reason to dote on what might have been. Israel, however, struggled with possibilities, visions hinged on "what if"; baby and mother lifeless in a bundle of blood; explanations of what happened and why; the father in a frenzy of grief and anger; the accusation he did not call for help soon enough.

Indignant at Van Loon's laxity, seared by the call of duty toward future hospital inhabitants, he broke the code of professional fellowship. The hospital administrator was sent a letter in clear, oversized script, so there would be no doubt about the clarity of its intent. Plain truth should prevail, he thought.

> "Dear Sir:
> I am on the obstetric service and have experienced a delivery which could have ended in a fatality. Since this may occur again, and I may be innocently involved, I request that you examine this particular case so I may know how to deal with it."

It was a polite note without specific accusations, one which an appeasing administrator could keep out of reach of official boards and state examiners if he chose a diplomatic course. Dr. S. B. Van Loon was not one to take kindly to an assault upon his professional honor. Short, with a pleasant potbelly nurtured by fine wines and marbled roasts, in a striped blue serge suit with ever present vest, he bespoke an association with power. "S.B.," he was called, really Samuel Baird, though in more polite parlance he was dubbed "Stocks and Bonds Van Loon." Most imposing was his stance when he felt a mother's pulse, reached with a flourish for a huge baroque gold pocket watch suspended from his vest pocket by a chain laden with gold insignias of prep school, medical societies, and financial institutions. The effect of his examination was to command instant cure. He gave the impression of a cheerful, composed, bon vivant who would not sully himself in an altercation but could call upon a gang of respectful hoodlums for his defense.

The administrator who asked to see Israel took but a few minutes to comprehend the circumstances of the young man's complaint. Dr. Van Loon was accosted, as if by chance, in the hospital lobby. An affable discussion followed, with indirect remarks about a young man, Israel Steingut, who was admittedly bold but should be watched closely lest he become obnoxious.

The administrator soothed Dr. Van Loon. "It's not serious. The boy is inexperienced and probably easily shocked. Obstetrics, as you well know, can jolt these youngsters. Leave it to me." Israel was recalled to the austere office to which he had sent his letter. "Son," said the administrator. "You unfortunately have been exposed to a harsh circumstance early in your career. I have spoken to Dr. Van Loon, and I believe he will perceive your insinuations as a warning."

"But he never comes when we call him! What happens if a patient dies?"

"They do, you know. This one didn't. No harm was done, and I would consider the situation closed if I were you. Of course, you could file an official appeal, which would open a can of worms. Dr. Van Loon has friends in this hospital, and there is always the possibility you would be eased out. I don't say he would do so, but you never know. Thank heavens he's not a vindictive man."

Israel left the meeting relieved. Soon after he wrote his letter he knew his audacity had betrayed him. Aunt Sophie might be disappointed, but Chiu the elder could very well have said, "You know what is right, Israel, which is all you need to know. See the truth in yourself and forget the rest of the world." The letter fulfilled his moral obligations.

Israel's appraisal of his courage was reinforced by Dr. Van Loon, who telephoned to request they meet in his private practice office. Dr.

Van Loon sat impassively, sunken into the back of a huge lounge chair. He enunciated distinctly and slowly, an oracle making pronouncements from his cave.

"I own this building," he said, "and have an internist and a surgeon working with me. I plan to form a clinic, small at first, and would like you to join us when you have completed your studies."

Israel blushed. This was his first offer, his initial contact with the combination of commercialism and medicine which he knew had to be addressed to be successful.

"What would I do?" Israel blurted.

"Surgery, of course. We will wait till you have completed your training. It may take several years, but I can be patient."

Israel's courage revived. He weighed pros and cons, called upon his suspicious and wary instincts. He had sent Van Loon a wreath of thorns for which he was offered a crown, an exchange which he felt drove him into a corner, where he must be alert and shrewd. Look ahead several years? It did not fit. The man disregarded time unless it was used for his benefit.

"Pardon me, sir," said Israel. "I wrote a letter which was tantamount to an attack upon you. I am glad the matter was resolved, but I don't understand why you offer me a position."

"That does require an explanation, doesn't it. First, let me say that you are proficient in your duties, sincere, and steadfast enough to become an excellent surgeon. The surgeon with me now is soon to retire, and if I may presume for him, he will be overjoyed to call upon a younger man's view point. Then again, there is the matter of guts. You are the only one I can recall who had the courage to broadcast what he thought was right. I've checked on you, and can think of no one I would rather have in my office."

Israel responded abruptly, as if Van Loon's statement was a superficial gesture which overlaid some darker meaning. "I shall have to think over the proposition carefully."

"Of course. And while you're making a decision, don't forget that lots of dollars flow through this office." Van Loon grinned.

Israel had been made an offer he could not readily discard, though the crassness of its financial summation nettled him. He worried over the emphasis on money, yet he expected adequate compensation for work conscientiously undertaken. How the aspect of finances was brought up, the tone of glee and self-assurance with which it was mentioned, as if this were Van Loon's heavy artillery to destroy all doubt, was mulled over by Israel. He was afraid of being seduced into a practice which devalued scholarship and medical curiousity to the level of a bad investment. "Really, why did he pick me?" Israel agonized,

"There are others who would not question a superior." The letter, the grievance he wrote, was a key issue. Certainly it took guts, but S. B. Van Loon was not the type to be cajoled or bludgeoned by someone's courage. Or was it courage? Reason blinked at Israel in a shot of pure white light. "He knows I'm smart. He knows I work hard. He realizes I might protest against inequity. He wants protest from a token saint, a do-gooder to place a halo over the lobby of his new clinic; and what he knows most of all is that I wouldn't dare hurt anyone, that I never go all the way. It's a patsy he wants, not a partner." That night Israel dreamed he was hovered over by the protective wings of a sleek black bird with curved claws.

Israel offered a spurious reason when he refused Dr. Van Loon's offer. He said he had an elderly aunt in need of help and wished to practice near her in the East. It was a half truth, though he held under consideration an internship in Albany, New York.

Having sniffed the sweat of cities and the manure of the midwest, upstate New York would present a subtle combination of both, with its forested rolling hills and picturesque mountain terrain beside small urban centers. Albany offered him a program in a surgical residency, of which he completed two-and-one-half years.

Israel looked apprehensively toward his coming of age at thirty as a watershed. Sophie was older and would eventually require aid though she proclaimed such insinuations to be insulting. Upstate New York failed him in a first attempt at practice, where, as he put it, even nature conspired against him by sending a vicious dog to chew bones on his doorstep. Israel entered his third decade with the rationalization that he had not yet fixed on a long term goal because he was supposed to wander, to experience the differences in people and places; yet he felt a growing pall of inertia which would lock him into permanent inactivity.

A series of trials and errors followed, such as employment in a compensation clinic where he discovered his chief duty was to oversee a long line of whirlpool baths and heat lamps which soothed bruised limbs. Most of those under treatment could have been given a bandaid or elastic wrap and returned to work in a day or two, instead of three weeks. Dr. Van Loon's offer, in retrospect, appeared first rate, but he was embarrassed to apply. Another effort expended in a tranquil village on the Hudson exposed him to an existence of night calls with snatches of sleep during the day. Here he was a medical doormat for a coterie of athletic physicians who loved boating, skiing, tennis, and womanizing. Israel covered for them, and as they enjoyed, Israel labored. Each changed practice situation gained him an increment of savings which he hoarded for the day of ultimate decision. With each bank deposit a cloud would dissipate and a lone sunbeam would speak to him in a palliative voice, "Dr. Steingut, your moment of glory has arrived."

Gradually his medical terrain shifted westward, to vistas of comfortable isolation and unabrasive clientele who he thought would not startle or disrupt his mood, restful as sows in the heat of the plains, peaceful as corn swinging in the breeze. Israel's imagination was distorted by his craving for placid security. No longer was he belabored by aspirations to battle for mankind or for himself.

During the major upheavals of the Vietnam conflict Israel buried himself in the medical department of a defense plant near Chicago. Occasionally he sewed a cut or repaired a tendon. Once it was incumbent he amputate a leg crushed beneath a steel girder, aware that years of superficial surgical exploits had milked his skills. He had no hope to secure a position in a large hospital, as he had not qualified for his Surgical Boards; and now felt too old to seek further training. At the age of forty-two, Israel gravitated to the lush and languid flat land of Iowa, where he might fulfill himself in a community hospital which cried out for his services, and where he might carry out a private practice in addition. It would be a life which permitted scholarship with introspection, unwarped by the raucousness of a polyglot population which exploded with anxiety and social hostility. Turmoil within him would be subdued if not eradicated. Iowa was to be the soil where he would settle and cohabit with nature and the solace of intellectual meanderings. Soon after, he met Carla.

Chapter 15

WHEN CARLA TALLIED the ledger of her two-year marriage to Dr. Israel Steingut, she noted the accrual of a small portion of riches. But the past few months were particularly disheartening. Yes, he was good, honest, a provider, and basically a gentle soul, perhaps he was too gentle. Her role had been that of a sponge, to absorb his misery and wipe dry for another day. Carla was tired of dependence and wilted attitudes. She longed to have someone resolute, one on whom she could lean occasionally, and Israel's lacerated past should have been forgotten by now, or subdued.

Dr. Steingut remained home during work days, two or three days a month. He used to make hospital rounds if he had a cold, or temperature, or during a snowstorm. Now he arranged for someone to cover his practice at the hint of a headache or abdominal cramps. By late afternoon Carla would return from work and find him slouched in an armchair, unshaven and unwashed. His head lolled. The odor of Kentucky bourbon blended with the stale stench of his breath.

"You've been drinking," she remarked without rancor.

He slurred, "It's for a cold."

"I don't have to tell you that liquor won't cure a virus."

He mumbled, "We don't know about these viruses. All I know, a cold makes me feel bad, and now I feel good. Don't you want me to feel good, my sweet?"

Carla washed and fed him as she would the child she planned to have when the time was right. She put him to bed, and as he stared upward at her he repeated, "I feel good, good, good." At least that was an improvement.

Israel complained about his patients. Entrenched hostility sought an exit, and often he found reason to be angry at some disturbed soul with irrational demands. Formerly, he stifled antagonism, calculated that he dealt with illness whose effects arose from a pool of personal problems. He was obliged to disengage himself as an individual and treat the illness, as it was apparent that the care of stressful situations was most efficient in a milieu of temporary dehumanization; a transformation of the feeling physician into an infallible automaton. But the cold blooded demeanor should be reversible. Israel's reactions toward explosive emotions were more complex, as he not only imbibed the patients' passions but developed an abundance of his own.

Carla's aging mother had seen Israel a week before. She ambulated stooped, over arthritic knees which refused to unbend. An injection into a particularly painful joint had been given, and Carla brought her back to Israel's hospital office to find out whether further treatment was indicated.

The old woman cried, "I think you made me worse." She pointed to a doughy mass of fat and fluid which bordered the inner side of her knee. "You made a lump. I never had a lump in my life."

"It's been there for years."

"Maybe so, but look at this." She sought out a thin blue line of vein, the least offensive of a host of old varicose vessels which snaked from toes to upper thighs. "Did you make that vein come out? I swear it wasn't there before your injection."

"It's nothing," Israel sighed. He was about to explain how she focused on a triviality with no relation to her pain or the treatment she received.

She continued. "Is that all you can do for me? I have a friend who went to a chiropractor, and..."

Israel held his open palm to her face, like a traffic cop who signals an unruly motorist to halt.

"I don't want to hear your suggestions for treatment. If you have pain I could have a consultant called in. Perhaps you need an artificial knee."

She gasped and rolled up her stockings with remarkable speed. "First, you wanted me to use a cane, like an invalid. Now you want to cut me open. You never give up, do you." She supported herself on the wall as she hobbled to the door.

Israel shouted after her. "Go see a chiropractor. And in the future take your complaints anywhere but here." He muttered "bitch" under his breath, and stared at the ceiling light. He saw a mirage, her gnome-light figure heavily clothed but for the exposed neck with ballooned veins. If he were a dog, like the one who once chewed bones on his doorstep, he would have gone for her jugular. He shook his head to banish an image so barbarous. Perhaps he should not have reacted like a drunk in a bar, or a schoolboy. All his life he had employed a strategy which enabled him to absorb multiple insults, called on intellectual tricks to attain a fake serenity in the midst of assault. Where he had learned to turn the other cheek he did not know, but no more. No longer would he force himself to remain calm. Human brutishness was his, too, and no one should expect that he hide his fury.

Carla chose an inopportune moment to approach Israel. He had gulped a double gin and was contented, and restrained. She should have known the pitfalls of artificially acquired bliss.

"You did not have to be so hard on my mother," Carla said.

"She asked for it, the bitch."

Carla was shocked by the courage of his assertiveness, rather than by what he answered. Had he not been drunk the statement would be refreshing, positive, one she could normally understand and detest. He was under the influence and it remained to be seen, post alcohol, if he would be so desperately honest in his opinions.

She tried to soothe him. "Mother is neurotic, hard to take, but *you* are a doctor."

"To hell with doctors," he screamed. "I am sick of standing by with a plastered tongue while some low down bastard tears me apart. I have feelings." He hiccoughed. "And I'll be damned if I let anybody make a doormat of me!"

Carla had supper alone, in silence, as she turned the pages of a detective story. Reading was impossible. She could counter his ugliness if she could formulate a plan with a modicum of hope, but old plans to rejuvenate Israel were obsolete, and hope would be as tenuous as a wheatfield in a swarm of locusts.

The sharp edge of stress blunts itself before the onset of another round of abuse and recrimination. During such days of comparative tranquility Carla posed the propostion that Israel ought to visit some of his old friends. He readily agreed, as he had sufficient presence of mind, intuition, or psychological insight to realize his future could become a shambles. The will to improve their relationship was fragmented, but not dead. "Do something," he told himself. "Lift yourself, or you will drown!"

"Israel," she said, "Whatever happened to Harry Pearl? You haven't seen him in ages." Dr. Steingut perked his head to one side like a wolf listening to the call of an injured moose.

Crazy Harry who was to race sled dogs in Alaska, the one who nearly caused the death of his doctor friend; that was a moment Israel could not forget; and he managed to come through the incident by the instinctual reaction of rolling from under the dog's jaws, animal versus animal. Israel was not averse to a visit with Harry Pearl, and Carla pressed him with subtle urgings, hints of the desolation which accompanies the loss of old friends, until he found the vitality to arrange a meeting with Harry.

In an interval of six months Harry Pearl had become a captive of urban Western culture. He had travelled to Los Angeles for a change of scene, and stayed three months. There he acquired a new woman, Francesca, near forty but with the countenance and figure of a local beauty pageant winner. She had so wanted to act, had the certificates in dance, gymnastics, and voice to prove it, that she insisted she was not too old for a career in theatre. She was filled with hope and cheer, attributes which Harry Pearl revered in close companions. "You are a hick farmer," she told Harry in a darling lisp which he swore arose from the lucious mouth of a second Marlene Dietrich. "I'll change my style," he countered, "if you will come back with me." He followed her instructions and guidance with the zest of a dog bred to follow its master. Harry Pearl welcomed Israel with genuine but controlled pleasure. The old raucous endearing shouts and backslaps were lost in his strident past. He shook hands with just enough squeeze to indicate he meant it. Mud-stained, torn, low-hung trousers were not his fashion. Israel was dazzled by pants checkered with yellow and black squares, with wide cuffs swishing over tan shoes, silver buckled. A turtleneck sweater with embroidered pockets gave the impression of an overzealous graduate of a charm school course. Israel felt poverty stricken; also curiously shy when he noted Francesca's tight jeans hug the bulges of her buttocks as she leaned forward to retrieve a diamond barette fallen from her head.

Do you still have your dogs?" asked Israel.

"No, that was foolishness. My little woman cured me. Now I'm in real estate, and by God I'll get Francesca on the stage if I have to buy my own theater. Did you know you must travel a hundred miles to see a good show? People hereabouts need art as much as anywhere."

Israel stammered in agreement.

"Tell him what made you aware of the better things in life," Francesca urged Harry. She then turned to Israel. "Ask him, Dr. Steingut. Make him tell you."

Francesca had induced him to attend sessions with a west coast consultant; not exactly a guru, certainly not a reputable psychologist, but an expert who delved into the mysteries of self-expression via body movement and incantations. He was a spin-off derived from techniques used in Europe and parts of Asia, especially applicable to Harry, whose jollity Francesca had analyzed to be a misplaced protective measure. "When you joke it's a huge cover-up," she would tell him, "and I want you to be the real you." Furthermore, she emphasized other features of Harry's uncultured life style. He was a slob, and perhaps a liar. She thought he had fabricated the value of his Iowa holdings; farms were for peasants. Granted there could be a peasant here and there who was successful, which she could not say since peasants don't spend their wealth; but where did she ever hear of a wealthy Jewish peasant farmer in America? Her relief on finding that Harry was not a fabricator, only eccentric, convinced her to induce him to seek help.

"Iz," said Harry, "I'd love for you to come out of yourself, feel your own electricity. There is only one way to do it. You need the treatment I had."

"In California?"

"You needn't travel that far. This guy I went to, his best student practices in Des Moines — it's not much of a trip, and it will pay dividends."

"What does he do for you?" Israel's curiosity was born of scientific interest.

"He gives you a phrase to learn and repeat, he teaches you how to say it. How! That's important. I can't tell you mine because its personal, and you will have to get your own. Then there are the exercises. I tell you, Israel, when you carry out the movements, properly, you feel like all the dirt is being washed out. You feel clean, fresh, smart." He held his arms for explanation in the style of a Balinese dancer. Francesca squatted and assumed the winged bird pose to reinforce Harry's tutorship.

She whispered, "Don't you feel the vibrations, Dr. Steingut?"

"I'm not sure," Israel mumbled.

"Of course you do," she said impatiently as she jerked her head to one side to permit the escape of demons she had permitted to enter her that morning.

Carla had spoken with Harry and Francesca, and was aware of the credo they would attempt to inflict on Israel. To attack Israel's emotional feelings was clearly a necessity, though his persistent antagonism toward any form of treatment had become a serious obstacle. Since psychiatry was an unmentionable word, an associated technique which lent itself to ridicule and thus less drastic, might be acceptable to Israel; I'm okay, you're okay; a guru; a dervish; a defrocked psychologist with a penchant for crackpot theories. She awaited her husband's return from the Pearl household with unbridled optimism. "It takes a nut to get inside another nut," she thought, "and Harry Pearl has unimpeachable qualifications." Surely he would not fail her, she concluded with the presumptious confidence of the positive thinker.

Israel entered with an aggressive scowl which had pre-empted any hint of his normal timidity. She sensed his visit with Harry and Francesca had been a lost cause. Now she had to choose between choking in his world and breathing freely in hers. He removed coat and jacket, hung them in the closet, deliberately, with care, as if he were embarking on difficult surgery. He boiled water and made a cup of tea.

Carla took the initiative. "I assume your visit with Harry was a bust."

"Exactly." He spoke into the teacup.

"I don't know why. They are fun to be with."

"Then you should have come along, instead of sneaking behind my back as if I were a schoolboy and you could arrange my fate with my teacher. It's so obvious it's stupid. How could you imagine the brains of the three of you could influence me!"

"Iz," she spoke apologetically. "I am trying to help the best I know how. I meant no harm, and I feel terrible that you see it as a devious scheme."

"The sort of trick you pulled would be an insult to a child. At least you could have chosen someone with intelligence to persuade me. Don't *ever* put me in Harry's class, or yours for that matter, when you judge I. Q. And don't call me 'Iz.'"

"Please, let's forget it. I promise I won't interfere with your precious thoughts again." Carla faced him, braced for collision.

"Alright, then," said Israel. "I suppose you want to know what you've done. You must want to know. I got there and met Harry, the fop, dressed like a well-heeled pimp; and Francesca, the whore, with aspirations to become a madonna of the stage. Greenbacks line the back of her eyes, and Harry is willing to break his back to put them there. What does he do then, but go into real estate, because she'd like to have a theater she can act in, even if it's built on a pile of manure. Come to think of it, her performance would be fit for a brood of pigs."

"Quit dramatizing," Carla asserted. "Harry may be crazy, but he hurts no one. Now that he has a woman who gives him some purpose, it galls you. If any treatment would do half as much for you, I'm for it."

"You would have me change like Harry, that excuse for manliness?"

"He can satisfy a woman." She put her hand to her mouth to countermand her retort.

Israel stared at the floor. "So that's what upsets you! I remember when you thought sex was like washing your teeth, refreshing but unnecessary, routine, a duty to perform and forget. Suddenly you turn into an unfulfilled Cleopatra. All you know of love comes from watching farm stock hump between feeds."

He cried as he lifted a chair and held it over her. Turning suddenly as if to smash his chair, he paused and set it down.

Carla's features were cold with determination. She stepped back and was barely audible. "Israel, I have thought for a long while of what I am going to say. I do love you, though you don't consider it possible now. I do not wish to hurt you, but we must separate, for the good of both of us. You should be alone, think out what you must do for yourself. Now I am an irritant. What I want to say is, I am leaving you until you feel strong enough to have me back."

She dialed a familiar telephone number, conversed in a few short, crisp phrases as if the dialogue were rehearsed, and hung up the receiver. Two bags packed, a note with her address left in the bedroom, and she was off to stay with a friend in the nurses' dormitory of the hospital.

Israel sat alone, shocked. He appeared catatonic, whimpered as she left, then broke into a wail. Alone in a vast secluded prairie in which to romp, he swallowed a jigger of gin, and another, many others until he fell asleep. Cold awakened him during the night. Unshaven, clothes rumpled and hair tousled, he gazed into darkness. Walls moved toward him, and he feared to turn lights on to verify the image. As he pulled his jacket from a chair he tore a sleeve, but managed to button up with one edge hanging below the other. He stumbled into the moonlight, a transplanted nightwalker in desperate flight, in Germany, exhausted in a ravine with the thud of boots at his temples. Dr. Israel Steingut was in a peculiar state of void, the emptiness within him in harmony with the vacuum he perceived outside.

He had already passed through town when he first felt the sting of the wind. Railroad tracks he walked beside glinted at him; two rows of vanishing steel projected solidity with their hardness and immutable precision; they pushed toward a known destination, a mechanistic testimonial to his failings. As he walked further, a crescent of flame rose and enlarged. It was a bonfire about which huddled four men, wanderers, like Israel, going nowhere in torn clothes, but alive with laughter, snarls, and hostility. They looked at each other with silent questions as the intruder approached.

Israel said, "I hope you don't mind my sitting by the fire. It is very cold out there."

"Naw," said a rotund, middle-aged man. "Here, have a spud." He held out a sharpened stick on which a wrinkled potato was impaled. "Watch it. It's hot."

Israel beamed his first smile at the unadorned directness of an act of fellowship. A bottle of wine was passed around the circle, but Israel did not drink. He ate his potato dry.

"Where'd you come from?" asked the round little man.

"Back there." Israel turned his head toward town.

"You on the road?" This from a young man in his thirties, with a swollen lip and dented nose. He had taken too much wine.

"What do you mean?"

"You one of us, a hobo?"

"I don't think so." Israel took note that his inquisitor inspected his ruffled but expensive clothes.

"I don't think so too. Why the hell are you stopping off here?" The young man was accusatory.

In an attempt to ease the tension, the round hobo interceded, "We're all in the same boat. If he's down and out he's one of us."

"Like hell he is!" The young man stood and pushed his imagined adversary. Israel's shoulder struck the rail as he fell. Both stood, separated by the little man. He was forcefully shoved away as a stub-handled knife clicked open in the hobo's hand. Israel was sharp, alive, ears tuned to a sudden breath or body movement. Eyes wide, semi-crouched and arms forward, stepping, dancing with body weight poised on toes, he saw only the blade. All else was extraneous. He guessed at the pattern of its excursions, pin-pointed the path of its tip. In an instant of aggressive overbalance by the hobo, Israel struck the unprotected wrist with his foot, and in a moment of reversal he had the man down with the knife at the young man's throat.

Decades of medical training were concentrated to a split second. Where to cut. One thrust and he could sever the jugular, or the great nerves to the arm, or up under the jaw to the vessels which feed the brain. The anatomy of violence lay before him more clearly than he had ever seen it on the pages of a textbook. Blood would not bother him now. Then he imagined the switchblade reshaped and shortened to the configuration of a scalpel. This was his personal weapon, and he was finely trained to use it; repay the patient who took from him without gratitude; punish the world that cast him in the role of a fool. He owed a debt to the spirit of revenge. Erase the debt, as his mother was erased by another expert knife user of his nebulous childhood. He was perched on a precipice of agonized confrontation, between barbaric retaliation and moral civility.

Israel's hate span was short lived. He recalled his empathy for those defenseless against terror. The hobo shook and writhed, moaned his entreaties, his forgiveness, and his epithets. Israel turned back into his structured world, where he held a scalpel which demanded restraint, where the helpless floater beneath him was the symbol of community malfeasance which he, the healer, was appointed to mitigate. Rising, Israel said he was sorry. He repeated it over and over. As he buttoned his coat he wondered what the devil happened to his torn sleeve. He walked the three miles to town quickly. Home he removed his jacket and shirt and washed. He rubbed his hands in soapy water repeatedly to feel the soft flesh of his fingers, instruments which he could will to do what he ordered. He was trained to control his fingers, and he vowed that no part of him should be permitted to become deranged or act without the superintendance of his conscious faculty. Carla was correct. He ought to open himself to advice, seek help. It was 5 A.M. when he phoned Harry Pearl.

"This is Israel. Dr. Steingut." He repeated his name till the subsidence of a raspy yawn and cough indicated he had Harry's ear.

"Iz, what a time to call! I don't make night calls. What's wrong?"

"Nothing to worry over. I want the name of the psychologist you said moved to this part of the country."

"Why? What's up?"

"Just give me his name."

"It's Joe, Joseph Harden. Maybe Dr. Harden. No, I don't remember the doctor part. Let me know how you make out."

Israel's first hour of sleep was fitful. He tossed with the excitement of a child given a creative toy. When he did sleep, it was prolonged and restful. In the morning he phoned Carla but had to leave a message as he could not reach her. As he paused, phone in hand, his eye was drawn to a bottle of gin half full on the table. Turning his head, he dialed a number in Des Moines and was surprised to receive an immediate appointment with Mr. Harden at four o'clock that afternoon.

Carla returned his call. She was doing well, though she missed their home. "Our separation is much better for you," she said, "and what better proof than your looking for help?"

"This psychologist sounds like a kook, but he's all I have." Israel sounded half-hearted.

"Who?"

"It's Joseph Harden. The one Harry Pearl recommended."

"Harden? Is that the one? Sure, he's a kook. Several of our nurses have been to him, and they saw through his mumbojumbo in no time. How can you get mixed up with that type?"

"You sent me to Harry Pearl."

Carla howled with laughter. "Sorry, I didn't mean to make light of it. So that was Harry's advice. What's the difference? You tried, and that's all that matters. You're just like the rest of the M.D.s, downright stupid when it comes to your own bodies. There has to be a more sensible way to get to the right man. In the meantime, don't give up. Remember, when you are ready, when the time is ripe, we will be together again."

Carla had encouraged and confused Israel. He acknowledged he must persist as she advised; what he searched for was a giant abstraction; and Israel had never been partial to the application of unscientific abstraction in the solution of problems. The process was akin to philosophy, where there was never an end point where it could be said, "This is the final, irreversible truth." Yet Carla imparted hope. Perhaps it was her unflinching voice and attitude, or her steadfast vivacity, or the intimation that she was not about to throw him out of her life. She wanted her Israel, just changed a little into a mate with a modicum of appreciation of the minor benefits which surrounded him. To be wanted, this was the watchword which sustained him, no matter what conditions he had to satisfy.

He would be more sensible, more selective according to his own precepts; no more hot tips, no pearls of wisdom from sources like Harry and his woman. This was Dr. Israel Steingut, who already had shown substantial evidence of his worth, who deserved the finest help available.

Where to go? How to go about it? He wanted expert, respected direction. There was a person he could call upon. Mike Hearn was the chief in a psychiatric hospital. Israel recalled that, in spite of his alcoholic past, whatever Mike did medically was unhurried, intelligent, and effective. He phoned to cancel the appointment in Des Moines and dialed Mike's number.

The drive to Crestline Mental Health Institute was a relaxed foray into a new phase of Dr. Steingut's life. Israel requested a month's sick leave from the hospital administrator with factual bluntness. As he drew near the immense square brick building, he was reminded of a prison, old and secure. Faces peered through iron grated windows. He shuddered. Out of hundreds of inmates, or patients, there must be a man, a doctor, who peered at the flat fields to wonder what he might have done to prevent his reaching this final home, this community of surveillance and enforced meditation. That is, if the ability to wonder was still intact. Cement steps which led to the entrance showed little wear, an indication that few came to pay their respects to these remnants of humanity. Israel stood alone at the thick oak doors.

He rang the bell and was greeted by Mike Hearn, who had been forewarned of his guest's arrival. Dr. Hearn's features were lined and molded in the cast of one who had forced upon himself a monastic existence. In a patched, clean white coat he slowly walked to his panelled office. A tarnished brass plate on his door was lettered: CHIEF MEDICAL OFFICER. Dr. Hearn was as stolid and genuine as the antique wood walls which surrounded him. He was no longer a secret drinker.

"How do you come to a place like this?" Israel expressed amazement.

"It's not hard. I could not get a job after I last saw you, but here I was welcomed. These people need an internist as much as anyone. More. No one pays attention to their ordinary illnesses. They too have hearts and lungs and all the other organs that fail them."

"Of course. Please excuse me." said Israel. He felt he had committed a coarse error. Mike had accomplished the most difficult of tasks, pounded the shape of his life to fit a bazarre niche which he accepted as his home. Did acceptance imply submission, or a healthy reduction of overbearing ego? Whatever the genesis, the man had the guts to diagnose the heart of happiness and take it into his arms, as a religionist embraces spiritual love.

Mike lived with his Swedish wife in a cottage near the hospital building. Shaded by poplars and stately walnut trees in summer, the white frame clapboards now showed through a camouflage of twisted bare limbs which enveloped the house and overhung its roof. Mrs. Hearn was country-style pretty, with rounded cheeks and blue eyes to complement her light hair. She was polite, a meticulous housewife, and intelligent. Like Carla she exuded resolute simplicity, and she engaged with ease in the men's conversation. Israel was intrigued with her, compared her to his wife, until he learned she did nothing but housework and attend women's clubs which catered to hospital patients. What a waste, he thought; and how could Mike be stimulated by her.

"What do you do for excitement?"

"We go to community plays twenty miles away; once in a great while, a movie. I write up interesting cases for the medical literature, and we read a lot." He added, "And you, Israel, what do you do?"

The question carried a brutal impact. Israel's remembrances of what he did were multiple flashes which burned out quickly. His work was patterned, not creative. He listened to music when his nerves were overheated. At a movie his thighs twitched with side to side spasms as if he struggled to prevent overflow of a full bladder. And Carla? He looked on her as a teenager views a beautiful woman, from a distance and with passionate affection, but filled with the inadequacy of the fool who aspires to that which he cannot control. Israel gazed at Dr. Hearn sheepishly, to convey he came as a supplicant, and not a boastful purveyor of success.

"Mike, I don't do very much. Practically nothing. I've gone down a long way since we were together. There's no zip left, and when I do get to do something worthwhile I stew over it."

He related what he knew or thought of himself, quietly and lucidly, as if he were recounting a narrative in a work of fiction.

Dr. Hearn said, "Iz, you are calling for help, and that's a great beginning. You are what I call a ninety percenter, one of those who finishes most of a project but always leaves a little hanging in mid-air. Yes, I know you are a good surgeon and endure to the end of a case. But it's still ninety percent, because the last ten percent that's left adrift is you. Whatever you accomplish doesn't nail down the satisfaction it should. Now I'm not a psychiatrist, but I've been here long enough to know you need help from someone with good common sense as well as top training. I think I have the man for you."

"Where? What must I do? Is he honest?"

"What do you mean?"

"I don't want to be strung along for years. I am too old for that. There's not much time."

"I can't say how long it will take, or how much good it will do. But this psychiatrist I met at a meeting in New York would understand you. That alone would shorten the process. He might take years, and he might give you some quick insights you could pursue yourself.

"He's in New York?"

"Yes, that's the trouble. What I would suggest is you see him, even for a few times, and let him direct you from there."

Israel felt himself knocking at a door of salvation which refused to open. Another failure. "How can I stay in New York? I can visit there, but I have a job."

Mike reassured him. "If necessary, he could steer you to another doctor nearby, though I doubt it. Or you might be one of those who could be guided by a monthly visit supplemented with intermediate phone calls. Or, you might have to move to New York."

On the road home Israel had to concentrate to avoid crossing the yellow line. If he went over the stripe he would find a sudden solution. A fractional turn of the wheel would transfigure him into a senseless broken body. He knew a great deal about broken bodies, at the hospital, his father, mother, war heroes. Heroes. They were mangled and fragmented by events they hoped to change. If he were to destroy himself, there ought to be some great positive logic to merit the destruction. The yellow line grew less threatening, settled to a painted strip which lay on a safe road as a mechanical marker. Israel was energized, invigorated enough to drive steadily for days. After a stop to gather clothes and necessities, his next stop would be New York.

Chapter 16

THE PROSPECT OF an extended stay in New York City appeared grim. Separation from Carla and hospital duties, his solitude, invested Israel with a flaccidity of will which begged for the stimulus to build his determination. Though he entertained visions of trails' end and goals attained, they were fleeting and unformed. He had to continue.

Initially he roomed in a hotel which rated itself clean and inexpensive. Forty-five dollars a day and cockroaches which streamed from the rim of the bathtub told Israel that hotels were no more reliable in their self-assessment than humans. He phoned Lin Chiu in Queens and was promptly invited to move to an empty room, if he did not mind the subway trips to midtown. On an early spring afternoon Israel moved, his only impasse a temporary one when his valise stuck in a subway door about to close. Two burly men helped free the valise, one a black Hispanic, the other with a Slavic countenance. Neither spoke understandable English. They pulled open the door and chuckled as they succeeded. Did they laugh in derision? Or in self-congratulation? They carried the suitcase to the center of the car where Israel could support himself between two poles. When he left the train, the Slav held open the door so Israel could pass through easily, an act of friendship by a stranger who knew the rigors of travel. The blight of New York lifted a little for Israel.

To the average midwesterner New York City is a strange foreign land, peopled with un-American Americans and crude foreigners who suck the wealth of the nation via welfare hand-outs and free lunch for the unproductive. They will agree that the city is exotic, if one means an overabundance of girlie shows. Perhaps it is the financial center of the world, but that's where the Bible says the money changers abound. Music, dance, theater, the arts are on the fringe of rational living, defused of significance by dirt and crime in the streets. Israel had heard so much deprecation of New York and the East, he almost believed it.

What he did see were city dwellers who were civil to each other, some with a roughness of expression, but with the same fellowship he had noted elsewhere. "Have a good day" was as favorite a phrase as in the prairie, on the tips of tongues of telephone operators and sales clerks; people were cheerful, helpful; toughs turned to coo at babies; a cab driver changed a flat tire for a woman motorist. And crime? He recalled the midwest where genteel youths with boy scout and church affiliations riddled an entire family at dinner with shotgun blasts; the scoundrel farmers he had met, who were the equal of any Wall Street stock hiker; the small wealthy banks in sleepy towns fleeced by their darling presidents; the prairie bond salesmen whose commissions amounted to extortion. Israel originally had run from the city to search for earthy truths in a pastoral setting, an imaginative quest which eluded him. Everyone, everywhere, had his peck of troubles.

Lin's apartment was in a twelve-story building, where he lived with his Chinese wife and one child. The space was small, even for a family accustomed to squeezed living conditions, and Mrs. Chiu said less effort was required to clean a small apartment. Israel was settled into what was called a study, where a chair and a pull-out bed nearly filled the room. No effort to pry, no embarrasing questions were put to Israel, and he said nothing relative to his wandering until Lin spoke of himself. With pipe in mouth, in brief fragments of recollection, he appeared to wish to open himself to a friend, like a well-bred oriental who had committed wrongs and sought to explain his mistakes. The young scientist had done well in his experiments with mice and rabbits, but he had succumbed to departmental prodding to produce dramatic results.

"I jumped too fast," he said. "My father warned me to go slow and I should have listened to him."

"I published a paper," Lin continued, "which described chromosome changes in mice after electrical stimulation of brain cells. The results were criticized, and who do you suppose turned on me? My superior, who had urged that I rush the article through without confirmation. He was the one who had me investigated."

"Investigated? You imply there was something shady."

"It's not that simple. I thought my approach was different, valuable, that others would be stimulated to further research."

"Then what was all the fuss about?"

"The article made the newspapers. Charges of sloppy scientific methods were made. My boss insisted his department maintained high standards, that he couldn't check on every little researcher under him, and out I went."

"Surely you can continue in another institution."

"I don't want to. I teach now, high school physics, and I love it." Lin wrinkled his face to a grin, for him an enormous display of contentment.

Israel surmised Lin had chosen wisely, else why would he be so satisfied. Simply put, Lin no longer wished to continue as a researcher with one ear cocked to the patronage of his superiors and the other leaning toward the media. If he had to fudge his results, cut corners to be his own master, the end was not worth the means. As Lin's father would say, an edifice built on sand will sink when the earth shakes. Israel thought Lin chose a strong foundation, and he wondered whether the earth would stop shaking long enough for him to make his own choice.

Dr. Joseph Warner had been informed of a patient from the midwest. Dr. Hearn had been in touch regarding Dr. Steingut. When Israel phoned, the secretary informed him that Dr. Warner was called to Texas as consultant in a murder investigation, that he would return on Wednesday, when he would surely see Dr. Steingut — a five-day hiatus in which Israel could see a show, walk at leisure, visit Aunt Sophie. Aunt Sophie was not an entertainment. She was a duty. In a nursing home in the Bronx, Aunt Sophie occupied a third floor room, where another resident slept in the next bed.

Sophie's legs were thicker, her abdomen larger, body flexed forward. She housed a big voice in an enlarged frame, both straining to cast an impression she could still join a picket line if she were asked. Israel embraced her. They cried, for different reasons. Sophie was genuinely happy, mindless of her physical deterioration and undaunted by her prospects. Israel saw in her the last hurrah, the passing of the strong and righteous.

She croaked, "I didn't want you to come here and see me like this."

"You look fine, healthy."

"Israel, please don't treat me as a child. We both know why I am here, what will be. Do not try to make me forget."

"Forget what?"

"That I was someone of substance. I am not afraid. When I go someone else will have more room to maneuver."

"You certainly have left your imprint. Just look at me."

She staggered to a halt and faced him with pressed lips. "I am looking at you, and I see trouble. Why are you here in New York?"

Israel told his aunt that Carla had left him and he was in New York to see a psychiatrist. He had determined to make an effort for himself, for his marriage. He would give up his job if necessary.

"Good," she replied. "You can get better jobs. Of course I never believed in psychiatrists, but I never needed them, and I don't claim to know everything. If a psychiatrist can show you the way out, then fine."

Before Israel left she offered what she thought was a meaningful piece of information, an addendum to the theory and philosophy she preached. Israel needed a push to overcome his inertia, and an introduction to success might be a productive stimulus. "When you were a boy," she recalled, "friends in Germany wrote to tell me how you and your mother escaped to the farm. Do you remember Johann Kurtzbaum, who took you to the train?"

"Vaguely. Mother spoke of him often, and his face stands out. I've dreamt of him. Blonde and blue-eyed. A boyhood hero."

"He lives somewhere on Long Island. The name is the same, and I understand he has been very successful. I never met him, but I wrote and called several times. It might do you good to see him."

"Why? It's been so long."

"He has overcome a past like yours. You could compare notes."

Johann, now in his sixties, never rid himself of the rolling gutturals of his German accent. He lay beside an Olympic size pool with the curvaceous outlines of a question mark. The structure was strangely uninviting, as its shape detracted from its swimming facility; and it was empty, forlorn, an impressive expanse of useless luxury. Johann's hair had been blonde, then gray, was now blonde again. A lean, wrinkled face, still handsome as a framework about sharp blue eyes, bespoke hours in the sun, perhaps sailing in the nearby sound, or jogging on secluded paths. Israel was shaken from his memory of the teenager who escorted him and Isolde through hazardous barricades; the young man whose racial derivation no German questioned because of his appearance and his utterly relaxed, carefree demeanor.

They shook hands and proceeded to a sumptuous living room. Kurtzbaum's family was on an extended vacation, their return date undecided, which made Israel suspect a separation in progress in this house also. Neither Johann or Israel were demoralized by criticism that those who saved themselves did so at the expense of many left behind; yet Johann Kurtzbaum was sad. He had cheated his visionary self to secure the comfort of materialism. Israel complimented Johann. "My mother spoke of you with pride. She called you 'the blonde Hassid.'"

Johann said, "I left them, with their dances and their prayers, and their denunciation of my saneness. I started in the textile business and worked my way up. Apparently the dealers were taken with what they figured was a circumcized Scandinavian. You can tell by my home I am not a poor man." He spoke with a hint of avarice about to enlarge into boastfulness, but Johann was too subtle to extend himself.

Almost as an afterthought he said, "I have a meeting of the S.C.H. tonight. Would you care to come?" He explained he was not totally immersed in a world of money and business. The Society of Children of the Holocaust was a group he founded to alleviate anxieties of young men and women whose parents could not disengage from their German concentration camp experience.

Meetings were held in the basement of a reform synagogue. Two dozen chairs were lined in neat rows, with an open area on one side which provided a dance surface if a light mood prevailed. On a narrow raised stage a podium dared the uninhibited to speak. Well-dressed, middle-class youths trickled into the hall. Several from an adjoining poverty-stricken neighborhood wore neatly creased, obviously worn clothes. They were the happiest of the lot. Kurtzbaum called for order and discussed a subject which had been on the agenda for weeks; a donation to be given to the Vienna Documentary Institute, which had for years laid the groundwork for apprehension of war criminals.

"Forget about those Germans," some shouted. "It's none of our business. Thirty-five years and we're still badgered for it. We get the pitch up to our eyeballs at home." Two thirds voted to send their hoarded dollars abroad.

A young man, tall, handsome, with sandy hair and blue eyes, approached the podium. He had taken his turn for exposition for his colleagues to probe and criticize. His topic was parental anxiety and pressure. They were enraged that their son wished to be an actor.

Israel smirked. He enjoyed what he had witnessed, but had reservations. Agreed, he was in the midst of the spontaneity of a revival meeting, but how long would the spell last after the participants returned home? The effect of their discourse thus far was positive, a haphazard unwinding of tight coils, a process he had not engaged in. Perhaps there were groups which could serve his special purpose. Impossible. Those youngsters hurdled living barriers, fought with their parents, cursed them, threw their minds and ideas into the battle to grind out a plateau of acceptance. Israel's encounters were populated with old spirits bottled within him.

The meeting was galvanized by the entrance of a young woman, dark and exotic, with a split skirt which bared her thigh to the hip. She strode toward Johann. Discussion ceased. Johann explained to Israel. "This is the one member we hoped would not come." As he spoke she thrust herself on him, kissed him on cheeks, mouth, neck, wherever she could plant her lips. He writhed to escape. Playful, she fumbled at his belt buckle to undo it. Her aggressive advances and Johann's frantic attempts to protect himself were the scene of a female rapist assaulting a victim. When she had had enough she attempted to repeat the performance on another and another, all mature men. Her passion was methodical and intrusive, without charm or grace. She forced herself on uncooperative partners as if she hated them by way of love.

Israel was confounded and amused. "What is happening? What's wrong with her?"

"She is finished. She can't be helped. It's the same every time and we're fed up. She's a whore," explained Johann. "Comes from a fine family who ended up in a concentration camp. Somehow they survived."

"Is that what bothers her, that her parents lived?"

"She says her mother screwed for the Nazis and her father was a Judas goat who led innocents into the gas chambers."

"Is it true?"

"Nobody makes the accusation, but the girl is certain in her own mind."

"But a prostitute!"

"Her parents broke up her impending marriage to a poor fellow, a musician. The girl left home. She's not a street walker. She's one of the expensive kind. And she never sees her parents, so I suppose she takes it out on us."

The young woman left as unobtrusively and unashamedly as she had entered, a child appeased by a session of play. The club members composed themselves as if nothing had happened, bantered in small groups about jobs, football, bargain shopping, and new restaurants. Next time, they said, she would be permanently excluded from meetings.

Johann offered to drive Israel back to Queens, but he refused. He boarded a subway car where a well dressed white man, obviously intoxicated, tried to prevent himself from pitching forward. A bearded black man in work clothes sat still and upright. According to prevalent rumors Israel expected the opposite; the black man should have been the one to career about in semi-stupor. Rumors destroyed individuality. They thrived on mass culpability, the antithesis of justice. Jews were victims as well as blacks and orientals, even Teutons. He imagined a convocation of humane Germans who waved greetings; good luck to Anna Grunstein, to a small-town bookseller, to a farmer, and to Axel. Israel gulped. Axel was a beast, not because he was German, but an individual gone wild.

Israel could not release the image of the Jewish-girl-turned prostitute. She, too, was an embittered victim of rumor, concocted by herself and entrenched until she was totally engulfed in its backlash. Perhaps the story of her parents was true. It did not matter. If she could have sat with them and asked, were you a whore, were you a Judas goat in the camps, it would have led to an answer which was arguable. Had she delved further, she could have come to the basic realization that self-preservation is not entirely evil when the alternative is total destruction.

Israel compared himself with the whore. He recalled flirtatious liaisons of his mother and the rigidity of his father. They were gone and he could not speak with them. To speak to himself about them was futile. In a way, that Jewish whore was better off than he. Reprehensible as her life appeared, she satisfied herself, chose her antagonists, and made a response. Israel had not made a response, could not clearly perceive an enemy to whom he could say, "You hurt me and I will act against you. I will execute the revenge to which I am entitled, and with which I will cleanse myself."

He dreamt a dark-skinned woman in a black silk slip unbuckled his belt and pulled down his pants. At first he was reticent to engage her, but as he changed his mind and was about to become aggressive, another woman approached. She was tall and fair skinned and plainly dressed in a cotton print to below the calves. Israel pushed her way, but as he confronted the darker figure, he found she was no longer alluring, as the women had exchanged clothes.

In the morning he worried about Carla. A woman like her left alone might act strangely, break the mold in which she had organized her life. It was unthinkable she might turn to prostitution, yet sex to her was a natural, gratuitous event, and not the romantic holy grail sought by other women. Besides, she did not have him to bolster and encourage, and there were others who needed the attention she loved to bestow. He had burdended her as surely as parents may inflict themselves on a child. If the child could break and run, so could she. Perhaps not. Carla lived in a small town under the watchfulness of prying neighbors. Then again, Carla didn't give a damn about neighbors, gossip, or any other restrictive social criticism. The worm of speculation bored into Israel and picked up speed. He asked Lin whether he could make a long distance call, private, with the phone pulled into the kitchen and the door shut.

"Is that you, Carla dear?"

"Of course it's me; and since when do you call me 'dear'? I like it."

"Carla, I think I've improved. Lin and his wife have been wonderful. Because of them I understand myself better."

"How? Understand what?"

"I feel more confident."

"Have you seen the psychiatrist?" She was almost shrill, as if she demanded a proper response to explain his heresy.

"I thought I should come home. I can cancel the appointment."

"Israel," she monotoned, "I want you to go through with our arrangement." She did not enlarge, embellish, or emphasize.

"Right, right. Of course, I'll see the shrink. I was only putting out an alternative. I am here, and I'll do what I have to." He paused. He had been subdued, was on the defensive, until the image of the dark Jewish girl revived him. "By the way, Carla, what are you doing with yourself?" There was some hazard in this question.

"What do you mean? I work, I read, I listen to music, even some of our classical records."

"Nothing else?"

"Oh, I go to a movie with the girls occasionally. Say! I see what you're driving at. Do I date or fool around? If I felt like it I would think of you and whoosh, the feeling would disappear." She chuckled. "Have no fear. Your wife is here. And how about you?" She countered. "I hear New York has a shortage of services, but sex isn't one of them."

Out of nowhere he fabricated a line of boastfulness, "Lin and his wife introduced me to a beautiful young woman with whom I talked at length. The sum total of our discussion ended with my thoughts of you." To lie was not his habit. He was accustomed to truth, explication, clarity, like a scientist who summarizes an experimental result. The conversation over, Israel was conscious of a glimmer of superiority he held over Carla. He was not compelled to tell all in scrupulous detail, to make himself vulnerable as an overturned turtle. Certainly he would try to see the psychiatrist, but he made no promise of lengthy commitments or an overhaul of his psyche. Sometimes a man must keep his thoughts and moods to himself. Strength of character included the ability to retire within a shell, alone but not lonely.

Finally Steingut found himself deposited at the foot of the mountain, which was his perception of the forty-story apartment building where lay buried the office of Dr. Warner. Joseph Warner, M.D. was the inscription on a bronzed plaque juxtaposed to a black arrow pointing downward. To the cellar? No grand building which housed distinguished tenants could be equipped with a steerage section, but Israel felt he was headed down into darkness, an ominous onset in a mission to find a savior. The illusion was soon dissipated. At the foot of the steps he was cheered by a wide corridor, sedate and pontifical, especially designed for an approach to one office. The Warner name again appeared on the door. Could he have been a Weissman, or a Warnofsky, since non-Jewish psychiatrists in this part of the city would constitute a severely repressed minority?

The office was plainer than he expected. Lights were shaded neon; appurtenances were comfortable and relatively inexpensive. Dr. Warner was evidently a photographer, or a traveller who revelled in snapshots which were enlarged and framed. Huge color photos of varied countries and peoples, Japan, India, Mexico, and Italy hung on the walls. One enlargement magnetized Israel. He could not turn away from the scene of Germany — an unruly forest at the foot of hills which rose and fell into the distance; low clouds cut off the upper limits of some hills. Before the trees stood a party of a dozen shrunken images which on close inspection were people in German mountain dress or peasant festival attire.

This was not the first time Israel had been attracted to a picture of his homeland. In the window of a travel agency he had fixed on placards advertising the Rhine and Bavaria. He had been fascinated, as he was now in Dr. Warner's office. Amorphous visions stirred his imagination, lured him into the scene on the wall as if he stood in the shadow of its trees craning to look into the hills. Israel had to remind himself he dutifully stood in the office of a psychiatrist whose ultimate goal might include a trip back to the womb. Yet his true journey to his source hung mutely on the wall. Without the embarrassment of delving questions, without external aid, his early life danced before him in amorphous shapes, teased him to come closer. He was addressed in a language of gummed recollection, cajoled, harassed. Parts of old faces, old dramas, were directed at him. Axel the soldier. His mother. Axel, again and again. A wave of rage enveloped him and he walked away from the picture, then returned to merge into its depth. The photo was his nemesis and his savior, what he had run from and to which he must return. It was as if he were starved, with food cached in a convoluted passage he must explore to survive.

Dr. Warner was not Jewish. He emigrated from Scotland as a boy and settled in New York to grow with the aroma of bagels and lox displacing the sweet blandness of scones and butter. The literary gems of Robert Burns were replaced with an accumulation of expressive phrases in Yiddish, Italian, and Spanish, invaluable assets for his New York University appointment and the polyglot population of his private practice. With a flagrant tuft of sandy hair at his brow and darting blue eyes within a lean, hawkish face, his quick small frame projected wasteless energy. He was impatient and intelligent. Israel knew he was in the presence of a medical dynamo who countenanced no dalliance, no contravention to the process of treatment, else the patient should be out hunting for another opinion.

"Dr. Steingut, I received a letter and a phone call from Dr. Hearn. He was very helpful, and as far as I can judge I will be a consultant in your case, as it will be difficult for you to undertake extensive treatment here." He spoke slowly, with controlled enunciation, as if he had practiced to rid himself of the rapid-fire speech expected of him.

Dr. Warner's abrupt, honest introduction clicked in Israel as a meeting of minds, a portent of a vigorous and prompt assault on his ailments. Quick results were preferable to what he had learned could be a painful, extended process. Dr. Warner was a proper choice who would respect the circumstances of Dr. Israel Steingut as a patient who must fulfill a duty to his wife, to Dr. Hearn, to the hospital in his search for treatment. Israel had already resolved that his destiny and any duty he owed to himself rested on his own efforts. Reliance on others would revive the ghost of his dependence, his ancient misery which he must surmount. To be coddled would be counterproductive, and he thought Dr. Warner would agree.

Israel said, "In the past weeks I have been away from my wife, my home, and my work. I seem to have gained more confidence. Perhaps I don't need to be here." Israel lingered on "perhaps."

"You may be correct, though we shall see." Dr. Warner, familiar with the usual themes of psychiatric resistance, persisted with finess and precision to attempt to crack Israel's newly-discovered cocksureness. In five daily sessions Warner extracted the pith of Israel's material and imagined existence, together with the overriding passion his patient expressed for the photo enlargement of a pastoral German scene. The photo took on phenomenal growth, until all else within Israel were footnotes to the major thesis he developed.

One afternoon Israel said, "If I go back to Germany, to my roots, do you think it will help me?"

Ordinarily Dr. Warner might recommend such a course of practical recollection after a year or two of exposition and self-effacing introspection on the part of his patient. Israel Steingut was not the ordinary patient, he was a mosaic of strengths and weaknesses, an intelligent and productive member of society with a creative spark which groped toward the core of his problems. Given the fact he could spend a maximum of a few weeks in the area without total interruption of his life-style, plus an unusually spirited insight thus far rigid against external penetration, Dr. Warner conjectured this might be a situation where his patient could be left to his own contrivances. Israel could try. If he failed, he would come crawling for help.

"Why," prodded Dr. Warner, "do you wish to return to Germany now?"

"I have a perpetual sense of having suppressed a major element of my life. I want to revive it, hold it in my hand as it were. When I came to this country as a boy I was instructed to forget, forget, and I did a good job of it."

"Is there someone you have in mind, someone you should not have forgotten?"

"Axel, the soldier," Israel blurted.

He had not been asked to free associate, to reach for whatever comes to mind. He was not pressed to choose a name amongst others in his sub-conscious. Axel lay there suspended above all others, ready to pop out like a head of steam breaking through a stuck valve. Israel sucked his breath in as he felt his skin warm.

"Israel, I know what you think. Your vision at present is somewhat imaginary, though no less potent and compulsive. Axel goes back a long time. Perhaps, and I advise this as an experimental trial, perhaps it would be best if you took a trip for a couple of weeks. It may actually shorten treatment time, even if you do not find what you think you will."

Israel rushed from the office as if he were a victorious underdog in a prize fight. He called Carla from a corner phone booth.

"Please wire me money in the morning, I have to catch a plane."

"Are you leaving me, Israel?" Carla's response was one of comic irony. "You don't have to run to Africa, or Pago-Pago, to get away from me. You can do that and live next door."

"I am going to Germany, to my roots."

"Sounds like a novel."

"No, no. I've thought of this for months, and finally I realize I must go through with it."

"What about the psychiatrist?"

"He's very helpful. He agrees with me."

"That's strange. I didn't think they worked that way. Are you sure he isn't trying to get rid of you?"

"If he was, he didn't tell me, and I don't care. You might call it a compulsion, an illogical impulse, but once I saw those pictures I knew I had to go."

Carla shrieked. "What pictures?"

"I'll tell you all about it when I see you." Israel was jubilant. He had latched onto a goal and would not compromise in its pursuit, no matter how tenuous his plans appeared. He was a gambler, a prospector who envisioned his mountain of gold barely beyond reach. "Wire the money," he said emphatically, "and I'll keep in touch."

Chapter 17

ISRAEL'S PLANS WERE nearly wrecked by what should have been a minor impediment. Lin Chiu solemnly introduced the importance of a passport, which takes several weeks to acquire. Suddenly, the fragility of his proposed journey became apparent to Israel. Fate was telling him to distrust his intuition and remain at home. A frantic search in a side pocket of his valise uncovered a flat packet wrapped in facial tissue. He found the document, still valid, which he had received two years before when he had anticipated a foreign vacation with Carla. His opportunity was not denied. Fate held out a block of time for him. The serendipitous exposure of his passport was as sure a sign to Israel as Moses' burning bush.

He could not doze on the plane to Berlin. The unbroken floor of clouds beneath were his fields of grass. Cumulous projections which pushed upwards were the growth of trees. Subdued throbs of jet engines were boyhood whispers. After he landed and had slept in a third-class hotel room he walked the streets, spoke to shoppers so amiable he thought he had come to the wrong country, or traveled in the fantasy of a pre-war time sphere. Gradually his native language took shape; the precisely accented gutteral sounds rolled from the back of his throat with staccato impact.

In a café he ordered coffee and pastry, marveled at the pungent aroma from his cup and the buttery richness of his dessert. These people know how to live, he mused. A brute of a man in a blue raincoat approached his table. Israel gasped in the remembrance of the face and figure. The pastry he chewed stuck as he swallowed. The stranger asked for a match, and none forthcoming he thanked Israel profusely and turned to another table. It could not be anyone I knew, thought Israel, since he would now be old and decrepit. Israel's personal history had become a hash of unfocused perceptions. Yet the vagaries of his past were not bizarre in his view, as his present was neither orderly nor directed.

A short plane trip and a bus ride took him to the home of his parents. The old street had not changed except for two apartment buildings artfully designed to blend with the quaint architecture of the private homes. In New York, new structures would have hovered as garish embezzlers of local culture, with massive cement blocks and huge aluminum bordered windows. "Be careful," Israel reflected. "Don't fall into a trap where snap judgements are based on external niceties."

The old home still inspired him. Israel was taller now, and standing at the base of steps leading to the door his eyes were level with the pearl button he used to push to alert his mother of his return. Chimes in the foyer would herald his entrance. The button returned his stare as if it dared him to reach out to it. Above the bell a large door knocker had been installed, possibly during the war when electricity was inconstant and batteries scarce. Should he try the bell or the knocker? It was a decision of some importance, for the old mechanism could drag him into a pit of nostalgia in which he had best not entangle himself. Hopes and solutions lay in the future and not in ruminations over what he might or might not have accomplished. He took the massive handle and banged it down repeatedly, more like a salesman with indomitable faith in his product, than a traveller returned to sentimentalize his youth. No one answered. With some effort he pressed the bell, but he heard no chime or ring when he put an ear to the door. For an instant he had an urge to stamp his feet, as he did in boyish impatience when the door did not open immediately on a cold afternoon. This was the home where he slept, ate, watched his father manipulate medical instruments, ran around furniture with his mother after him. Inconsequential nostalgia; a lifetime ago; not to be doted on or he would be hooked with the bait of homesickness.

Perhaps he could talk to a neighbor and find out when the occupants could be expected. As he turned his head toward the adjoining house a distant glint blinded him. At least two streets away low sunlight reflected off a glass storefront. Israel imagined the light ray to be a laser beam shot from a gigantic mechanism of combat. He thought he heard the glass burst with sharp cracks, accompanied by the musical tinkle of falling splinters. Fanciful raucous voices rose at the far end of the street, gutteral cries accented by whacks of flailing sticks. Israel craned to verify what he envisioned, but saw only a van in mechanical difficulty, which had sputtered and backfired. There were no flailing truncheons, shattered glass, or milling crowds. He was disgusted as well as relieved. Further investigation of his old haunts would be tantamount to self-inflicted punishment.

The railway terminal, the same one to which Johann had led him and his mother, was reached in a half hour's walk. Strange, to take long unfaltering steps without having to detect an assailant from a doorway on the opposite side of the street. What should have been a curious sense of freedom was diluted by the effort he had to make to assure himself of safety. Yet passers-by greeted him politely; some slowed as if to engage in friendly banter. Israel walked faster when he was approached, avowed he did so because he was in a hurry and not because of fanciful memories. After he purchased his ticket and waited for the train, the small traveling bag he held seemed inordinately imbalanced, as if he relived the day he was a small boy who carried an unwieldy box.

A gentle boy of six who sat with his mother on the train across the aisle offered Israel a lick of his half chewed lollypop. Israel withdrew a wrapped caramel from his pocket, dangled it, and raised his eyebrows to signal the mother for permission. She nodded her assent, and the boy grasped his gift and plunged it into his mouth to replace his previous delicacy. He nodded his approval. His black hair and deep brown eyes were the genetic complements of his mother's prominent cheek bones and darkly creamed complexion.

"What is his name?" Israel asked.

"David. David Schwartz," replied the mother, chin forward, with the ease and abruptness of accentuated pride.

Their conversation was subdued and shortened, as other passengers sat two rows away; but Israel satisfied his guess that she was Jewish, and married to a businessman, both the offspring of families who had safely emigrated from Germany yet returned after the war. Yes, they liked living here. No, there was no trouble at all. Good neighbors were everywhere. A distinguished gray haired man passed down the train aisle, shoulders back and chin in, with head rigid in that imperious stance which sends onlookers scuttling to one side. The mother gazed at him intently as he approached, duelled him with her large, expressive eyes. For an instant his demeanor cracked. He glanced at her swiftly and recanted, but in that split second when two worlds were about to collide, one shifted course to find its unpolluted trajectory.

"Are there still Nazis here?" Israel posed the question studiously, as if he sought an historical perspective.

"A few old ones remember yesterday's glory, but can't do a thing about it." She paused. "And some young ones suffer from an overactive imagination." Israel's eyes widened. He did not understand her meaning.

"There are always those who seek power and don't have the brains to acquire it except by force. They are the trouble makers, but we know how to deal with them. Surely you have the same hoodlums in America."

Israel recalled questions his friends would ask. "Can it happen here?" He would stand aside at such discussions, retire to a corner and listen to a record, or in his home would excuse his disappearance into the kitchen to slice the cake or serve beverages. He had retired from a political world which beckoned him to engage and confront. The stiff militarist who walked in the aisle had also retired from the fray, but somehow his arms, his darting eyes, were receptive to rejuvenation. What could ensue if the old man were to come face to face with an adoring youngster who knew the old dreams and could nurture new ones?

The mother scanned Israel. She was serious. "Don't worry," she said as if she had defined his struggle to awaken from indecision, "we are alert and we complain if we have to. There are few of us left, but they hear us as if we were millions."

The millions were a memory, thought Israel, a voice out of the debris of decades, and what the populace heard was a distorted echo. Reverberative sounds cross fields, bounce off mountains, and return to points of inception. Their audible intensity may be doubled or tripled, but soon the reverberations recede to a stillness deeper and more frightening than before; and confusion is the final effect of persistent echoes. The spirit of this mother must be steeped in the courage and bravado of an Indian warrior to live in this land; or she could be blinded by the optimism of the Jew who stumbles toward survival.

Israel left the train before his companions. He stood and handed the mother a bag of caramels. "From a medical view, sweets are not good for your son," he said, "but used with discretion they will not harm him." They nodded to each other in silent transmission that she possessed a wordly caution gathered from the past and forged for the present. No harm would be permitted to come to her son.

The sleepy village where Israel was to board his bus was unchanged. It was the gateway to his old hiding place, where barriers against his movements should now be lowered. An early haze irritated his nostrils, and he felt the atmosphere thicken and enclose him so he could not go on. A devastating lethargy whispered to him he had done enough, gone far enough. Shaking himself, he mobilized the energy to continue. Nearby was an inn which would serve as a temporary haven to retrench and review his plans. Before going to sleep he went downstairs to a side room with several rough wooden tables, and ordered a stein of dark beer which he sipped like brandy. Three men in work clothes sat at an adjoining table. They spoke in low growls about the advantages of dairy cattle over those fed for slaughter, about a breed of pigs notorious for eating its young, about the weather and its effect on depth of soil moisture. It all sounded like the talk he heard in Iowa when farmers gathered in village bars after chores. To work the land was a binding, universal pursuit, as was medicine and surgery. Soil, and people dependent on it, suffered the same concerns everywhere. An American president had spoken of guns and butter in the same breath, but they were worlds apart, placed in the ludicrous apposition of growth and destruction. In spite of the complaints and travails of the farm talk he heard, Israel sensed a confirmation of the future. No matter the problems, times would be better. Israel detected hope in their lamentations.

The morning was bright and invigorating, so that he boarded the bus which was to be the final leg of his travel, with freshened vigor. The vehicle was driven by a talkative, rotund, elderly man with a flamboyant white moustache which he continually stroked as he smacked his lips. He was the counterpart of the town band leader who enjoys his rendition no matter what the crowd thinks. Sitting up front with no one else in the bus, Israel engaged in converstion which finally turned to an old farmhouse past the top of the hill, on a route the bus formerly by-passed.

"I know the hill you mean. We have taken this route for twenty years. I can let you off wherever you wish." He was proud to accomodate his traveler.

Israel described an exact location according to the rise and fall of the terrain and the twists in the road. "I can get off at the farmhouse."

The driver tugged at his moustache with unusual ferocity. "But there is no farmhouse where you say it must be. Hasn't been one on that spot for longer than I care to remember. You must have been very young when you were last here." He remained silent, as if he recalled the mirage of an old house virtually isolated from other farms, with the wierd, capricious rumors which circulated about its occupants. No one now cared about those people, their home, the piece of enshrouded land out of the mainstream of village life and secreted in a haze of tales of a time best forgotten. That is, no one cared except his passenger, a short, sensitive, scholarly man who spoke German with a strange admixture of accents as if he had learned it elsewhere.

Israel said, "I visited an aunt here once, and I wondered what happened to the place."

The driver, frustrated that he was not asked to impart definitive information, observations, scenic descriptions and explanations, responded in a biting tone. "No one who lived here is around anymore. If the war didn't get them, they died of old age. And if they were young and smart, they moved away. Please don't ask where they went. A strange lot they were; didn't mix with the villagers at all." Politely he severed the flow of questions his bus driver's instinct informed him were certain to follow. Nasty incidents of old days were not a fit subject for conversation in a monotonous job where he engaged in banter for the sake of amusement. The morning was too salubrious to burrow into dark memories.

The bus jerked to a stop. "This is where you want to get off." The driver was curt. The countryside he had passed through was a dowdy panorama of scrubby acreages and run down homes. Now he stood on a paved road. Houses were large and built of cedar and brick. The poverty-stricken agrarian nature of the land had been rejuvenated into lively tracts fit for country squires. Sleek horses cuddled beside stout barns. Here and there a few pigs or a cluster of fat cattle appeared to be the hobby stock of an entrepreneur farmer rather than the lifeblood of a nation's food supply. After the bus pulled away, Israel turned to find the dwelling and land which had been both his haven and his entrapment.

There was no farmhouse. Set back a hundred yards from the road a huge two-story cement structure squatted on its concrete pad. A flat, cropped lawn could not disguise the role of the structure as a nucleus of material production in a center of agribusiness. One side of the edifice was devoted to the storage and sale of fertilizer. The remainder hoarded machines for the manufacture of plastic sheets and bags. Israel tried to find a spot of sweetness, a point where he could stand unaffected by the pungent odor of decayed manure, and out of range of the throb of machines. At the rear of the building he forgot the smells and noises. He walked about the edge of the concrete foundation and patted his toes on the earth as if his foot were a divining rod. Somewhere two bodies, Anna's and his mother's, were buried.

Israel wandered about the grounds with no item of reference to guide him, until he spotted a huge tree with twisted, broken branches, which stood free from the shadow of cement superstructure. He recalled how he had climbed it to impress someone, the girl he cavorted with; recalled the whoosh of a knife thrown into its bark as if he desecrated living skin. As he paced off from the base of the tree, he tried to calculate where he had dug the burial pit that hurried tearful night. Uncertain distances shrank, vague paths retraced themselves, until in his mind's eye his finger pointed to the building's cement wall; for it dawned on him the graves were embedded under the steel reinforced concrete of its floor. Israel forced himself to enter. He passed rows of bags filled with nitrogenous waste, to find anyone who might know what had happened to the earth that had been worked over during construction. The search would be frustrating, as there could be no recourse against his injured dignity. No one could be punished for an act which only he perceived to be desecration of the dead. An old man bent over ledger books on a metal table appeared a suitable candidate to question.

"How long is this building up?"

"About fifteen years." His gnarled hands relaxed as he dropped his pen.

"Did you see it from the beginning, I mean did you see the earth dug up by bulldozers?"

"Yes." The worker hurried to explain, as the inquirer could be a government official full of peculiar notions about plant safety or proper drainage. "I saw every shovel of dirt, inspected the footings, the pipes and wires, and was especially careful about the steel reinforcement in the concrete. You see, I had to report back to the boss; sort of a second check on the builder."

"Never mind that. Was there anything uncovered in the digging?"

"What do you mean?"

Israel hesitated. "Like bodies, skeletons."

The old man wiped his brow. "Wait here, I'll get the boss."

"Stop!" Israel exclaimed. "The boss can't help. I want to know what you saw."

"Nothing, nothing like that," the old man stammered.

"I am sorry I disturbed you, truly sorry." Tension had subsided. There were no answers, no discernible expectations from such questions. His void was best left unexplored. Imagine the horror on being told of old bones dumped on some stinking waste pile, or ground up for food or fertilizer. Perhaps they, the bodies, were still under the weight of the factory, imprisoned yet secured from wind and erosion, in a plot resistant to all but the eventualities of nature. He felt relieved to have come this far, to have investigated every possible route, in itself an act of attainment. The graves were but symbols, and he could not imagine himself weeping over a mound of dirt. Let the bodies, the murder and death, the spirit of perseverance and loyalty, remain as abstracts which he could mold, and from which he could imbibe courage.

The town was clean, larger than it used to be, and busier. More cars and vans, and at times a truck rattled down the main street. One carried refrigerators. New brick, and rustic plank façades adorned the houses, and though there were no tall apartment buildings a few duplexes detracted from the lazy isolation of a farm community. In place of the book store a clothing retail outlet sold work clothes. Down the street the renovated movie house displayed a billboard which advertised a film with overt sexual overtones. In that respect, thought Israel, the world remained static. The old low budget pictures posed as the artistic interpreters of sex. He could discern no difference, nor was he interested in finding any, between artistry and pornography. Israel stood with one leg on the brink of middle age and the other in the fullness of adolescence, a boy inspecting the billboard in search of that minute bit of color or curve which might titillate him. As usual his eagerness went unrewarded, though he was aware of a call to youth and excitement. He was too old for pictures and needed reality to sustain him. He missed Carla.

It was late in the afternoon, too late for inquiries. Besides, he was not sure what plan to follow. Two streets from the main thoroughfare he found a clean frame house with a room-for-rent sign. An elderly couple came to the door and showed him the attic, spotless, angular and slant-roofed, with a comfortable bed and burner to prepare beverages. The room had been transformed from a rough storage area to a neatly-papered, comfortable room with the clean smell of pine oil and the shimmer of afternoon light through gauze curtains. It was a model of German household efficiency, with the caress of peasant design to impart protective comfort. There is in everyone some deep, constructive goodness, thought Israel. In bed, staring at the cheerful, flowered wall figures, he tried to envision Axel, how and where he could be found, a task weighted with uncertainty and failure.

Israel needed a stroke of luck, and finding one he proceeded to capitalize on it. When he spoke to the old couple who boarded him he surmised they were retired farmers who knew everyone in the village or in the fields, and who were anxious to divulge what they knew. Anna's farm had been close to theirs, though they rarely had spoken to her.

"And what happened to that farm?" Israel asked the old man.

"All we know is that one day the lady was there, and the next day she was gone, with all the others."

"But I understood she was sick."

"We suspected, but we didn't know. She could have run away, as so many did. It was the war, you know."

"Someone must have worked the land after she left," Israel probed.

"No, it wasn't that way. There was no order, no neat progression of events; only bombs and Allied soldiers. For a few years the land was parcelled out to neighbors and new families who came to farm. Then the plastics company bought the property from the town, and after renting it out they built their plant on it."

Israel explained his probing, that he was a distant relative of Anna and had undertaken a nostalgic binge of discovery. The old folks were satisfied with the lame excuse for the droves of questions put to them. Remembrance was their only remaining field of competence, and any younger individual who wanted their help showed a degree of respect they thought had vanished. Israel was their resurrection. A band of intimacy was quickly achieved, so that inquiries regarding the anti-aircraft crew which had been stationed nearby did not appear outlandish.

"A lazy bunch, those soldiers. They did nothing but live off the fat of the land." The landlord and his wife spoke in unison as if their bias had been formulated in previous discussions.

"Surely some of the men stayed after the war," quizzed Israel.

The old man sat in a rocker, poured himself a brandy. Memory, precious memory, had been challenged, and he had to prove his alertness, in detail if possible.

"There was one soldier who settled in town after the war. Worked as a mechanic for a while. His name, his name, let me see, Alec, Emile, Axel. Yes, he was Axel. He had some dealings with Anna. But he is gone now, probably out of the country. His aunt lives in the village. Must have been a fine fellow to bring an aunt to live with him. So many were homeless in those days." Information poured from the old man. "Go two streets north of the movie house and you will find her little apartment, in a brown and white house on the corner. His aunt is Miss Schusswig. Don't upset her. She is not as old as we, but she had a hard life and lives on very little income. In fact I don't know how she manages."

"Tell me," said Israel, "how you can be so sure this Axel was the one who knew Anna?"

The old man was overjoyed to piece together obscure information. "Because that's the same soldier who bought produce from me and sold it to his buddies. He did the same with Anna, though we all kept quiet about it. That man must have done well for himself, not that I blame him. War does strange things. At first you are told to fight the enemy. Later you find your enemy is poverty, and no one has to tell you how to fight it."

Israel located Miss Schusswig. Again he confronted someone aged and stooped, with a thin, hesitant voice and the demeanor of a sick rabbit frightened to emerge from its hole. Age and desecration were Israel's companions. This journey into his youth could leave him also bent, stiff, and frightened. To give up the search and go home would be his simplest solution, though the alternative of a psychiatrist's couch to clarify his childhood could be abysmal. He had to continue his rendezvous with the infirm and near senile, those who were a misstep away from the grave.

Miss Schusswig was not the fountain of information Israel had hoped. In spite of his polite insistence she hesitated and whispered nothing of factual value. When he mentioned Axel, or the soldier with the anti-aircraft battery, the one who sold produce to the military, she became flustered and withdrawn. Israel guessed she teetered at the edge of fury, a reaction the old lady could no longer evoke. It was too dangerous to goad her against her will, as she might suffer a stroke, or call the police, and he was not interested in responses to German authorities, or revival of his emergency medical skills. At this stage he wished to forget he was a doctor. Seeing her living conditions, Israel deduced that Miss Schusswig obtained money from someone to live in her middle-class apartment in a well regarded neighborhood.

Returning to his room, Israel said to his talkative landlord, "I don't wish to pry, but I am fascinated that an old woman like Miss Schusswig can live so well without taking in boarders. I did not think her government subsidy could sustain her."

"It's outside money, my boy. Outside money makes the difference. Every month, on the eighth or ninth, she goes to the bank. Why? Because she gets a check in the mail the day before. We even know where it comes from. America. We've met her in town several times, and she boasts that she has what we don't, a rich relative who isn't stingy."

Israel rushed to a calendar. Until now time had passed by him as a wandering dream without accountable hours or days. Suddenly he was obliged to pin down with numbers the days of the month and hours of the day. This was the third. He investigated and learned the mailman's route went up the main street and a right turn toward Miss Schusswig's dwelling to make his calls about ten in the morning. Mail was left in an open box in the hallway, and after the postman left a two-minute interval passed before Miss Schusswig's arthritic joints could propel her to the sealed envelopes which linked her to distant lands.

First she had to descend a small flight of steps and maneuver through a curve in the hall, which gave Israel fifty-five seconds to inspect the mail without projecting himself into her line of vision. The situation was subjected to mathematical calculations which included the speed she progressed, the distance, the length of the curve in the corridor, and the angle of vision when he would be at risk. Once he wished to be a scholar of mathematics, but he never imagined he would use his skills as a thief. He would not harm the old lady, but her nephew Axel would be another matter.

The mailman must have been an infantry sergeant, for his comings and goings followed the precision of an atomic clock. Israel paced the opposite side of the street and discovered he could easily reach the mail box unseen after the delivery was dropped. The first day he retrieved a large yellow envelope postmarked Berlin and unsealed. To reach inside would have gone undetected, but he resolved then and there that he would retain his honesty and not mutilate, steam open, or otherwise inspect contents meant to be private. Clues ascertained from the exterior of mailings he felt to be privy to general inspection. A letter was of the secret essence of an individual, though superficial scrutiny could not be offensive.

No mail was delivered to Miss Schusswig the second day. On his third vigil all he had to examine was a folded advertisement from a newly-opened butcher shop which featured bargains for chickens, pork, and weiners. On the eighth of the month the postman lingered. Israel hurried to the box to find it crammed with assorted sizes and shapes of envelopes. Quickly he riffled through the pact. The arrhythmic shuffling gait he listened for was about to round the curve in the hall. One small bit of paper, thin and inconsequential, nearly missed inspection as he fumbled through the odd-sized pieces. It's stamp was U.S.A., with an illegible postmark. The antennae of his senses extended in multiple directions; ears strained toward the stairs; eyes swept the corners of the envelope; fingers juggled the unwieldy batch of papers. In the few safe seconds he could count on, a blurred imprint on the left upper corner of the letter glowed as a distinct pattern, as if he were accustomed to the halo of fog lights. He could read, "A.G." and below it "Arundel, Indiana."

His uplifted mood bordered on hysteria. Here was a place to go and someone to look for. A well-defined goal, not a whimsy or a hazy quest, presented a stark challenge which was plain and clean in concept.

A factor of excitement made him bounce along as if he were poised to soar. He had breached the bounds of ethics to achieve what he sought. For once he had justified means to gain his end, put himself outside the pale of good-boy behavior.

The main street of the village was busy in the air of festivity which precedes a weekend. Israel jostled through a crowd of women in a brightly-lit shop to purchase sausages, a magazine with semi-nude pictures, and two bottles of wine. One he presented to his landlord, a going-away present. He said. "Don't worry if you smell burning wieners tonight, as I will celebrate in my room." The wine bottle held high indicated what he would drink. In his room he wrote on a card the letters and place he had stolen from Miss Schusswig's mail, repeated the information to himself and tore the paper to bits.

Now he could read, or devour, his magazine. Captivated with the lure of bared bosoms and torsos in suggestive postures he wondered why he had always looked with disdain on such remarkably stimulating images. Wine and the spicy aftertaste of sausage, which invariably produced headaches and nausea, now combined to generate a pleasant, diffuse tingle. The bawdy magazine pictures complemented the vibrant stimuli of his taste buds.

He envisioned himself a burly youth of past eons perched beside a fire with his captive woman, his dinner the fresh meat of his kill. A warm erection surprised him with its intensity and persistence. The magazine dropped from his hand. Home, his own bed, and Carla, supplanted the photos of nude bodies and spread thighs. He twisted and turned, tried to sit upright, but the rub of overlying sheets conspired with his contortions to irritate him further, until he relieved himself in ejaculation. The old cultural guilt which used to overwhelm him was puny and fleeting. "Why not," Israel told himself, "I enjoyed it."

In the midst of explanations to his landlord regarding departure and the plethora of arrangements to be made for his trip to America, the tug of duty diluted his accomplishment. When he saw a growth of pink tulips in bloom he knew what he must do. Israel purchased a huge bunch of tulips, had their stems bound in colored ribbons, and carried them to Miss Schusswig.

He said to her sweetly, "I hope you enjoy the flowers. They are a small token of appreciation." She accepted them casually, gently poured water in a vase, and placed the stems into it. She turned to him. "Did Axel give you these for me? He does so much for me, you know."

Israel stammered, "No, *I* got them for you." At the moment he had expunged Axel from the event but she brought her nephew back into focus. Israel was on the brink of explanation, why he was there, what he planned to do, but he said nothing lest Axel be warned that Helmut Steingut was on his trail. And even Axel must have some kindliness in him to care for his aunt with such diligence. Nor was he, Israel, the epitome of honest intentions. He doubted himself, his ideas, his acts. Was he the practitioner of compassion bringing flowers to the little old lady, or was he lowered to the role of schemer? Sins could not be expiated with a gift of beauty. His attitude hardened. He had almost mired himself into inextricable indecision. If revenge was to be judicious, sentiment must have no part in its execution.

Israel was fortunate to book a flight for Chicago leaving in forty-eight hours. Visitors who had milled about streets and highways had returned to jobs and daily routines. The country resembled a huge vacation resort after Labor Day. Israel, too, had a job awaiting him, but it would not be routine. What he set out to accomplish was suffused with a dream-like quality, and he would inform no one. To convince himself he did not act out of an insane motive, he wished to solidify ties with his adult past. Two letters were sent off, one to his psychiatrist, the other to Carla.

Dear Dr. WARNER:

I wish to thank you for your indulgence in my case. Knowing how reluctantly you agreed that I make this trip, I believe your intuition served you well when you consented. I found what I looked for, not a person in the flesh, but the information I need to take me further. My life, more to the point my immediate future, opened to me like the petals of a flower. Thus, I shall not be coming back to see you, though I must admit you were the catalyst that awakened me. I thank you again.

Yours truly,
Dr. Israel Steingut.

When he reviewed the phrase "like the petals of a flower," he tore up the letter and rewrote it. Though he had drawn the metaphor subconsciously, easily, Israel surmised gushy allusions would be judged fanciful by a psychiatrist. Not so bold as to give an impression he had cured himself, he nevertheless wished to display his energy as rational, the basis of a normal, successful pursuit. To Carla he wrote:

My dear wife,

In the weeks I have been away from you I have been extremely busy, though I thought of you frequently. Having made the necessary arrangements, I shall be flying back to the States. Perhaps you wonder whether I have changed or been transformed into that man you want to see, full of the joy of life and freed from the worries which plagued me. Yes, I think I have changed, but not in the way you might imagine. Germany has been a Godsend to me (now how could I ever say that!), since the country and its people have opened me up like the petals of a flower seeking the light.

Amongst many interesting people, one I found out about especially intrigues me. I believe if I could meet him I would unravel the knot which has bound me all these years. If and when I see him I do not know exactly how I will react, but I have a pretty good idea of what I must do. It should not be long, perhaps a month or two, before we are together, but I know you have the stability and patience to wait for me while I follow to conclusion this last, greatest hope. I love you very much, and whatever happens, even if I fail, I shall come to you and you will perceive me in a different light. I shall write, but it may be several weeks before I am settled.

With much love,
Israel

He did not erase the bit about petals of flowers opening to the light, since it was his true sentiment, which Carla should find refreshing. She always thought of Israel as too sensible and pragmatic, with no leaning toward romantic fluff.

Carla, upon receipt of the letter, opened it carefully with a dull knife slid through its edge to avoid mutilation of its contents. She had reconstructed several versions of his extensive travels. Once, she doubted he would return, but his dependence on her was a major influence which would drive him into her arms. Another woman? Not her Israel. He was too old, and she was too attractive. She could not imagine his spirit revived and activated by a woman his own age. But was he off his rocker, completely haywire, acting out some fantasy he had picked up on a psychiatrist's couch? The possibility that he was irrational was strong, and she would attempt to intercede, though she had no idea where he was headed. His letter hinted at vaguely desperate notions, as if it were a recitation of an unformed dream, and Carla did not appreciate the solution of pragmatic problems with dreams.

Still, he showed a degree of gumption, an aggressiveness she had not been able to instill in him, and which she judged to be a positive factor in his favor. Of what importance could be the man he was supposed to find? Israel was coyly secretive in his explanation that he could not divulge more to his wife because he did not know the answers to his own questions, yet he appeared positive enough in pursuit of his strange search. Apparently he was more possessed with his goals than he cared to admit, which cast a pall of evasiveness and possible danger over what could be an insane caprice.

Carla sought information from Dr. Hearn, she called Dr. Warner in New York, checked every airline with flights from Germany to New York. She overlooked, however, direct travel to Chicago. She had to grip herself, confirm her own steadfastness, to subdue the unaccustomed anxiety which threatened her. She was forced to wait for him to founder. Whatever happened, she was determined to help him. She reassured herself he would return to the old days when he put his head on her shoulder after a difficult surgery which made him doubt his ability. Perhaps she should have encouraged Israel to remain home, with all his foibles intact. She had managed him before, and could steel herself to do so again.

Chapter 18

THE AMERICANIZED GERMAN population of Arundel, Indiana, had built a town reminiscent of the Fatherland only by its contrasts. Instead of picturesque, winding streets, cobblestones, and structures of architectural dignity, Arundel was square, squat, and polluted by a malodorous haze. The perpetrator of its ugliness was the Pathmark packing plant, to which the community was wedded and enslaved. Surrounding farms were bountiful oases of production and rural beauty, with neat acreages tilted on rolling hills of lush grass. When Israel walked to the edge of the plant and examined its expanse of brick and concrete blocks sooted with leavings of a projectile bellow of smoke, he suffered the urge to get the hell away; where the terrain was unsullied; where he could practice in a modern medical facility and breathe sharp, clean air. Then he saw the farms, not dissimilar from those of Iowa, and he realized the dirt and grime of the village were the refuse, the excreta, of the town's activity. To walk away into the sweet fields would be a simple solution, about as permanent an evasion as that of an escaped cow that wandered from the slaughter house.

Israel was consumed by plans, plans, plans. Logic, manipulation, mathematical precision, the what, where, and how of things occupied him. He was a virile animal on the trail of a spoor which he sensed was acute. The odor of the plant, which would have nauseated him, became pungently invigorating. Wood-slatted trucks rumbled to the rear of the plant and unloaded interminable cargoes of cattle and hogs, munching, grunting, and defecating on their way to the knife. If only those beasts knew what they were to become, as he had known when he witnessed the slaughter of his mother. The beasts unloaded from the trucks did not know; but he knew, and he did nothing. Now he would manage differently. Prepare and attack rather than submit. Keep the body firm and the mind agile. Patience, patience to build, to accumulate power! In his room he did push-ups and exercises, he jumped rope to increase lung and heart capacity. When fate called he would be primed for instant action.

The initials A. G. on Miss Schusswig's letter could prove an enigma. Probably the original name had been changed, but Axel must be employed here, as were all others in Arundel except for a few shopkeepers and bank tellers. To install himself inside the plant would not be an insurmountable project for a man of his background and training. Years ago he had worked in a defense plant, so that with some embellishment of his dossier he could pass as an industiral surgeon, a euphemism for a general practitioner who treated a multitude of cuts, bruises, and sprains.

Israel, who disdained sartorial elegance as a factor in human relationships, had his suit pressed, bought a tie with two diagonal white stripes on a bed of pastel blue, and wore a beige shirt. In the plant, he opened a door labelled "personnel," and stiffly confident, inquired of a secretary whether he could meet the chief of the medical department. He oozed authority. No one had visited the office impeccably dressed since an undertaker arrived to remove the body of the largest stockholder stricken on this very spot.

Miss Evans was underfed and underpaid. She was lean and leathery, with the look of a pioneer, but her appearance was a bluff, as she trembled when she faced prestige.

"Shall I call Dr. Groothaus?"

"Please do, if you are certain he is head of the medical department."

Dr. Jan Groothaus was a liberal, hard-drinking Dutchman with a slight accent. He had to be a drinker, or otherwise flawed, to have banished himself to Arundel.

"Sir," Israel was forthright, "I am a surgeon who practiced in Iowa. I would like to apply for a position on your staff." He placed his credentials on the desk, state license, American Medical Association, and Fellow of American College of Surgeons, pocket-worn cards of identification and status. "In the past I have had experience in industrial medicine."

Dr. Groothaus sucked in his breath and asked no questions. He needed medical help desperately, as the only applicants he got in response to frequent advertisements were submitted by foreigners and chronic misfits. Here was a man of character, and Dr. Groothaus did not care why he trudged into this foresaken hole so long as he was steady on his feet, could recognize a normal heart-beat, and could sew a cut. Salary, duties and schedules were discussed, with time apportioned amongst three doctors, including the newcomer.

"It is just a routine," said Groothaus, "but we will have to see your medical diploma and original state license."

Israel had anticipated the request. It was part of his plan. If he wrote home for the documents, Carla would be on the scene the following day, with hard-headed persuasion and custodial fervor which might be too realistic to resist. She might mistake his determination for delusion.

Israel explained, "My documents were destroyed in a fire, but you can send my photo and license number, which the state will verify. In addition, I have my passport for proof of identity." He displayed an easy, natural confidence, without a hint of salesmanship. Never had he lied regarding his qualifications. His skills did not reside in his papers. The one deed he abhorred was to misrepresent his capability or fudge on contractual obligations.

Dr. Groothaus led Israel to an adjoining office and asked whether he would like a drink.

"No thank you," Israel said, "but you have one. I don't drink in the day."

It was the perfect answer for Dr. Groothaus. He could not stomach another staff member with his own problems, yet this applicant was no bible-spouting teetotaller, a distinct hazard encountered in this part of the country. "Fine, I would like you to join us, and I shall try to make it pleasant for you. Start tomorrow if you wish, but don't hurry if that is inconvenient."

"Tomorrow is satisfactory." Israel had thought he might delay his appearance a week or more to minimize an overanxious projection, but the plant was so bogged down with routine employee examinations there was no need to be coy. He would charge into his duties, keep his eyes open, and get to those files. After that, well, there had to be a degree of flexibility in any plot.

Upon leaving the office he turned to Miss Evans. "You have been exceedingly efficient. I shall be working here, and I appreciate your kindness." She beamed with thanks, which Israel judged a promise of good rapport from a useful aide, according to plan.

Israel and Dr. Groothaus carried the medical load of the Pathmark Packing Plant with ease bordering on boredom. Dr. Singh, who cared for the night shift, was a ghostly figure, a depressed, conscientious East Indian who entered and departed unseen. Duties of the day which formerly were a shambles of inefficiency were methodically organized. Israel set aside times for routine examinations and coordinated them with immunization injections. He rearranged the surgical room so that cuts and blisters could be attended with dispatch, and he suggested Miss Evans update the filing systems with cross indices. Any worker could be located by job and age group, as well as by alphabetical sequence. Dr. Groothaus was positive he had snared a genius.

Israel brought up an item of modern industrial medicine. "We should get into the plant and watch the men at work. Efficiency experts don't know half what we do about the prevention of injuries. They don't have the knowledge of anatomy and body movements. With a little common sense, we could predict the hazards."

Groothaus could not possibly disagree. Subjected to an aggressive medical spirit, he began to relish his duties. A new creative light enhanced the dull discipline of preventive medicine. "I hate the sights and smells in the plant. You take whatever time you can spare to study conditions at first hand."

Each day Israel walked in a different area of the work sections. He wondered how anyone with civilized attributes could adjust to the abominable surroundings. Animals were electrically stunned, drained of blood, ripped open and sawed into parts. By the time various cuts of meat and bone reached their respective conveyor belts, they were impersonal reminders of a clean butcher shop, or the week-end roast in a housewife's kitchen. Somewhere between docile animals in a field and the canning tables, brutality had been suspended. Israel traversed slippery floors bordered with troughs through which oozed a stream of blood; he watched intestines hosed out and packed in barrels; inspected the agile motions of men who stripped carcasses of skin and fat, each with his specific act of separation. With a swipe of a razor sharp knife a layer of fat would be detached, with an accurately gauged thickness left intact for a proper gravy. The speed, the deft dancing hands of the knife wielders, were an executioner's choreograph. Here was the line of division, where the differential between a kill and a morsel to cheer a cultured palate were delineated. Axel was in this department, where barbarism adopted the face of propriety. He belonged there, as his unmatched skill with the knife was a symphony of motion.

From lists of eight hundred employees Israel retrieved three with the initials A.G. One was a woman. Another, aged thirty-two. His trump file card showed an Alexander Grover, age fifty-eight. Not old enough. The age discrepancy unnerved Israel, as if figures and statistical analysis were based on a strange system of logic. Axel had to be in his late sixties. But if he had changed his name, so could he fabricate his age, as finding employment would have been complicated by many factors, not the least of which would be his longevity. When the packing plant hired a worker, it looked forward to a long period of captivity.

"Miss Evans," Israel remarked in passing, "when you hire a man, can he fake his age?"

"What do you mean?"

"Can he say he is younger than he is and get away with it?"

Miss Evans hesitated. A good secretary is wary of interrogation or investigation. "Actually, there were times when we were very busy, and if an older man applied we did not check as long as he was fit for the job. You know, doctor, age isn't everything." She brushed back a straggled tuft of hair to emphasize her philosophy.

"Of course, Miss Evans. Thank you."

"Why do you want to know?"

"It's purely medical. Someday I might want to collect data for an article on preventive medicine in a packing plant." He smiled at the facility with which he could lie.

Had Israel wished, he could have gone to the files and apprised himself of all known particulars regarding Alexander Grover. Intentional delay proved more rewarding, as it imparted a peculiar exhilaration of cat and mouse play, with the mouse cornered beyond reach of his hole. Dr. Singh inadvertently forced the issue. One morning a carefully inscribed note lay on Israel's desk.

"Dr. Steingut, please have a look at one of our older employees, Alexander Grover. He cut his index finger. Though tendons are intact, he has an ugly swelling. I put him on antibiotics, though you may wish to substitute another medication."

Israel completed his early morning duties. He worked slowly, methodically, listened at length to the sounds in his stethescope as if they were harbingers of new discoveries. After the last routine examination, he threw the stethescope on the table and shouted impatiently, "Miss Evans, have Alexander Grover see me immediately!"

A gray-haired man with sunken eyes entered with a hand held immobile on his abdomen. His shoulders were broad and sloped, like that of a rapid-punching pugilist. The back was ramrod straight, and he stood at attention except for the flexed arm. Few wrinkles marred the pink skin beneath three days' growth of black fuzz. But his eyes bespoke his age, or that he had taxed himself in a life of excess; sunken eyes of subdued cruelty, with pale blubbery bags pulling at their lower lids. His spotless butchers' coat overlay an open-throated shirt.

"Are you Mr. Grover, Alexander Grover?" Israel did not look up from the file card he held.

"Yes, sir." The response was sharp, as if it followed a command. Israel strained to the quality of its inflection. "Yes" was thickly intoned and could have been a cumbersome "Ja."

"I understand you cut your finger several days ago."

A long arm unfolded to expose granite hard fingers with ragged nails. The index finger was bent to a claw.

"It's an infection alright. Dr. Singh was right. Please raise your sleeve." Israel inspected the limb and palpated for swollen lymph glands. A roseate streak on the forearm lost its color as it merged into an old scar over the wrist.

"How did you do it? I mean the cut," Israel asked.

"I don't know. It never happened before."

"It is possible your reflexes are slower than they were."

Grover was indignant. "I am just as good as I ever was with the knife. I am the best they have on my job." The anger of his response impaired the caution of his articulation. Israel was certain he knew the accent; guttural trumpets blared, booted feet stamped past. Israel squeezed the flesh of his thigh to compose himself.

He chose a professional manner. "We shall have to change the antibiotic to a form of penicillin. It is most effective by injection." As he manipulated the syringe he held it rigid, but floundered when he plunged the needle. The glass cylinder had become a precious instrument of multiple capabilities. Before, it was a mechanical adjunct of medical treatment. Now it was a container he could fill with ammunition. When he completed the penicillin injection Israel barely heard the appreciative thank you his patient expressed. Words were lost in a din of murderous possibilities which sloshed through his consciousness.

"Are you German?" asked Israel.

"I lived there many years." Israel did not pursue an obviously equivocal answer. He watched Grover's expression of passive innocence. Enough was said. It was a beginning.

"I will recommend you stay off work." Israel appeared indulgent.

"Doctor, please keep me on the job. I can slice with my left hand."

"I should think you'd be happy to rest at home with your family."

"I have no family, and I like to work. I must work." Grover spoke with desperation. This was the type of employee the plant loved and respected. Loyalty was supplemented with an evangelical attitude of self-sacrifice towards his duty. The Axel Israel knew did not give a damn about duty, and he surmised that a constant expenditure of energy could be a cooling remedy to one who lived with the fires of hell.

"Let's try to get you another job," Dr. Steingut interceded. "You cannot use the knife safely with that wound." He shouted through the open door, "Miss Evans, could you see that Mr. Grover is put on some easy task, where he does not need to use his right arm."

Miss Evans rustled the papers she held and made a phone call to a plant supervisor. She fought for Dr. Steingut's wish. When she entered the examination room she flaunted her prowess. "Doctor, I did it! Mr. Grover can be placed as a temporary inspector." Grover accepted his position as a partial victory, and as he left he took long, confident steps.

Israel called to him, "Before you go, make appointments for daily visits. We will have to give several injections before you will be out of the woods."

Israel did not doubt he would be obeyed. Rather, his attention was riveted to the propulsion of those long powerful legs in their apparent hurried exit from the room. One foot lagged slightly; its toes dropped in indecision, then reversed forcefully upward to conceal their disability. To Israel the almost imperceptible limp cast a sinister quality. He reassured himself that he was unafraid. The spent vision of a boyhood wrestling match reminded him he had once taken advantage of that limp, when he threw Axel to the ground in an instant of glory accompanied by the urge to kill; crude boyish emotions deluged in an aftermath of guilt. Now he was more mature, yet he trembled with elation. To curb his excitement he went to a movie.

Arundel's single movie house, struggling to stay alive, pandered to all tastes with double features which coupled themes of violence and love. Like a soldier on a spree, Israel stayed for both films. The directors were inept and the actors totally miscast, so that he knew he was exposed to the clinkers of the picture industry. He thoroughly enjoyed both films. The misrepresentation of actors was a turnabout of reality in which he was personally enmeshed. Axel Gans had become Alexander Grover, a staid English appellation which could be applied to a church-going family man content to live in an isolated village. And what of himself? He had changed his own name from Helmut. Was he the studious scion of Old Testament scholars who lived by the book and debated intricacies of Hebrew law, or was he closer to a Helmut, hard and venturesome, indomitable and fearless? Some of both, he hoped. Names were deceptive, appearances deceptive, and trust in the logic and benignity of the human condition the greatest deception of all. He was startled by his negativism. Not everyone he had known was untrustworthy. He counted on his fingers the compassionate ones, those who could soften the abrasive edge of his fears. And there was Carla. He no longer thought of her as a compassionate figure on whose shoulders he could weep, but he wanted her close to him. He wrote to her:

Dearest;

At last I can report that it won't be long, perhaps a week or two, before I am free to tell you where I am and when I shall see you. Soon we should be together, a moment I hope you have longed for as much as I. Note I talk of being free. Until now I have searched for the ultimate liberation, from myself. Most of us, and you are a rare exception, are a tangled mass of ambitions and anxieties, so that it is difficult to organize ourselves before we know where we are headed. I believe my vision has cleared. For once in my life events have shaped themselves to fit my goal. One obstacle remains but I am certain I shall overcome it. I feel like the surgeon who has cut deeper than ordinary reason dictates to eradicate a growth. Let love rest till we meet.

He signed the letter with endearing felicitations and drove a hundred miles on a Sunday afternoon to mail it. The trip was an unnecessary precaution, as Carla could not read the postmark. Once she knew that he was safe, and firm in her belief he was a rational man who had become temporarily unwound, as most rational men will, she determined not to imagine ultimate possibilities. The allusion to the surgeon who cut deeper than necessary might mean more in anyone but a surgeon, who will tend to emphasize his audacity with operating room metaphors. Israel was acting like most members of his profession.

Next day he met with Alexander Grover for his fourth injection. The streak on his forearm had faded and the receding swelling of his fingers permitted near normal movements.

"Take off your trousers," Israel said.

"I can take it in the arm, doc. There's plenty of room."

"No, this one has to go in the rear end." Grover unclipped his belt and dropped his trousers to the level of his upper thighs.

"Please take them off." Israel was curt. "You may not faint, but if you should, you would trip over your pants." Grover removed his trousers. Limbs and buttocks bared, he would receive the contents of the syringe with resignation. Israel examined the ragged scars on his forward leg.

"That was a nasty gash. How did you get it?"

"It was an accident; a fall from a ladder."

"I could swear I've seen old war wounds like it, old shrapnel wounds."

As the needle slid beneath the skin it shifted and bent in the squeeze of a violent buttock contraction. "Am I hurting you?"

"No, no, not at all." Grover appeared nonchalant.

As the patient dressed, Israel ceremoniously turned his brass nameplate on his desk and held a finger on it as if he called attention to its letters. Grover had heard the doctor's name muffled by the secretary, but pain and concern for his job displaced ancient memories. But in plain view, with Israel's finger poised over it, the dark metallic inscription "Steingut" rose from its base like a bird of prey drawn to a victim. He clinched his belt and marched out with care to avoid a limp.

Israel had pressed through a stage of confrontation into the arena of active aggression. Though out of his element, in the midst of ideas foreign to him, he was convinced there was nothing to do but attack. Instead of "How do I love thee, let me count the ways," he thought in terms of "How can I kill him, let me count the days." Since he was in an ideal situation, physician treating patient, he was privy to a multitude of choices which he gathered into two categories. Fast and slow. The coup de grace could be given by an injection for a suffered heart attack. Nothing so gross as a blow on the head in a dark recess of Arundel's streets was to be considered, since he could not stoop to mundane brutality; and Alexander Grover or Axel Gans had been a highly trained practitioner of mayhem, which, like bicycle riding, does not entirely evaporate for lack of practice. Israel decided he wished to return to Carla as a virile specimen of manhood, not a carved up carcass.

The slow approach would be safer, more agreeable. As strong brandy must be sniffed and sipped for the fullness of its bouquet, so must he savor the gradual demolition of his victim. For example, he could diagnose a disease in Grover which required persistent treatment. A series of medications could be instituted to achieve a cumulative effect. Impossible? Nothing was impossible with study and analysis, processes with which Israel had been successful. There was only one danger in a time-consuming approach. It was not risk of apprehension, as he would canvas all possibilities with the discrimination of a loaded computer. The major hazard was his psyche. A plague of indecision might descend on him in mid-course. Should he falter in a drawn out process, if the pangs of humaneness and civility intervened, he could fail.

Alexander Grover did not show for his next visit, and as Israel was about to ask Miss Evans to summon his patient, he was interrupted by a most opportune phone call. The conversation and its aftermath proved a welcome interlude within an arena of intertwined tensions. Only last night he felt his pulse to determine why he was flushed, as if he had stepped out of a hot bath. The artery at his wrist bounded beneath his finger with the unmistakeable thud of high blood pressure. To do away with Axel, or Alexander, would be no achievement if severe illness were the price exacted.

The voice on the phone was that of Dr. Groothaus, though it was almost unrecognizable in its boyish excitement. "Dr. Steingut, before you do another thing, come to my office. Please!"

Israel rushed in. "What is it? Is there something wrong?"

Groothaus beamed. "Israel, I'm not drunk, and I feel well. Very well. For years I've had a dream, a stupid one I thought, till you came on the scene. It's no dream now. I can see it clearly." He swept his hand about the room.

"I'm relieved. You weren't yourself for a minute."

"Of course not. I'm someone better than myself. I want to leave this meat factory and open an office in town, and I want you with me. I tell you, it can work. The people need good care, and with you doing some surgery, we can give it to them."

Israel gazed at his boss, the wrinkles at the corners of his parched lips, the pot belly weighted with the effect of barrels of beer consumed. Instead of revulsion or rejection, he was excited. Groothaus was a good man, a fairly competent physician, and honest. This would not be an associate to lean upon and learn from. On the contrary, he would be dependent on him, Dr. Steingut, the one who sought relief by whimpering on his wife's shoulders. Israel was the recipient of a heartfelt compliment, which, if accepted and acted upon, could be a turning point in his life. But there was unfinished business, and who could tell if Dr. Groothaus would want him after it was over?

"I have the greatest respect for you, Dr. Groothaus. You have been kind and considerate. But I have a wife who is a nurse, and I would have to convince her to make the move. I believe we would do well together. Give me some time to think it over and complete some business on my mind."

Groothaus had gleaned his employee was married, though he had the impression that permanent separation, perhaps divorce, was pending. "Take all the time you need. Just don't forget me. I need you, and I think you need me." To Israel the assessment was true as well as fortuitous. It was time someone needed him.

The interlude with Groothaus turned sour as Israel returned to his office. Seized with convulsions of doubt he entertained whims of irresponsibility and cowardice. Alexander Grover, temporarily forgotten, was his nemesis, and the course laid out for his punishment must not be reversed. Israel had him summoned to the examination room.

"You missed your last appointment. Never mind, I was busy anyway. How do you feel?" The hand and arm were practically healed, but Grover complained of fatigue and weight loss. He couldn't eat, was nauseous, even vomited once.

"Perhaps it's the penicillin." Israel's examination discovered no cause for the symptoms.

"You are older than is shown in your file, aren't you?"

"A few years. But I've done my work as well as any of them."

"It doesn't make a particle of difference to me. I simply wish you to know that I know. And you are German. Did you not serve in the German army?"

Grover's sunken eyes swelled outward. "Well, yes! How did you know?"

"By your accent, and your bearing." Israel pressed. "And you were in an anti-aircraft unit. Don't ask me how I know. It was near a farm." He was on the verge of describing the farm, the women and boy on it, particulars, details in preparation for his final thrust about a knife plunged into a woman's vagina; if he could express it all without breaking down.

Grover forced himself erect from his sagged stance and interrupted. "Sir, my past is my own business. I assume my arm is better. I would like to go."

Israel managed a grin. "Axel, the treatment was a success. I am sending you back to your old job." Grover did not flinch at his German name. If anything, Israel imagined he detected his rigid expression sag with relaxation. Was it defiance? Or the relief that accompanies the elimination of subterfuge. Israel had placed the full measure of justice on Grover's back, yet it appeared to lighten his burden.

Other than a routine inspection of the plant when he had started work, Israel studiously avoided visits to its interior; the bowels of the place he termed it. The sight of blood had repulsed him, in surgery too, though he had to live with it there, distracted from its impact by the healing business at hand. Huge sections of the plant were deluged with sloppy, smelly puddles of gore, which normally would have deprived him of an evening's appetite. He proclaimed to Miss Evans, "I will make daily visits to watch the men work, a sort of time-study appraisal. Please arrange my schedule."

She was amazed. "But doctor, you yourself told me how you hated to go inside. You were positively squeamish about it."

"I am after an inspection of movements and materials in relation to the prevention of accidents. Like Grover's. That's the department I shall be in if you need me. When are they busiest?" He lied fluently.

"About 11 A.M." She replied. "when the split carcasses come through the line."

"Good. I'll do a little each day, perhaps twenty or thirty minutes."

In one morning Israel familiarized himself with the maze of doors and catwalks which overhung elongated tables equipped to transform confused animals into cartons of labeled cans. He blocked out machine noises and unaesthetic sights, as his attention was focused on one face. For a long ten minutes he stared, before Axel, in a reprieve from constant cutting, saw the motionless figure above him leaning forward with a hand on the pipe rail of the narrow catwalk. On the second morning Axel ceased to wonder why he was the center of medical attention. He was on the receiving end of a voodoo rite whose result he could not guess except that it was intended to be offensive. Axel worked rapidly, made his cuts with the clean sweep of a beheader, as he cursed beneath his breath in German with each swipe of the blade. Several glances upward assured him he was not the object of a fleeting inspection, but a focus of protracted voyeurism.

In the evening Axel Gans usually fried chicken breasts in butter and herbs with thinly sliced potatoes, or prepared hamburger with garlic and onions. Lately he submitted to a fare of Swiss cheese sandwiches washed down with cold milk—anything to fill the stomach—and flopped into bed with the hope he would be refreshed in the morning. Work and more work was his salvation. Sleep did not come easily. Aspirin helped, then sleeping pills which he bought on prescription given by Drs. Singh and Groothaus. He dreamt he was a slick-haired general in a natty uniform covered with medals and giving orders to his troops to fire. As the guns blasted, their glinting steel barrels bent downward.

When Israel noted Axel's hand waver in an attempt to separate the fat from an unusually large pork back, he extended his watch. Axel appeared weaker, not in the decisiveness of his strokes, but in the way he shifted his feet to maintain balance. He was thinner, too, and though his eyes had been regressed, the swollen sag of his lids infused a quality of terror into his fatigued appearance. Israel mumbled to himself subconsciously, "Get weak, you bastard, fall down. It will be easy to kill you then."

He quickly recanted. Nature would roust out the elderly for death or replacement. He did not have to do anything but watch. Intently. There was more retribution in this than in the blows of an axe or knife. The executioner remained unsoiled while self punishment took its toll. A righteous act of prolonged suffering was being inflicted on the culprit. Then why, thought Israel, did he feel uneasy in the role of a virtuous conqueror? Perhaps he never could become a masterful, heroic figure. His antagonist was old, tired, and sick. He needed a doctor, and not a magic potion to ward off Israel's incantations. Axel might be the prey of unnatural pressures, but there were a few medical tricks which could delay the finality of voodoo mischief. Israel questioned his own detachment as he passively watched a man die.

In a half-hearted fling of desperation Israel stood at his catwalk position twice that Friday. He stared resolutely at Axel, who stared back in defiance. Israel made the exaggerated effort to clarify a mass of doubt. The doubled watch was a duty to himself, so he could say he tried everything, though he entertained no illusion that Grover would succumb to intensified effort. To Israel's astonishment Grover did not appear at his work station on Monday. "The plan worked," Israel mused. The murderer's recollection must have revived, sharply honed as a razor and pointed inward to his vitals; a boomerang of justice returned to exact its due. Dr. Steingut checked to be certain Grover had not reported in. He scrutinized work sheets, medical files, made frantic excursions into the plant.

For three days Grover's spot on the trimming line was taken by a tall young man who sang as he sliced, a contrast Israel found disruptive. Joy had been associated with morose plans, not song blared out on the meat line. "What I am doing," he told himself, "is so finely organized it is endangered by any diversion." The next step was obvious. He would visit Axel, in private, and determine a final solution when they were together, alone. In the starkness of such a meeting there would be no distraction.

Israel approached the neat frame house on a block otherwise filled with unpainted residences. It could have been a small house in Germany. Axel always had been handy, and he had probably improved the property gratuitously. Leave it to Axel to paint, touch up, repair a roof or fill cracked cement. That was what he had done for Anna on the farm; a superficial gesture of benevolence; yet great pains and back breaking labor were put into his projects. Israel noted the sturdiness of the stairway as he bounded up; no cracks; evenly painted; with a fresh smell; a mark of German culture. He knocked on the door and heard a distant, garbled sound of acknowledgement. He entered and strode into a small bedroom coved off a prosaic living room. Had he been a frequent visitor, Israel could not have been more brash.

Axel filled the iron bed with his gaunt frame clothed in blue pajamas, clean but faded by multiple washings. They looked at each other with the equanimity of a patient and his visitor meeting according to a pre-set schedule.

Israel spoke, "When you did not come to work I worrried about you. That is why I am here."

Axel was casual. "You must be a good doctor. You care about your patients."

"I do. Some, more than others. Tell me, how are you getting along?"

"Pretty well. Of course I don't eat like I did, and I suppose that is why I am so weak." He stared at the ceiling.

"Too bad," Israel commiserated. "Perhaps I can get to the bottom of what ails you. Let me examine you." He opened his bag and lifted out a stethescope with several small instruments.

For a moment Axel hesitated. His eyes wandered about the room as if he would discover a new way out, suddenly gather his strength to spring to safety. The effort was taxing. He lay back in resignation. "Go ahead, doc. Do what you want."

Israel placed the earpieces of the stethescope to his head. He understood the invitation, "Do what you want," as clearly as any urging in his dreams to avenge himself. But automatically, even as he conjectured how easily he could kill a helpless man, his hands succumbed to the patterned motions of a routine examination. Heart, lungs, abdomen, were listened to and palpated. If there is a magnetic field of medical sanity, Israel was its captive. Only when he reached to Axel's genitals, when he was haunted by an image of ripped out testicles and an amputated penis spurting blood, did he swallow hard to subdue the ferocity so alien to him.

Israel finished his examination and washed his hands. "Mr. Grover, I find nothing to make you so sick. However, something must be going on that needs further investigation."

"I will not go to any hospital, if that's what you mean."

"You will die, lying here without food or care."

Axel closed his eyes. "We know about death, don't we? And if we know it well enough, it is a friend." He smiled at the depth of his erudition.

"Why did you kill her? I saw you do it." Israel turned away as he sobbed.

"It was the war. I was young. I went crazy. I wanted her, and she led me on." The words tumbled out softly as if he recited in his sleep. Israel reeled and grasped Axel's throat. "Go ahead, squeeze," murmured Axel. "I don't care anymore."

Israel backed away. He wrung his hands. A dog once could have had him by the throat, but the brute avoided the kill. Let it go, this business of killing. The man is terminal and he suffers. I am glad he suffers. I am a doctor, but I will not weaken. I will not force myself to help him, but I won't kill him.

"So you wish to die," said Israel. "Die, then. I won't make it any easier. You always were a coward."

Axel propped himself up. "I was a soldier. A German soldier. I did things that seemed weak, but I did them for me. I believed in myself. I was not a coward."

"You have responsibilities, such as none but a coward would shirk. There is your aunt, Miss Schusswig, who depends on you. Perhaps you have not stuck to your rules as well as you think."

"Naturally you know about her. It didn't take long to figure it out. She won't need me, only my money. I've made a will to take care of her if someone sees to it. That doesn't mean I've changed. I always helped out; Anna, your mother, you; but I came first, I had to be appreciated. I can tell you my aunt will appreciate me." He raised himself on an elbow and cocked his head to the side, a coquettish gesture of entreaty he knew would not fail. "Dr. Steingut, you can do it for me."

"Do what?" Israel was alarmed at a request which he might find impossible to refuse a dying man.

Axel spoke rapidly, with more vigor than Israel had judged he could summon. "You take care of my will. You don't have to do a thing. Leave your address, and when the time comes, my lawyer will have you sign a paper so my benefits and pension will go to Miss Schusswig."

As Israel walked through darkening streets, a column of plant smoke spiralled upward to overshadow the evening light. He had to turn a corner. Another angle of the sky came into view. Smoke had drifted aside, exposed a scimitar moon sharp and clean against an azure backdrop. It was the clearest night he had seen in Arundel.

"Of course I'll give him my address. It doesn't compromise me, as I have him under my thumb. He will die soon. *Kaputt.* Nature is full of ironies, but it never misses in its ultimate justice. Rich moguls become sick and suffer the aches of the lowest wino cramped in a corner of a cold stairwell. Look at Axel. His aplomb, his deviousness, his vanity can't save him now."

Israel gave Dr. Groothaus a week's notice of his departure. Miss Evans was inconsolable; another man who depended on her office skills was to leave her side. Israel was not perturbed by his going, though he placed a burden on his colleagues. "I must be firm. I got what I wanted from them, which makes up for the favors my patients and friends got from me." He was packed two days before he would leave, with an open suitcase and a carton of books in the center of the room. He phoned Carla that he was soon to be home. After a few phrases, time schedules, health good, how he missed her, he requested she have ready a bottle of good champagne. Carla shrieked with joy and kissed the telephone.

Next morning Dr. Groothaus, anxious to display his mental acuity after a night of intemperance, spoke to Israel. "You know that fellow Alexander Grover? I put him back on the job. He came in looking a mess, but he practically burst into tears to convince me he had to work. If he can handle it, and it's what he wants, I figured it's best for him. I will watch his progress."

Israel was dumbfounded. An event supposed to be rigidly ordained had become twisted into circumstance he could not define or control. Only a few days before Axel could not get to his feet. Israel rushed to the catwalk inside the plant; torn by the flash judgement that he had made a monumental medical miscalculation. No, he had not been inadequate. A mysterious act of fate had turned against him.

Axel was at his position, moved his knife arm with the rhythm of a mesmerized skeleton. Skin folds hung from his cheeks. Thin as he was, drooped layers of neck tissue simulated an overfed double chin. His eyes were half shut as if he excluded from his vision all but the cleft he must slice between muscle and fat of a carcass. Balance was maintained with spread legs and bent knees, and at intervals he leaned forward to support his body weight against the work table.

"I have not been mistaken. I was not wrong," Israel muttered. "He will die. Perhaps it will take longer than I thought. Death is playing a cat and mouse game with him, exactly as I planned; and he will suffer, though I must admit he's tough."

Israel reported to Dr. Groothaus. "I have seen Grover. Apparently he can do the work, so I suppose you should keep him at it. He's the kind who would be unhappy off the job."

The brisk sunlit morning of Israel's departure was rent by secretarial tears and shouts of colleagues' good wishes. Miss Evans stopped sobbing long enough to hand Israel a small package he could hold on the palm of his hand. "This is from Dr. Groothaus. He isn't here just now, but he wants to see you."

Israel peeled away cardboard and protective layers of tissue. A rectangular watch with lizard strap gleamed through the morning's smoke. Nonchalantly he placed the gift on his wrist and checked the time whenever he heard a footstep. Groothaus dashed in and took his hand.

"Please don't thank me. It's a token of remembrance. Not that we won't see each other again. We will." He drew Israel into his office. Coffee and doughnuts were on his desk, a rare portent of some festive occasion. "Have some, Dr. Steingut." Israel ate between "thank yous" and "I didn't deserve it," but Groothaus was immune to his expressions of gratitude.

"Do you know where I've been? I just looked at a piece of property we can renovate into an office. Arundel hasn't seen the likes of this one. It's on a corner, and a bargain. I tell you, Israel, I should have done this years ago. But then, I didn't have you."

"As I said, sir, I'll try. I'm not certain I can make the change."

"Never mind. Just think of the work you'll do. Anything you want, and I'm not the type to interfere. And think of the money. Don't forget the money."

In the car, Israel raised the sleeve of his left arm to make his wrist visible. When the road stretched to a lonely paved strip, free from oncoming traffic, turns, or signals, the watch spoke to him of good times and the consolation of a large bank account. The gold case reflected the light of confidence, and the black lizard strap hugged his skin as a mother hugs a child. Israel no longer mused over the probability of Axel's demise. He reiterated, like the refrain of a song, "Somebody wants me, needs me for what I can offer, and is willing to pay what I am worth."

Chapter 19

CARLA PREPARED FOR Israel's homecoming with exhilaration. About to reach for a recipe to unravel the mystery of hearts-of-artichoke, she saw through the window a car with strange license plates. She dried her hands and tucked her blouse inside the work jeans in which she cooked, gardened, or repaired a kitchen drain. According to her calculations, if the out-of-state plates, Indiana she thought, announced Israel's arrival, he had come prematurely. Israel had driven through part of the night, slept beside a twenty-four hour hamburger emporium, and resumed his journey in the early hours of the morning.

They met on the sidewalk. Israel eased himself out of an insect-smeared compact as Carla nervously rearranged her hair. Both beamed with anticipation. She opened her arms and rushed to him, but he either reeled from fatigue or stepped aside, she did not know which. Instead of a lovers' embrace and warm kisses frantically applied to as many parts as his lips could reach, she received a peck on the mouth. She was about to return greetings more suited to months of stifled passions, when Israel blurted out.

"Carla, darling, I want to make a new life for myself. A new practice is waiting for me in Indiana, only for me, and you can find work there."

Carla delivered the embraces she had hoarded though her wild energy was subdued by the rush of his proposed plans. Initially she felt he was off on a second flight of fancy, another straw man dredged from his psyche, to be set up and brought down in an imagined field of glory. Now, like some medieval potentate, he would travel with an entourage, Carla. But he remained steadfast in his explanations and conclusions, immensely practical, confident of success. His intransigence bothered her more than his plans of relocation, as Israel should have been contented to return from a period of wanderlust and submit to a healing process. With time, she could manuever him into acceptance of their lot.

After an early dinner, at which his consumption of double portions and a bottle of wine suggested he had been fed on leftovers, he embraced her with the vigor she thought had been lost. He belched frequently, a relief he had never permitted himself. They should talk for an hour, he said, before they made love, and he launched into a description of his visits with Lin Chiu, the psychiatrist, Johann Kurtzbaum, his trip to Germany. She must realize he had changed. That he was an enigma to her, capable of bizarre, daring exploits, was plain to Israel.

Carla interrupted. "Did you visit your old haunts in Germany? I sensed that was your real purpose."

"Yes, I had a very definite purpose in mind."

"You mean the German soldier?"

"Yes."

"You found him?" She was electrified.

"I did. In Indiana," he said as if he had been tranquilized.

"Oh my God, you killed him!" She bolted to her feet.

Israel did not respond directly. He circled the room with hands in trouser pockets, compact and self-contained, unperturbed, with the air of a college professor who posed a problem to his student.

"Damn it, Israel, what's wrong with you? You've taken some sort of horrible revenge and you act as if you did us a favor. I want to know so I can judge whether I can stand with you."

"No," said Israel quietly. "I committed no murder, not even any violence, though I wanted to."

Carla went limp with relief. She hugged him and laughed. "Of course you wouldn't. Not my Israel." She tilted her head and teased, "Did you chicken out?"

"I did not retreat. I got what I wanted."

"Don't misunderstand me," she apologized. "I wasn't thrilled by your wild idea of fun and games."

"I did it. I finished him off."

"How? How could you?"

"I literally watched him die. He was alive when I left, but he was going fast. When he knew who I was, he became sick."

"I bet you offered to help him. Didn't you?"

"Of course I did. That's what made the scheme perfect. I gave him a choice, and I can't help it if he chose to punish himself."

"Then what did you get out of the whole business? Where is the revenge you counted on?"

"I was the catalyst. I stared at him while he worked. It was as good as shooting bullets into him."

"Bullshit!" She exploded. "He was probably sick. By the way, how do you know he's dead?"

"That, my dear girl, is a *fait accompli*. If he hasn't succumbed yet, he will soon." Carla knew the case he built for himself was not debatable. If the thought of success gave him such assurance, it was best not to destroy his delusion of victory. After a time, she mused, he would settle into old habits of indecision. Then she could deal with him as a malleable human being, flawed but sane enough to accept her consolement. "Now about this job in Indiana," Carla said, "are you certain you want to take it?" Israel described the town and Dr. Groothaus, a true gentleman who recognized surgical capability and was willing to reward it.

"I never heard you define your ability in terms of money. You would leave a hospital with a good back-up for a country-style practice that is outmoded?"

"But they need me. Dr. Groothaus needs me."

"You mean he will line your pockets."

"Why do you describe the situation in such a crass way? It's true, in part. But I object to your insinuation that I am degrading myself. Ideals have no substance, no impact, unless they are respected, and the only respect people can show comes out of a wallet. You have too many saintly notions about medicine. I don't want to be a saint. I want to be normal, get paid for my work, and suffer the consequences if I mess up."

Carla retreated. She had to reassure her husband who was thirty years too late in the discovery of his reborn spirit. Was his spirit true, fixed, a base to build on, or was his tirade a blast of wind trapped and bagged in his eccentric journey? Instead of calm acceptance, he suddenly sought a new, vibrant set of conditions. He had misplaced the time-sequence of his life-style, escaped from tempestuous puberty directly to immature adulthood. Now, out of character, he was filled with fire and determination, and she did not know him. Unforeseen qualities in him had surfaced, attributes of vigorous, successful men she had met but could not love. If this was the real Israel, she too would undergo basic alterations if they clung together. Carla thought of herself as a tough, well-knit piece of fabric which might not withstand the dissemblage and patchwork inherent in an accomodation to Israel's startling new fashions.

"Is that a new watch?" Carla remarked in what was to be a meaningless shift of converstaion.

Israel never wore jewelry. If he replaced a watch it would be a practical step to guarantee accurate time. Patients were expected to keep appointments and meetings were to be attended on the minute less the traffic of the mind become congested. A fancy gold watch which signalled wealth, or beauty, detracted from its sole function.

Israel held his wrist at arm's length and turned his hand to catch the light's reflections. "Dr. Groothaus gave it to me as a gift. That man respected me."

"With no ulterior motives?"

"None. He helped me and I did my best for him. He was my friend, not just some boss. He's no greedy moneybags,"

"Israel, I'm glad you found him." Both were silently pleased. He had not yet become a medical entrepreneur, a commercial purveyor of surgery for dollars. Notwithstanding the untoward turns of his transformation, some ideals remained to be nurtured and perhaps rejuvenated.

"If you go," Carla said, "when would you leave?"

Israel was exuberant. "Give me a week to rest and pack. I'll phone Groothaus tonight we are coming."

"Not we, you."

"What do you mean?"

"When you left you were plain Israel. Now I see a Dr. Steingut whom I am not quite sure I know. After four months wandering about by yourself you should get along without me for a few more months, or a year."

"A year! I told you everything, laid it out for you. Both of us can do well, and I see no special glitter in your job, or this house, to hold you. You are not the princess type; strictly rural, that's what you are! And since I've accomodated to the territory, you can."

Carla whined, almost begged. "Israel, you still don't understand. It is not land, or a house, or geography that interests me. It is you. You have a different outlook, another set of principles, and I must adjust to them. Perhaps I am to blame. I don't know. There are gaps to fill between us, and I must find out if we fit together."

In a long phone call to Dr. Groothaus, Israel requested he watch for a four-room apartment. His week was spent in sporadic packing and driving Carla to the hospital, though two evenings were saved to dine out and enjoy a movie. On the spur of the moment they would engage in sex, wild, untrammeled liaisons of newlyweds about to be separated by war. Problems were glossed over by an act of erasure.

Israel's car was packed, with boxes of books strapped on the roof. He looked at his watch. Eight A.M. She held him to her and cried.

Israel was composed. "When you are ready to come, let me know."

"I am not sure," she whimpered.

"I'm looking for a four-room apartment. We can furnish a den for a second bedroom."

"For children?" She eased the words through tears.

"Either that, or you can use it for yourself when you become angry with me."

As he drove off the car radio played a rare, old Benny Goodman recording. His fingers on the steering wheel tapped to the beat of subdued dreams. His mind dissolved in an amalgam of past bewilderment and future infallibility. The open road was a jungle path, and he was on an overdue safari. Wild beasts, snarling dogs that ogled the curves of his throat could not stop him. Perhaps he would have to maim or destroy, but his actions would no longer reflect revenge. They would arise from the covenant between man and nature, eat and be eaten, live well and die gracefully so that others may follow in the empty spaces. Israel Steingut fancied he had begun his tribal rite into maturity. All he had to do was kill his lion and present its hide to his woman when she arrived.

After four days of disillusionment, days packed with the shock of awareness and recrimination, Israel returned home. He had gone with ferocious expectations and returned disgruntled and depleted. Dr. Groothaus was drying out in the alcoholic unit of a distant hospital. "Israel, it must have been a sham, a mirage," said Groothaus. "Twice a year, at least, I sink this low. I failed to tell you because I didn't remember. You know that man, Grover? He dropped dead on the job. Maybe that's why I went on this tout. Get out of here, fast. Don't even think of this stinking town."

On the road, Israel turned to look at his watch, but it was difficult to read the dial. The inclination to tear it off and heave it through the car window had to be squelched. Groothaus was not to blame. He remained an honest man. Israel Steingut was the fool, who jumped to believe what he wanted to hear. He too was in the category of a drunk who had hit bottom. If he did anything, it would be in the nature of upward mobility. Mike Hearn did that.

Revenge was no longer an issue. He missed the feeling, conscious or unconscious, that there was a supreme injustice he had to correct. He longed for his cause, yet he was not burdened with it. The exorcism of revenge had left a void which he could accept as a permanent anesthetic of the spirit, or which he could fill with ordinary bits of living, his wife, his home, his duties. He had escaped humiliation and death as a child, and since he was faced with a second beginning, he could do it again. Israel was buoyed by submerged pride which revealed itself above the surface, the pride of a survivor.

Carla again met him outside the house, where he clasped her in a long, warm embrace. It was as if he crawled from a rough sea to clutch an outgrowth of rock. There were hours when he moped, though he did not drink or take medication, hours so intolerable to Carla that she called the hospital to inform them Dr. Steingut was back. "They want you as soon as you can make it, this afternoon if possible. They're swamped." Israel left with knees bent like an old man, worked through most of the night, and returned wide-eyed and elated. His mood was euphoric and hopeful.

"I think I can hang on here," he announced.

"Yes," said Carla, "and you can start your own practice in town." The simplicity of her advice jolted him.

He placed his hand on Carla's shoulder. "I can help you." she said.

"No, that's not the way it's going to be. You say it as if I were your son. If you need to be giving, get yourself someone really dependent on you. Someone young, and small, like a child." At a distance they confronted each other with knowing smiles. Without analysis or even conscious recognition by Carla, the dam of Israel's resistance had parted. He was certain enough of himself and his future to stand upright in a house of divided loves. He had been cleansed sufficiently to live with in reasonable harmony.

When Israel lapsed into moods dredged up by the spectre of revenge, or guilt, or self-effacement, he would step outside and walk toward the open fields. Originally he had come to escape dirt, congestion, and urban hostility, against which he had to armor himself with enforced watchfulness. This place had been his hide-out, just as he had hid on a farm in Germany. Now it was no longer a cove of retreat. It had its own character, its independence and distinction.

He would look out on the landscape, flat, unexciting, but giving of clean, new growth. His own tumult was subdued and the dullness of the land was restful.

ABOUT THE AUTHOR

Bernard Diamond, himself a surgeon, was raised and educated in New York City. Iowa was his home for many years. He is the author of several plays which have been performed by theater companies and he has also written technical works for his medical colleagues. This is his first novel.

ABOUT THE BOOK

This book was typeset in Caledonia on a photocomposition system. W. A. Dwiggins' Caledonia is based upon the eighteenth-century Scotch Roman family of typefaces. It is one of the most readable and ageless typefaces found within the modern typographic library. Jean Wagner of Columbia Publishing Company set the book in type. Quentin Fiore designed the book's cover and interior. It was printed and bound by Thomson-Shore, Inc. in Dexter, Michigan, on acid-free Warren paper.